THE CANNON AND THE QUILL

BOOK 2: PRINCES OF THE WORLD

BY THE SAME AUTHOR

The Cannon and the Quill, Book One: We All be Jacobites Here*

Jester-Night (Book 1 of the Ambir Dragon Tales)

Minor Confessions of an Angel Falling Upward*

Watch Out For the Hallway: Our Two-Year Investigation of the Most Haunted Library in North Carolina (with Tonya Madia)

Roommates from Beyond: How to Live in a Haunted Home (with Tonya Madia)

*Part of the Stanton Chronicles

THE CANNON AND THE QUILL

BOOK 2: PRINCES OF THE WORLD

PART OF THE STANTON CHRONICLES

JOEY MADIA

New Mystics Enterprises
Leavittsburg, Ohio

The Cannon and the Quill Book 2: Princes of the World

Published by New Mystics Enterprises, Leavittsburg, OH 44430
www.newmystics.com

ACKNOWLEDGMENTS

A hearty Huzzah to Jonathan Edwards and Port City Tour Company/Beaufort Escape Rooms for commissioning the walking tour, stage show, and escape room on which I've based this series.

Thanks to the Beaufort Pirate Invasion, North Carolina Maritime Museum, Beaufort Historic Site, Japan's "Passage of Dreams," *North Carolina Travel*, and all the other venues that asked Angus to tell his stories for their audiences.

Cheers to all the pirate re-enactors with whom I have worked. You are my true and trusted mates. Lots of rum and coin to ye all!

To Baylus Brooks, Captain Horatio Sinbad, and other historians whose diligence and passion have made it possible for this story to be steeped in history while also being a fantastical journey into the unknown—I offer you my deepest thanks and respect.

To illustrator extraordinaire, Chuck Regan.

To my four beta readers, whose suggestions and feedback made this book better.

And, most of all, to my love, my lass, my real-life Ailish. Tonya— There's no one else I'd rather sail 'round the world (or be safely quarantined) with, especially in these Times of Pox and Plague.

DEDICATION

To Eric Vasbinder, my real life Blackbeard.

We have told our stories in many different ways, in many
different places.

Cheers and huzzah for the ones still yet to come.

PART ONE:

BLOODIED CLOAKS AND SECRETS

As Duncan MacDonald passed the deep blue waters of Loch Voil and crested the final hill that brought him within sight of his cousin Rob Roy's cattle farm near Duncan's modest cottage in the Highlands of Scotland, he grasped tightly to the dark green, bloodstained cloak that lay across his saddle and tried to gather his thoughts.

During his return journey from the Caribbean, a weeks-long odyssey full of hardships and obstacles of which he was barely conscious, he had played the events in Commodore Benjamin Hornigold's fortress office in Nassau repeatedly in his head.

Edward Thache's clear distrust—no doubt from senses honed from years under combat conditions as a privateer and pirate.

Angus's excitement at seeing a familiar face from home—a face that drained of color as Duncan pulled his pistol.

Hardest of all to remember, though, were the final moments of his mere hours in Nassau as he grabbed the bloodied cloak as proof of the horrific deed he had done and taken passage off the island…

Taken together, it was all a sight more than his tired mind could bear.

And so, as any man in his position would, he drank. Drank until he passed out upon the rum- and ale-stained table of whatever tavern or galley he happened to be sheltering in at the time, the coarse woolen cloak that marked forever his guilt always by his side.

Kicking his horse into a trot—no sense in trying to buy himself another handful of minutes after he had come so far—Duncan flinched as a sizable crowd began to spill from the entrance to Rob Roy's home. No doubt some well-hidden lookout had sent a signal as man and horse approached. Things had most assuredly gotten worse since the departure of the Old Pretender, James Stuart, in January after a string of defeats at the hands of King George's defenders the month before. Because of their primary role in the battles, the dangerous loyalties of the MacGregors and their associated clans were no longer a matter of question.

The sooner the rebellion was over, the better for them all. It had brought the Highlands nothing but horror.

To Duncan most of all.

Looks of concern and distrust at a possible intruder turned to smiles of welcome as those at the farm identified Duncan's well-known black and red tartan, affixed over his shoulder in the ancient Highlander manner. As he scanned the faces of the nearly two dozen individuals now assembled in the yard, Duncan felt his chest clench and his hands begin to shake.

Among them was Ailish, Angus's long-time companion and Duncan's second cousin, such a look upon her face that Duncan considered throwing the cloak upon the ground and riding hard for Glasgow, never to know the rolling hills of the Highlands again.

But he knew too well his duty and that he could not shirk it.

Which was how he had gotten into this damned miserable mess in the first place.

"Aye, mae coosin' Dooncan! Waelcoom hoom, big yin!"

Rob Roy had separated from the crowd at the moment of recognition to greet his trusted assassin outside the farmstead's split-rail fence. "Waev missed ye. Oi, wae haev." Patting the rider's leg, Rob dropped his voice. "Tael mae the deed is doon," he whispered, his eyes going cold in the asking.

"Aye coosin," Duncan answered, handing Rob the cloak. "I haev brought ye proof a' the deed. An' a list a' names a' traitors tae give our laird an' king. Haev ye any ale? I am perched."

"Ye mae drink yer fill," Rob whispered, running his hand over the new set of stains set into his brother's cloak. "We baest bae joinin' the oothers."

Getting down from his horse—so much better the delay that would come with walking instead of riding, no matter how brief it would be—Duncan watched his cousin, whose hand had not left the bloody stains. It was clear that Rob, hard and pragmatic though he was—after all, he had turned over two Jacobite leaders in February to try to quell some of their enemies' wrath—had harbored some small doubt that his nephew would actually die.

"What tale a' the deed shood I tell?" Duncan asked. "Oor doo ye intaind tae hide the cloak an' say noothin' aboot it?"

Rob shook his head. "Thair's noothin' fer oos in hidin' anythin' 'atall. Angus died in saervice tae the rightful king an', althoo I saent ye tae fetch the lad baefore harm coold coom his way, hae was killed in a fight wit' a pirate. Thair's nae point in causin' unnecessary grief."

A chill spread out from the center of Duncan's back. Could he look Ailish in the eye and speak those words with conviction?

And exactly when was grief by any means *necessary*?

"Dooncan... whair's the brooch? The acorn an' the oak leaf?"

Duncan shook his head. "I doan knoo a' any brooch, coosin. I brought what proof I could."

As Rob opened his mouth to argue, the inhabitants of the house were upon them.

Ailish was first in line.

"That cloak," she said, putting out her hand to touch its fouly darkened areas. "That baelonged tae Angus. Dooncan, what doo ye knoo?"

As the women gathered around her, James, Rob Roy's eldest son, took her by the shoulder. "Ye need noot worry, Ailish, lass. I am haer tae coomfort thee, nay matter what's baen doon."

I wish it haid baen ye, ye schemin' bastard, Duncan thought, his hand going unobtrusively to the claymore at his side. For he had known the truth about James's role in the entire regrettable mess before he had left Scotland for the Caribbean.

Yet, still he went, so loyal was he to the cause.

"Ailish, lass," Rob said gently, offering her his hand. "Dooncan has soom news, an' it weel bae damnably haird tae hear..."

Jake Givens, part-time podcaster and maritime aficionado, reached for his microphone through the thick, persistent fog as he heard the first of the series of beeps that signaled the start of his weekly podcast, Jake's Maritime Mysteries.

But the microphone wasn't there. And now that he thought about it, there *weren't* any beeps—at least not the type that signaled the start of the show...

So where the hell was he?

"Lay back, Mr. Givens. You have a visitor, but, seeing your agitated state, I'm beginning to wonder if it's..."

As the voice above him blurred into a drone, Jake managed to open his left eye just a little, finding his right one completely blocked by something soft yet scratchy. Lifting his right hand, he felt the pinch and pull of an IV taped to the back of it.

A hospital. Right. He'd been beaten up. Badly, it seemed.

Through a haze of viscous eye muck, he could make out a nurse and a young Hispanic man standing beside her. The man looked less than happy at hearing the nurse's words.

"Like I said, Nurse..." he glanced at her nametag, "Allen... I'm with the FBI. Tech Specialist Tino Alvarado. And as I also said, I need to question this man, who was the sole witness to a very serious crime. A threat to national security. Now, if I have to get a doctor, or place a call to our Newark field office, I will, but maybe it's better for us all if—"

"Suit yourself," the nurse answered, raising her hands in surrender. "My shift's about to end." Having a pang of doubt before walking away, Nurse Allen leaned in close to Jake. "Is there anything you need, Mister Givens? Any way I can make you more comfortable before I disappear?"

His curiosity peaked by the words *FBI*, *witness*, and *national security*, Jake was anxious to be rid of the nurse before she changed her mind or, worse, someone with real authority came in and enforced her initial recommendation.

"I'm fine. Thanks for everything. You've been great."

Pursing her lips and looking back and forth at the two young wise guys, Nurse Allen exited the room, her shiny white, orthopedic shoes squeaking as she went.

Before the door had closed, Tino was placing a chair beside the bed. "Mister Givens... Jake... what can you tell me about what happened to you?"

Leaning his head, which had now begun to throb, into his pile of pillows, Jake thought back... Getting ready for his show... the arrival of Mr. Minever, the mailman, with a package... from Dr. Kirstine MacGregor... a thumb drive.

Then... the thugs. A pair of them. Looking for what had arrived. As if they had *known*... known about *everything*...

Tino put his hand firmly on Jake's shoulder as he launched himself up from the bed—or attempted to.

"Easy there, Jake," Tino said, easing him into the pillows. "You set off one of the alarms on those monitors and our little chat is over. I'm not authorized to be here."

"But you said..."

"What I needed to." Glancing at the door, Tino leaned in closer. "Look, Jake. I am a close friend of Kirstine MacGregor's. I know what was on that thumb drive. Some of it, at least. And given what's happened to you, and the fact that Kirstine is missing..."

A bolt of pain shot through Jake's head, having nothing to do with the beating he had taken. "What do you mean, missing?"

"Come on, dude," Tino said, shaking his head. "Don't be dumb. You know exactly what I mean. As in... nowhere to be found. Not work, not home. Not answering her cell, the GPS on which is disabled. Not sure she'd know how. So someone else—whoever has her..."

Jake gritted his teeth as he used the sidebar to pull himself up into a painful half-sit. Trying to catch his breath, he said, "It's my fault. I pushed her too hard. I never should have asked those questions about codes and all that on my show."

Tino laughed. "Do you actually think you could make Doctor Kirstine MacGregor do anything she didn't want to? Believe me, you can't. And you didn't. What she showed me, she went after on her own."

"So what do we do... Tino, right?"

"Glad you asked. And, since we're gonna be working together, you can call me Haxx."

Working together... with an FBI agent... to find Kirstine... whom he was fairly sure he loved...

It all seemed and sounded just about perfect to Jake as the exhaustion from his exertions gave way to a dreamless sleep he didn't try to fight.

Angus MacGregor—although he had been using his mother's clan name of MacKinnon on his uncle Rob Roy's orders—was counting his share of the *Marianne*'s recent take when he heard two men talking about a thick-brogued Highlander who had recently arrived in New Providence.

Shoving the coins back into his bag, which he hid in a blanket in the middle of his hammock, Angus ran outside to question them.

"Where did this Highlander gaet off tae?"

"He's up with Hornigold and the officers," one of them replied.

As Angus reached the door, he heard the familiar voice of Duncan MacDonald beginning a Highland toast.

"Hair's tae oos," the Highlander shouted, as Angus burst through the door, saying, "Wha's like oos?"

Without skipping a beat, Duncan answered, "Gey few, an' thaer a' deid! Angus, mae lad! Yer lookin' half a man!"

Hugging the visitor without restraint or shame, despite the men staring at the exchange, brows raised and eyes full of questions, Angus asked, "What are ye doon hair, Dooncan? Coom tae fight fer the cause?"

Duncan drained his glass and looked Angus in the eye, his lilting tone turning solemn. "Baen fightin' fer it, Angus. Caen ye say the same?"

Angus watched as Commodore Hornigold, clearly attuned to the change in mood, drained his mug and said, "We should leave ye two alone. I would like to assess the sheets and cordage on the *Marianne*, Mister Thache, if ye would be so kind as to accompany me?"

Picking up the cue, Edward Thache, who had emptied his mug before anyone else, said, wiping his beard, "Aye, Cap'n." Setting down his mug and turning for the door, he stopped and turned back. "Ye need anythin', Angus—anythin' at all—ye just holler, ye hear?"

Putting his hand on Angus's shoulder, Duncan said to Edward, "Nae need fer concern, Maester Thache. The lad's wit' family noo."

"Aye," Edward said, exiting with Hornigold and closing the door behind them.

Angus found the lack of belief beneath Edward's answer more than a little puzzling, but he moved past intuition to focus on the man who had come such a long, long way to see him. "Tis good tae see ye, Dooncan. I haev saent many a laetter an' nae haird a—"

Angus felt his tongue thicken and words fall away as Duncan moved in a flash to lock the door and draw and cock his pistol.

"Ye close yer hole now, Angus, ye hair mae?" he said, pointing the pistol square at Angus's chest. "This is goon' hard er easy fer ye, Angus, boot it is goon' either way, ye goddamned traitorin' coo."

Angus felt his breath catch as he closed his eyes tightly against the unfathomable action before him and he heard the pistol fire.

When the expected pain of a metal ball ripping through his body did not come, he opened an eye just enough to see Duncan, through a haze of grey-blue smoke, bending over, his hand clutching his shoulder, his unfired pistol beside him.

Tossing his just-fired pistol onto a nearby table and pulling a second from his sash, which he cocked and pointed in a single motion at the wounded Highlander's head, was privateer turned pirate, Angus's once-again savior, Samuel Bellamy.

"I doan understand," Angus said, the shock of the last few moments overwhelming him. "Where in Heaven did ye—"

"I would rather not say in front of *him*," Bellamy answered, moving his pistol closer to Duncan's temple. "I am sure ye understand my marked lack of trust, Mister MacDonald."

Through gritted teeth, the Highlander replied, "Aye, that I doo."

Angus, barely able to stand, managed to make his way to Hornigold's chair, collapsing into it while saying, "I owe ye mae life, Maister Bellamy. I think that is twice oover noo..."

Sam smiled. "It is I who owe ye, Angus. I made a pledge to ye when I saw the oak and acorns, and I fully mean to keep it." Turning his attention back to Duncan, Sam said, as Edward began shouting outside and banging upon the bolted door, "If ye expect to have yer wound sewn and dressed before ye bleed out on the floor, ye had best be explaining to us just what the hell yer on about here. Angus, my friend—if ye can find your legs, kindly unlock the door."

Fifteen minutes later, for an audience that included Sam, Edward, Hornigold, and a few others that had come to constitute an inner circle of sorts at the fort, Duncan finished his explanation.

"It seems mae family has thrown a stone at mae door," Angus said, feeling much older than his years. "An' tis all the doon a' that hackit roaster, mae numpty coosin James…"

"Aye, lad," Duncan said, as Bellamy threaded a hooked needle and prepared to sew his shoulder. "Hae fooled oos all, I tael ye true, froom yer ooncle tae John Erskine, tae the rightful king himself, James Stuart."

As Sam set to work, Edward stood to his imposing better-than-six-foot height, his eyes full of fury. "As far as I am concerned, there has been an attempted murder on one of our own. The punishment fer such an offense is hangin'. Why bother sewin' the shoulder, Sam? Tis a waste a' thread. Someone fetch a rope."

Above the din of enthusiastic agreement, Angus yelled, "I was at the end of the pistol hae aimed an' I say hae should live."

As the gathered men stared at him in confusion—none more so than Duncan MacDonald—Angus smiled. "I weel explain when I get back. I haev tae fetch mae cloak. Uh… Maester Bellamy, would ye bae soo kind as tae stop sewin' Dooncan's shoolder 'til I raeturn? I naid a bit a' his blood."

As a cold rain fell upon the sleeping ships anchored in neat, bobbing rows along the slips of the London docks, scarcely a soul was stirring. Several ships would be weighing anchor at first light, which was several hours away, and their crews were getting their last sound sleeps for what would be weeks or months.

It was the perfect time for a meeting his co-conspirator had chosen to hold in the utmost of secrecy, the cold, driving rain be well and truly damned.

As former lord, now former earl, Henry Bolingbroke stood in the shadows of the bow of a tall three-master, trying to ignore the rancid smells wafting up from the barrels that surrounded him, he attempted to take the measure of the endless misfortunes that had befallen him in the prior eighteen months.

Such an assessment was hard to do full justice given the pain and discomfort, both physical and mental, he was feeling, made all the worse by the weather.

How could he have guessed, situated as he was as secretary of foreign affairs under Queen Anne, who had died nineteen months earlier with no clear successor, how his fortunes would decline upon the ascension of the damned German, George of Hanover. His prior dealings with James Stuart, the so-called Old Pretender—a nickname bestowed upon him because of his oft-shouted claim to the throne while operating in exile from France—had only made wicked matters worse. Stuart had made him promises of new opportunities should he relocate to the Old Pretender's base of operations in Lorraine. Promises that fell to shreds as they lost battle after battle, making the sting of losing his position, title, and lands at the onset of the Hanoverian's reign all the harder to bear. He had eagerly agreed to lend his contacts and resources to the true king's rebellion and it had cost him big.

At the start of his defection, all was well. Good as his word, James gave Bolingbroke the title of earl and sought his advice on most—if not all—matters concerning his cobbled-together court. How could he foresee how the campaign in Scotland the previous winter would go so terribly wrong? God and the prophets—not that either existed in the mind of Bolingbroke, so the pox on the Papists as well as the Protestants—could not have foreseen the endless calamities, misjudgments, and defeats that would befall the constantly ill James while he was in the Highlands.

Logic be damned... Upon his return to Lorraine in February—scarcely a month ago—James had placed the blame in turn on each of his assembled circle of advisors, the most heavily though on Bolingbroke, who had his earldom and position as secretary of state taken—nay *ripped*—away.

So he had returned to London, waiting on these diseased and dismal docks in a bone-aching rain, ready to forge his latest alliance.

Such were the ways of a political creature such as he.

"Henry, my old friend. Over here, man. Come in out of the rain before you drown!"

Peering through the thickening sheets of rain toward the whispering voice, Bolingbroke saw an open door and a lit lantern a dozen feet away. Catching himself in a half-hearted prayer to God (he had spent too much time with the Papists), he willed his sizable bulk toward a welcome respite from the rain.

Launching his bulk, head down, through the doorway, he found himself in a warehouse holding nothing but dozens of rows of damp and bug-infested pallets haphazardly laid over with moldering, rancid straw.

So this was the fabled holding pen of the slaves brought in by the Royal African Company prior to their auctioning off.

My God, he thought, although the sight before him reaffirmed his position that there could be no such entity, or else places such as this would not exist.

No wonder his former friend, Jonathan Swift, had so much to say about the lack of morals amongst the English.

"You look positively shocked, Lord—or is it Earl?—Bolingbroke."

Holding a handkerchief he had earlier dabbed with lavender tight to his nose, Bolingbroke replied to the man he had come to meet, "It's just Henry, for the moment."

Closing and locking the door, Bolingbroke's latest and most unlikely co-conspirator turned up the wick on the lantern. "Step closer to the flame, Henry. Better to see your face and you can warm yourself. You truly look a mess. Certainly slimmer than you were when last we met."

And when was that? Henry wondered, putting his hands toward the smoke-blackened glass of the lantern. "Ah yes," he said aloud, "I remember now. You were amongst the rogues overseeing the pulling of furniture from my home when your good laddie Georgie had me exiled. Isn't that right, Lord Colson?"

Andrew Colson, deputy governor of the Royal African Company and longtime confidante of the ever-ascending Lord John Carteret, who ran the RAC and had the ear of the king—for he was one of the few amongst the nobles that spoke a word of German—grimaced at the tone of Henry's voice.

"It is, Henry. I admit it. But it is also poor form to dredge up seedy memories of past betrayals when you so desperately need to discuss current and future ones, would you not admit?"

Henry was experienced enough to force a smile and nod. His fortunes had turned even worse in recent days. He had no sooner arrived back in London, through a circuitous and secret route, than Parliament had issued a series of stern proclamations against any and all leaders of the barely breathing Jacobite cause.

To remain one would be suicide. He needed Colson's help to salvage whatever little prospects he had managed not to lose.

"What can you do for us, Henry? That is the primary question. After all, there is no *quid* without a *quo*."

"True enough. I therefore offer this. I can give you Lieutenant General Hamilton to start. And other names thereafter. I know their hiding places, their rendezvous points, and who those persons are here in England that are still offering aid to their operations."

"Then that shall be the start," Colson answered, turning the wick a little higher and producing paper, quill, and ink. "Though I am sure, once you are dry, fed, and given the proper position, you shall give us plenty more."

At the feet of the newly arrived visitor, a sizeable pool of thick, fresh blood was morphing the ornately patterned tiles beneath it into a sacreligious mass of forbidden symbolism as it spread along the entrance hall of the monarch's favorite palace.

They had been at it again.

Cardinal Giulio Alberoni, lifting his red robes to the middle of his shins as he moved around the edge of the no doubt still sticky spill, noticed two sets of pale red footprints—one male, one female—leading toward the throne room.

This, too, was an all too often occurrence.

"Your majesties!" He waited outside the door, something to which he was rather unaccustomed, although he knew better than to enter the throne room at times when there were not previously scheduled audiences.

The king of Spain, Philip the Fifth, grandson of France's Louis the Fourteenth—and the central reason for the thirteen-year War of Spanish Succession that had culminated in the Treaty of Utrecht, forbidding a single man to sit on the thrones of France and Spain—was an amorous man, and, being a pillar of Catholic morality, devoted only to his spouse.

Which was why, upon the death of Philip's first wife, Maria Luisa, two years prior, the Cardinal had arranged for the king's marriage on Christmas Eve that same year to Elisabeth Farnese, whose father was the hereditary prince of the Italian city of Parma and whose paternal grandfather was an elector palatinate. Her mother's sisters had been queens of Spain and Portugal and a consort to a Holy Roman emperor. Centuries earlier, in the time of the Borgias, her ancestor, Giulia Farnese, accurately called *La Bella*, was the mistress of their patriarch, Rodrigo, who ruled the Vatican under the title of Pope Alexander the Sixth.

Cardinal Alberoni, ever the strategist, like so many of his brethren working in the Holy City of Rome and around the globe, had not only solved the problem of satisfying the conjugal needs of the king, to whom a select handful of powerful members of the Court tasked him with looking after. He had also won the alliance of the newly crowned Queen Elisabeth, a fiery personality who in less than a year and a half had already proven herself a formidable power behind the throne of Spain.

In turn, she was, of course, fiercely loyal to the man who had made her ascension possible. Trusting a Cardinal was easy for her to do. Not only had *La Bella* been mistress to a pope—she had further used this advantage to see her brother Alessandro named a Cardinal in 1493. History would remember him as His Holiness, Pope Paul the Third.

Yet Cardinal Alberoni's position was far from comfortable and easy. Philip and Elisabeth shared a joy of the hunt and their habits afterward were, as demonstrated by the blood in the palace entrance, less than up to standards.

They were also given to spontaneous fits of passion, at times within the throne room, which is why Alberoni now lowered himself to waiting for an answer. He had learned the hard way—his cheeks still flushing hot in scarlet shades that matched exactly his cassock at the thought of the odd angles and violent motions of paired flesh he had inadvertently seen just a week ago.

"Your majesties!" he called again, his impatience growing beyond its bounds. "I have news of Capitan Machado, my king. Most urgent news."

This last bit was a lie—or a stretch at best. Although Amaro Rodriguez Felipe y Tejera Marchado, commander of the king's ship *Ave María*—referred to by most as Amaro Pargo for the way he pursed his lips like a fish—was known by all to be a favorite of Philip's, the news was not urgent at all.

It was worth a little lie, however, to be alleviated from the insult of having to wait not fifteen feet from a pool of blood, shed no doubt from the slit-open torso of some filthy, unholy beast not half an hour before.

"Ah, my good Cardinal, come in, come in!" Philip was now at the door, his powdered wig askew and his hands busily tucking his shirt into his pants. "The queen and I were just cleaning ourselves after a very vigorous hunt. We bagged quite the pair of stags. Sorry to keep you waiting, Your Eminence."

To just which hunt the king was referring, Alberoni did not care to know.

"You have news of my faithful servant Amaro, *si*? Come in and sit so our queen can hear it as well." Philip made a sweeping gesture with his arm, indicating a chair by the royal dais. "Has he sunk many English ships? Or better yet—captured a ship full of pirates? What does he call them? Ah, yes… *cerdos*—lousy piratical pig-swine!"

"Please, Philip. Do not be a bore. The Cardinal does not care for vulgar, lowly language. He is, after all, a pious man of God."

Alberoni looked upon the visage of the queen. Her youthful face—she was only twenty-three, a decade younger than her husband—was still long and thin, her rose-bloom cheeks a perfect complement to her light brown hair, although she was already showing signs of a fattening around the middle from the daily indulgences of a pampered life at court.

And, as God assuredly knew, from the very start, she had indulged. As part of the marriage agreement, she had insisted on having her choice of the best jewels the crown could offer, leading in part to the delay of the voyage from Spain's holdings in the New World of the twelve plate fleet ships under the command of Don Juan Esteban de Ubilla that had been wrecked by a hurricane the previous July.

No wonder she does not want to talk about Pargo, the Cardinal thought. Ubilla, the most respected among the capitan-generals of the royal Spanish navy, had been the hot-blooded young man's mentor. Were anyone other than Alberoni made aware that the chosen queen's demands had contributed to Ubilla's fate, it would place a strain on the king's relationship with Pargo that the Cardinal could ill afford.

Before Alberoni could answer, Philip was up and out of his chair. "*Mio Dio*, my old friend—tell me the news! And then, please... have someone clean up the mess we have made. The fun is over. I am feeling fully embarrassed by our folly. Silly, really. I do not know what happens to me at times..."

Watching the queen's face darken at her husband's turn of mood—an increasingly frequent happening that more and more members of the court were finding it hard to ignore, Alberoni smiled. "He is on the hunt, Your Majesty, and most confident that he will soon capture a prize worthy of Spain and your respect."

Philip sat back down. "Most excellent, Your Eminence. Send him a letter relaying my thanks and anticipation of a great presentation of treasure. Now, if you will excuse the queen and me, we are very tired and must be off to bed."

Once again looking at the queen as he made his bow before taking his leave, Alberoni saw her eyes turn skyward—but only for a second. Regaining her composure, she winked at him, in assurance that all would be well.

Alberoni turned to go, only then allowing himself to smile.

He had chosen well indeed.

A s Duncan MacDonald gingerly maneuvered a new shirt over his sewn and bandaged shoulder, he watched with curiosity and no small amount of fear as Angus ran his hand over the newly made bloodstains on his father's woolen cloak.

Bloodstains he took no small pleasure in making directly from Duncan's wound.

Despite the dire circumstances, and bypassing a wagonload of irony, Duncan had the somewhat absurd thought that Rob Roy would be proud of the man his nephew had become.

"What are yer plans fer mae, Angus?" Duncan asked, carefully affixing his tartan over his wounded left shoulder with a Celtic knot brooch overlaid with a raven, the symbol of his clan.

Removing his own brooch from the cloak—his father's oak leaf and acorns, symbol of the House of Stuart—Angus handed it to Duncan.

"Bring this cloak hoom tae Ooncle Rob an' tael haim yer work is doon. I am daed an' nae longer a concaern." As the men in the room started to stir, Angus put out his hands, silently requesting their patience. "If ye doonae, ye mae as well bae hanged bae this lot. An' I knoo the difficult position ye wair in."

Duncan lowered his head. "Noot joost mae, Angus. I saw the cloud coom o'er yer ooncle's eyes. He haid nay choice. King James made himself clear on't… An' he daemanded names a' oother traetors tae the cause tae boot."

"Names a' those who oppose us ye weel haev," Angus answered, the tension rising in his voice. "Mae coosin' James… I naid ye tae keep a close eye on haim, Dooncan. An' keep him away froom Ailish if ye caen. I knoo the lass is sore wit' mae an' it mae bae one day ye caen tael hair a bit a' the trooth. Tael her I died weel. Boot fer noo…"

"Ye shall bae daid. Wit' honor. I promise ye." Duncan put out his hand. Angus did not hesitate a moment before taking it in his own.

"All well and good," Samuel Bellamy said, shaking his head. "But there is the matter of now having to hide ye from sight, Angus… Or, at least from those who would tell your uncle or our enemies that might find some gain in it that ye are still alive…"

Angus, seeing Commodore Hornigold and Mister Thache nodding in agreement, smiled. "It saems that nom de guerres are goin' tae bae mae lot fer noo. Angus MacGregor daed in Scootland. Angus MacKinnon died hair today. An' in his place shall arise… Conall MacBlaquart. If ye caen arrange fer me tae bae upon a ship that weel take mae away fer a good long while, there are very few who knoo what took place in this room."

"I will make it so," Hornigold replied. "I am sure we can count on loyalty and secrecy from those who have sworn their allegiance to our young republic. As for you, MacDonald, I shall expect ye on a ship by nightfall as well. I will furnish ye with a list of names of pirates loyal to George and I expect ye will put it to quick and deadly use. Because, although Angus's plan is sound, his leniency is more than I would give and this is your chance to earn it. I am sure these men agree."

"Aye," Duncan answered. "Yer damned weel right tae ask it a' mae. I weel see yer wishes doon."

PORT ROYAL, SOUTH CAROLINA, APRIL 28, 1716

There was nothing like the slow coming down after the intense bloodlust of battle to make a man see with renewed clarity the path that lay before him.

Colonel James Moore could see things clearly now indeed.

As his brother, Maurice, talked through an interpreter with a council of Cherokee who had aided in a thorough defeat of their common enemy, the Creek, Moore turned his thoughts to the future. It would not be long before he was able to bring to a swift conclusion the Yamasee War now that the Cherokee were committed to their side. *The enemy of my enemy is my friend* was a human truth on which Moore had learned to rely during the Tuscarora War five years earlier in the Colony of North Carolina and it was bearing out again on the battlefields of her southern sister.

Staring at the dried blood on his hands before shifting his gaze to the three dozen half-naked corpses splayed across the field on which they had fought, Moore had to admit he wished that he were home. He missed the Albemarle. That was where his future fortunes lay. His closest allies, Edward Moseley and Jeremiah Vail, were slowly taking control of the area, strengthening a key alliance with the lieutenant governor of Virginia by negotiating favorable tobacco prices for their crops while the rest of the Colony of North Carolina suffered. They were also secretly supporting the lead Lord Proprietor, called the Palatine, John Carteret, a ruthless man who, in exchange for their loyalty, was arranging for his proprietor lackey in the Albemarle, Baron William Craven, to do *their* bidding in a reverse from the current arrangement.

Which was the single reason that he still backed their play. Moore was anti-proprietor to the depths of his soul. Why should the American colonies be ruled by a group of hereditary aristocrats growing fat on a gift made by Charles the Second fifty years earlier to those who helped him regain the crown his father had so clumsily lost in conjunction with his head?

It did not appear remotely fair. And Colonel Moore was a man who valued what was fair.

Take the Yamasee War. Twelve months prior, a group of vicious savages slaughtered ninety settlers over perceived injustices in the fur trade. They had to be perceived—savages had no rights, and, therefore, were owed no justice. No *fair*ness.

Ergo, he had answered the call on behalf of the families of the slaughtered settlers and those that cowered in their cabins instead of pursuing their God-given rights as White men.

He had been writing the butcher's bill on their holy behalf ever since.

"Colonel Moore, have you a moment, sir? For an introduction?" Moore, pulling a rag from his pocket and cleaning the blood from his hands, stood and smiled. Before him was the newly appointed deputy governor of South Carolina, Robert Daniell. A man who had already been and would increasingly be useful to Moore's ever-larger causes.

"Daniell, it is damned good to see you. We have handily dispatched the enemy!"

If Daniell was in any way uneasy at the carnage all around him, he did not let it show. "So I see. I have come to expect no less, Colonel Moore. That is why I did not fight you when you turned down the position on the Indian trade council. We need you right where you are. If you continue to excel, there shall be no need for five men in a stuffy meeting hall to control these savages through the appearance of diplomacy. We shall simply dictate terms."

Moore nodded. He did not care at all for politicians, but he was growing fond of Daniell, who would soon be the de facto head of South Carolina, once the current deputy governor, a malcontent named Charles Craven who had made the mistake of provoking the proprietors—including his own brother William—one too many times. He was due to sail for London any day to defend his actions to the Crown and no one expected him to return. "You want something of me, is that not right?"

Daniell pointed to the man beside him. A man who looked as though he had seen both the sea and the slaughter of men, as had Moore. In other words, a man he could possibly trust. "This is Colonel William Rhett. He is—"

"No need to give me his history," Moore said, extending his hand, which Daniell's companion took with a firm and confident grip. "I am well versed in the exploits and accolades of the colonel. All good men of Carolina are. Your defense of Charles Town in aught-six was masterful. And your business acumen. Well... let me assure you, sir, my associates and I have studied your methods closely."

Moore was referring to Colonel Rhett's escapades in the mid-1690s, when he captained the *Providence*, sailing the route between the Carolinas and Bahamas, acquiring great wealth by not being choosy concerning on which side of the law his trading partners stood. With the aid of his wife, he had managed to accumulate a healthy war chest by the time a Dutch buccaneer named van Hoven captured the *Providence* in 1699.

Rhett nodded his head. "I am flattered, Colonel Moore. Your military successes are known to me as well. I look forward to our working in tandem."

Moore raised a brow. "Why, this is excellent news. Most excellent. And I suppose to be expected. It was the shrewd maneuvering by yourself and Nicholas Trott against Charles Craven that paved the way for our mutual friend Daniell here to rise to his imminent station. I am not sure we could have won the war so quickly without your intervention. And, as you may know, myself and my associates have had dealings with the outgoing deputy governor's brother, William, another of these proprietors. Still in all, we have little use of a sailing man in our present campaign…"

"We must think of the future, James," Daniell answered. "This war will not go on much longer. Meanwhile, the pirates of the Bahamas are fast becoming a rather vexing problem. Colonel Rhett has been selected to head our efforts where these rabble are concerned. Our mutual allies are most anxious that what is currently but a fleabite not be allowed to fester to a puss-filled open wound. Together, I am confident you will do great things. Now, if you will excuse us, we have a meeting with poor Charles to complete the transfer of power."

"Give Craven my best, my friend," Moore said, smiling. "May his voyage home find favorable winds." As his visitors walked away, his brother Maurice approached.

"Who was that with Daniell?" he asked.

"Another newly appointed ally, brother. One perfect for our needs."

"**H**oist, mae lads! Like ye mean it! If she falls, it weel bae a helluva long night gettin' 'er tae go back oop!"

Rob Roy MacGregor was watching carefully as a burly knot of Highlanders strained their muscles to raise the frame of an entranceway to his newly expanded barn. Things were going well for the on-again, off-again outlaw, whose deal with the rightful king James Stuart and with the Duke of Argyll had saved him from financial ruin at the hands of his nemesis, James Graham, the First Duke of Montrose.

As he watched the dozen men raise the heavy, white oak structure into place, he shifted his gaze solely to one in the middle.

Duncan had been favoring his shoulder since he had returned. Rob had asked him about it a few times over a mug of heather ale, to which he replied that he had caught a chill in it during the rough journey home from the Bahamas. Just a few nights ago, certain Duncan was lying, Rob stopped just short of asking him to remove his shirt and prove it.

Were he wrong, the already strained relationship between the two cousins might just snap, at a time when Rob could ill afford such an upset of his carefully balanced cottage of cards.

As the hammers began to swing, driving the spikes that would secure the addition to the existing frame of the barn, Rob turned to the sound of fast-approaching horses. Three men were coming over the hill, not bothering to pause to identify themselves to the sentries Rob had posted. They knew the man in the middle well, as did he. It was John Erskine, the former earl of Mar and leader of their unsuccessful battles against the false king's forces—led by Rob's new ally, the Duke of Argyll—the previous November.

Rob's head began to hurt. As shrewd as he could be in all matters political, the past year had been an axe a little too sharp to manage without drawing some of his own blood here and there every time he had to wield it.

In the case of Angus's death, it was even more than he could stand, but, the deed having been carried out as instructed by Duncan, he had to see it through. He owed Angus and all their fallen kin and comrades nothing less.

"Eh, John," he said, forcing a smile. "What brings ye hair tae Balquhidder? I haer tell yeel bae taken yer tail tae France."

Remaining atop his horse, the only sense of superiority he had left over the lying, manipulative cattleman before him, Erskine shook his head. "Nay, Rob. I am nay turnin' tail. I am left wit' nay a choice. The British Parliament has passed a Writ of Attainder fer treason again' mae. James weel give mae protection an' I weel help him continue the fight. I knoo what ye haev doon, an' ye managed tae convince the king it's right."

Rob ran his hand through his lengthening beard, dragging out knots with his chipped and battered fingernails. "Ye give mae reason tae think on what ye say, John. I haev always admired ye. Yer courage. Yer clarity a' vision. Boot watch yerself in France. Yer thinkin' yer loocky, boot things are mebbe noot what ye think they are."

Expecting Erskine to turn and leave, Rob changed his stance, placing his hand upon the pommel of his claymore, as the former earl climbed down from his horse and approached him.

"I mean ye nay harm, Rob," Erskine said, spreading his arms wide. "I only wish tae express mae condolences o'er yer nephew. 'Tis nay mickle what ye had tae doo. An' o'er a plot bae yer eldest, noo less. I see James thair, enjoyin' a cold mug while everyone else toils. Hoo caen ye—"

"I caen 'cause I ha'e tae. Mae family business bae noon a' yers. Baesides… yer the wee hen that ne'er laid away. Donnae play the innocent former laird wit' mae, John. I ha'e plenty moor fraends thaen ye doo."

Erskine retreated a step. "Troo enuff fer the moment, Rob. Boot wae booth knoo how the tide caen turn. Watch yerself. Deils abound."

As Erskine took the saddle and turned to go, Rob spit on the ground before him, mumbling to himself, "An' ye as weel, John." He then turned back to watch the work on his barn, now the biggest in the shire.

Louis. Louis. *Mon Dieu*, child! Leave that cursed mongrel alone and *listen* to me!"

For the past seven months, Philippe the Second, Duke of Orleans and Regent of France, had been cultivating a relationship—which meant cultivating his meager patience—with the heir to the throne, six-year-old Louis. It was a constant struggle for the fidgety boy's attention and loyalty, made easier only when he had banished the meddlesome Cardinal de Fleury from his role as Louis's tutor—a role he himself was now endeavoring to fill. All while forging an alliance with Britain and her allies and undoing the harsher policies, such as censorship, of his uncle, Louis the Fourteenth. The royal printing presses were hard at work from dawn until dusk replacing books that the former king had ordered banned and burned.

Opening a volume of Moliere's collected works, one of which, *Dom Juan*, Philippe had begun rehearsals for the previous week at the Comédie-Française, in of course the title role, he read aloud, "'It is not only for what we do that we are held responsible, but also for what we do not do.' Do you understand this, Louis? It is advice we must heed from the pen of the great Moliere."

Louis, who had managed to dislodge a length of piping from his brand new velvet jacket, began winding it around his squealing canine's neck. "I just want to play with my dog. And I am *hungry*…"

Slamming the book down hard enough to make the boy cry out like his dog, Philippe yelled, "You are always hungry! And if you kill your dog with that string as you seem to mean to, I will tell you… I will be most happy, for perhaps then you will learn what you must to be a better king than those that came before!"

As the boy's cries increased to the point of almost being screams, scaring away the dog before he could do it any actual harm and further fraying Philippe's nerves, the duke heard a knock at the open door.

"If you are above the age of six, you may enter," he said, creating as much distance between himself and Louis as the room would allow.

"Aye, mae duke… I see I ha'e caught ye at an eel moment. I weel moost happily return at a later time."

Recognizing the subtle brogue of John Law, a financial wizard and someone he most wanted to see, he said, "I will call the guards if I must to prevent you from going. Hold just a moment,

John, and I shall have this wailing nuisance—I mean, of course, our future king—removed." Passing his guest as he headed for the door, Philippe shouted down the hall. "Marius Adenot! Your presence is requested with all due haste by our blessed future king!"

Within moments, a handsome young man was at the door. He had answered such a call often enough in the past several months to know exactly what "Your presence is requested with all due haste by our blessed future king" actually meant.

Get this brat out of my sight before I kill him and take the throne myself.

"Marius—this is John Law. He is in the process of setting up the Banque Générale Privée for us. It will change a great deal in a very positive way for the finances of France."

Marius bowed low, his skills as a former footman serving him well. Turning to Louis, whose crying had reduced to a mere trickle of tears at the sight of Marius in the doorway, he said, "Come now, Louis. We have to get you ready. You and the duke are going to the Palais-Royal tonight to see the Comédie-Italienne. I hear that Riccoboni's players are most excellent."

Louis scrunched up his face. "But I want to—"

"Play with your dog," Marius and the duke said together. Marius continued alone. "So bring him along and do that for now. But then we must get you ready. Duke Philippe arranged for these players to travel all the way from Parma."

As Louis took Marius's hand, John Law turned to the regent. "Is that right? I haev haird ye haev baen taeken tae elevatin' the culture. I would like tae attend, if I may."

Watching Marius and Louis exit, Philippe motioned for Law to sit in a chair by his desk.

"He seems a good lad, this Marius Adenot," Law said, pulling a sheaf of papers from his jacket. "Apt tae doo yer will."

"He should be," Philippe replied, taking the papers. "I make it possible for him to enjoy a prolonged and most energetic—so I hear—dalliance with a certain young temptress named Eleonore Fouquet."

Law raised a brow. "Fouquet? A relation, nay doubt, a' Nicolas, the viscount an' former finance sooperintendaent tae Louis the Ferteenth."

The duke smiled. He had chosen this Scotsman well. "The same. So you see how useful our young Marius will be as we launch the Banque Générale Privée. So much more than a footman and nursemaid that boy will be, at least for as long as he holds the attention of Eleonore Fouquet. Although, from the way she smiles any time she is here—which is more often than legitimate reasons would dictate—I do feel confident that time is on our side."

Baron. William. Craven.

These three words had begun to feel like a rotting tooth in Lord Andrew Colson's jaw. Ever since the New Year's ritual at the Mammon Lodge, when Craven had accepted the demon's kiss of blood and become a full-fledged member, Craven had seemed a different man.

Or was he something else entirely?

Although this transformation was the essence of the ritual, in which the recipient accepted the help of the powerful entity that answered to the name of Mammon in exchange for doing the infernal monster's bidding, Colson had never seen such a marked and thorough change. He certainly had experienced nothing even close when he had endured his own initiation. Then again, no former initiate had ever been as unmanly and skeptical as Baron William Craven.

Colson had to give Lord Carteret credit. He had seen something in Craven that Colson had not.

It was too bad he would have to betray his friend and benefactor. But the time had come for a change.

Leafing through his papers in preparation for a meeting of the shareholders of the Royal African Company, Colson realized he had not read a single word. It was no matter—he knew what he wished to say. The papers full of accounting columns and strategic objectives were mostly just a show, giving him something to do as the most powerful lords in London, among them Craven and Carteret, made their way into the room.

"Ah, Andrew. Early as usual," Lord Carteret said, patting him on the shoulder. "When I finally decide to let go the reins, the RAC shall be in able hands indeed."

"Although we pray that is no time soon, My Lord," Craven said, sauntering up beside them in a bright red coat, ostentatiously long and fancy lace protruding from its brocaded collar and cuffs.

Ignoring Craven as he always had, Colson stood to full height in an effort to remove Carteret's hand from his shoulder. Looking his (on paper) superior in the eye, he said, "I of course agree with that sentiment. If you wish to call the meeting to order, I have the monthly reports to make."

"I shall, Andrew," Lord Carteret answered, "although—and I meant to tell you sooner—there is a change to the agenda. Baron Craven will have the floor for the entirety of the meeting. He has much to tell us about his considerable progress in the Carolinas. Progress that will further strengthen the RAC's assets and allow us to meet head on the challenges to market share caused by our neighbors, the East India Company. I would have kept you better up to date, but the Family is working with a new contact—one that prefers to deal only with the baron and Edward Moseley, and their gang of colonial thugs. Leave your reports with our secretary and he shall see they are copied and shared."

Hiding his anger at this clear affront and deviation from protocol as best he could (*meant to tell you sooner, my freckled backside...*) Colson placed his papers on the table. "Whatever is best for the Royal African Company, My Lord." Impressing himself with the evenness of his tone, Colson—dismissing the dangerous idea to leave—took his seat.

Sending Craven to the front of the room to prepare, Carteret leaned in close to Andrew, whispering in his ear, "What do you have in process with the fallen and fickle Bolingbroke?"

Plenty, Andrew thought, *not that it's your business*.

"Very little," he said aloud, shaking his head in faux exasperation. "The man moves like molasses. He is easily sidetracked with a plethora of doomed-to-fail endeavors. He is fickle, as you say. Once I have his list of contacts, rest assured I shall inform you."

"Excellent, my friend. And no hard feelings about Craven's new prominence here and at the Lodge, eh? No doubt Mammon's attention will once more be focused on us both. Craven is fresh and eager. Mammon's newest toy."

As Carteret walked toward the front of the room, calling the meeting to order as he did so, Andrew began to ponder Carteret's words. "*Will once more be focused on us* both."

So the leader of the Lodge was feeling the slight as well.

It was a feeling to which he should become accustomed.

For there was so much more to come.

There were few things more deadly or invigorating than a sudden squall rising up amidst a battle on the water, and Samuel Bellamy was relishing every second of the rush of adrenaline sweeping through his body at every crack of thunder or boom of the guns.

"Keep 'em hot, men!" he yelled as the Spanish frigate *Fidela* sought to bring nearly half of her thirty deadly cannon to bear on the six-gun sloop that Commodore Hornigold had given Bellamy to command as a test run for a more permanent appointment as soon as the opportunity arose.

An opportunity that he just might be in the midst of seizing.

Which is why he had taken a chance on the chaos of the storm. In fair weather, his six-gun sloop would not have had a chance in hell of taking a frigate like the one grappling with the swells before him. But *Fidela* was slow and heavy, unable to navigate as efficiently as the pirate's sleek, maneuverable sloop, and so he had taken her into his sights and ordered a pursuit.

As the *Fidela* fought the waves, Bellamy turned his glass toward the sound of snapping sails and a shout of concern from his men. Two ships were approaching. One was the *Marianne*, Hornigold's flagship, upon which Edward Thache served as sailing master and William Howard as quartermaster. They were a trio unparalleled in the Caribbean, although Sam, with the help of his own sailing master, Paulsgrave Williams, was quickly developing a reputation almost equal to those he most admired. Forcing his eye to focus farther through the gale to identify the other vessel, Sam felt his heart skip a beat.

"Damn it all," he muttered, identifying her as the *Ranger*, commanded by the cutthroat Captain Vane. He wondered how hard it would be to let an "errant" cannonball smash his rival's mainmast to splinters...

Before he could further consider such a serious action, Williams was at his side. "Look smart, Captain Bellamy. *Fidela* will be getting into position to destroy us as the storm starts to slacken. Whatever small advantage we have had will soon be utterly lost. It appears Captain Hornigold has arrived in the nick of time."

As Sam nodded in agreement, he heard the sound of the *Marianne* firing the cannon at her bow, and a moment later the sound of explosions and dying men on the decks of the frigate *Fidela.*

"Shall we follow her success with a volley of our own?" the chief gunner asked, the tone in his voice begging for a yes.

Sam, somewhat sadly, could not comply. "Stay the guns, Mister Morris. Another direct hit and there won't be anything left to salvage." As the longer *Marianne* came to rest beside his sloop, Sam offered greetings and thanks to her commander and her crew. "I fear ye saved us from a bite too big to chew with the storm so suddenly easing. If it had only kept up strength, we no doubt would have had her."

As Hornigold's officers readied their men to board the Spanish frigate at the sound of her captain's orders to hoist their white flag in surrender, the commodore tipped his tricorne. "I admire your strategy and fortitude, Mister Bellamy. So much so, that your crew will enjoy two thirds of whatever spoils—"

Hornigold's words were lost as a volley of cannon fire was let loose from the deck of Charles Vane's ship. Sam could hear one of the projectiles as it whistled past his sloop.

Hornigold was moving from starboard to port across the quarterdeck of the *Marianne* to confront the approaching raider. "Are you mad, man?" he yelled. "Hold your damnable fire! The prize is ours. Ye have no claim to her, Vane. I order ye to withdraw!"

As the *Ranger* forced herself between Bellamy's sloop and the *Marianne*, all of the officers on the trio of ships pulled their pistols, readying—and some even welcoming—a fight.

Tensions had been mounting the past three weeks, as Vane and his rabble had taken several English ships, in contravention to Hornigold's orders and the agreement of the republic of pirates he was struggling to forge.

"I don't take ordahs from ye, old man," Vane said, spitting a thick, green glob of God knew what on the *Marianne*'s starboard gunnel, not two feet from where Hornigold and his officers stood. "As a mattah a' fact, I 'ave taken ta defyin' 'em every chance I get, or 'aven't ye noticed. Now, ya gives me that greasy frigate or I will ordah me men ta fire these guns, an' this time it won' be jus' a warnin'."

Edward Thache cocked his pistol, pointing it squarely at Vane's forehead. "Just give the order, Captain Hornigold, an' we will gladly gut these vermin."

"Stand down, Edward. All of ye. Stand down." Hornigold stuck his pistol in his belt and indicated again for his hesitate crew to follow. "Give the order, Mister Bellamy, to your crew, if ye would please."

Not understanding Hornigold's position and contemplating defiance, Sam heard the click of additional pistols and muskets on the *Ranger*. He would have to trust his commodore. The last thing they needed was any further demonstration of the lack of cohesion among the Caribbean pirate crews for the amusement of the Spanish, who had arrayed themselves along their decks wondering to whom they would be surrendering.

Their captain would no doubt report what they saw to Madrid.

"Ye heard him, men. Lower your weapons."

As movement and muttering filled the space around him, Sam noticed a crewman on the *Ranger* pulling a pistol from his belt.

It was Joseph Stanton.

"Angus! Angus, ya bastard! I see ya there, hidin' behind yer bodyguard. Move aside, Mister Thache. That dirty blackguard owes me fer destroying my family an' I am ready fer payment in full."

The *Marianne*'s sailing master moved position not an inch.

Sam stepped closer to the gunnel for a better view—and angle, should the shooting start—as Angus moved around his bulky protector, stepping fearlessly into the path of Stanton's pistol.

"Tis noot 'blackguard,' Joseph. Tis MacBlaquart. Conall MacBlaquart. I am nae longer the numpty lad who forced ye intae that alley in Boston. Althoo, given the chance, I would surely doo it again."

Since the incident with Duncan MacDonald eight weeks earlier, Angus had begun to grow a beard. He was also getting extra rations of food and physically demanding duties to help him build muscle and fill out his frame. He had been away from New Providence, mostly on the *Marianne*, with increasing frequency, learning more of the duties of the brethren of the sea. For those that only knew him in passing, the changes were enough to begin to disguise him and his nom de guerre was starting to stick.

Sam was also working with him on diminishing his brogue, although far less progress was being made in that particular area, much to his disappointment.

"Keep yer heid, mate. I doan think ye ken what yer doon," Angus continued, showing an impressive amount of fortitude in the face of Stanton's pistol.

Then again, Sam thought, *tis becoming a regular occurrence with this willful son of the Highlands.*

In answer, Joseph moved his thumb to cock his pistol, but Vane stayed his hand. "Leave off now, Joseph. Can ye see 'is eyes? Tis somethin' changed about 'em." Taking the pistol from Stanton, Vane aimed his glare at Angus. "Don't know what 'appened ta ye, whatever yer callin' yerself, an' I don' much care. But I don' want bloodshed here tahday. None of us do, save for this damned 'othead 'ere. An' one day, of *my* choosin', 'e shall get 'is revenge. I want that Spanish frigate, an' I am gettin' what I want." Spreading his arms in a sign of peace, he next addressed Hornigold. "That agreeable ta ya, Gran'pa?"

Damned clever of you, Vane, Hornigold thought, nodding his head. He was all but sure the wily rogue had staged the incident with Stanton ahead of time. As he ordered the crews of the *Marianne* and Bellamy's sloop to make way, he tried to control the shaking in his legs.

Charles Vane now had the upper hand and hard pressed was Hornigold to stem the carnage that was certainly soon to come.

PART TWO:

FROM PEACEFUL FARMER TO PIRATE

Laden with sugar, bananas, and rum, the French merchant vessel *Marie Louise* had been at sea less than eight hours when her chief mate, Alexandre Colombe, spied what could only be flames in the darkness not far beyond their bow.

Ringing the ship's bell, Colombe had barely removed his pistol from his sash when the master of the vessel, Jean-Paul Bisset, was up the ladder from the hold and standing beside him, spyglass in hand.

"What eez it, Colombe?" Bisset asked, taking in a sharp draught of air as he also spied the steadily approaching flames.

"Do you see, *mon capitaine*, why I rang zee bell? Such a sight could only mean one zhing. Shall I summon zee rest of zee crew?"

Capitaine Bisset, a veteran privateer who had seen plenty of bloody engagements during the War of Spanish Succession, placed his spyglass in its holder and shook his head. "*Non*, Alexandre. The larger show of force, zee worse zees weel go. You must remain calm."

As the two dozen men on the approaching periague began to release a series of high-pitched shrieks that might make a lesser man's blood run cold, Capitaine Bisset smiled. "Zey are just trying to scare us, *mon ami*. Do not let zem succeed, eh?"

When the large canoe reached them, Capitaine Bisset called down, "Rogues! I know who you are, an' what you want! There ees no need for zees show! Come aboard an' we weel see to your needs."

Alexandre leaned in, the look of concern on his face further deepening the already pronounced lines at his mouth and brow. "*Mon capitaine*, will you surrender so easily? If the men should see such a cowardly display..."

Bisset pursed his lips, tilting his head and squinting his eyes in a show of contemplation. "Alexandre. You are *très* bold, eh? But you are also perhaps correct. It could be I am being too hasty, eh? After all, there are not many of zem an' we hold, for now, zee high ground, as eet were. Very weel—summon zee rest of zee crew. *Rapidement*, Alexandre! Do eet!"

As his chief mate disappeared below, Bisset straightened his collar and coat before placing his hand on the hilt of his sword. God willing, this would not go as far as his having to remove it from its scabbard, but Alexandre's remarks had necessitated going in another direction than what Bisset had first envisioned.

While the men in the periague lit more torches, Alexandre and the fifteen members of the *Marie Louise*'s crew crowded onto the deck.

"*Mon Dieu!*" one of the crewman muttered, getting a good look at the men in the boat below them. "Zay are savages! Look at zem! Zeir wild hair, zeir painted, half-naked bodies! *Mon capitaine*, I beg of you—give zem what zay want an' let us be on our way! I have a wife, two leetle girls…"

"I know zis, Pierre," Bisset replied. "But I cannot be weak. I am tasked with a great responsibility. Our holds are full an' zee owner of zees ship must not be disappointed by thinking we are *lâche*, eh?"

No man on board the *Marie Louise* was willing to admit to cowardice.

"*Très bien* zen," Bisset replied, placing his hand more firmly on his sword. "We shall do our best."

As the crew on the merchant ship muttered amongst themselves, steeling their resolve for whatever was to come, a tall man in the bow of the periague called up, "I demand to address the captain of this vessel!"

Bisset raised his arm. "I am Capitaine Jean-Paul Bisset! Zees crew an' zees ship are my responsibility, as is eets cargo. With whom am I making parley?"

The man in the boat drew his sword as he raised his torch to illuminate better the flag that flew at his bow. "I am Samuel Bellamy, of Nassau, New Providence. I intend to board this vessel, Captain Bisset, and relieve her of half of her goods, plus my needs in sheets and cordage. Ye can see from my flag that I am a pirate, as are my companions, and we shall not be denied."

And so it begins in earnest, Bisset thought, wondering if the responsibility he continued to carry was becoming too great for the meager rewards it brought.

"Capitaine Bellamy, we weel not give in to such demands. Zees ship an' eets cargo are bound for France. We may be fewer zan you, but we are brave an' unafraid. Much blood weel be spilled in your tiny leetle boat before this night is through."

"Very well, Bisset," Sam answered, handing his torch to one of his equally savage-looking crew and pulling another flag, this one solid red, from the bow of the boat. "Being French, ye know what this is, and what it means."

Indeed the capitaine did. The *joli rouge* meant no quarter. It meant Bellamy would take more than he needed and more lives than he would otherwise prefer. It meant that instead of Bisset returning to France with half his cargo and light on cordage and sheets, but with his crew and ship intact, he might not return at all.

"*Oui*, Capitaine Bellamy. I know it weel. For I flew it many times as a privateer for my beloved France."

"Then what say ye to it, sir? Do ye give me what I demand of ye, without further fuss or fight, or do I hoist this *joli rouge* in place of the bones and black and do what I must to see my mission done?"

Just as I knew it would be, Bisset thought, barely succeeding in hiding a grin. *Oh, what leetle has changed in* le monde *since zee supposed end of zee war*. "*Très bien*, mon capitaine, you have convinced me. Let us enact our transaction so we might both be on our way. I weel send down a ladder for you."

Bisset knew well enough what Bellamy's series of birdcalls to the darkness behind his boat that followed the acquiescence meant. A well-armed pirate ship would soon be joining them, ready to take what Bellamy demanded. With luck, they would not ask for silver or gold, nor would they take his ship.

As Bellamy climbed aboard, the crew of the *Marie Louise* parted as if they had rehearsed it a hundred times, revealing a sinewy, elaborately tatooed Chinese male coming up from the entrance to the hold wielding two vicious-looking straight swords with both edges honed to razor-sharpness.

In an instant, every pirate on the periague had pistols and muskets trained on the man, who showed no sign of heeding their implied command to halt his progress or die.

To everyone's surprise, on both the merchantman and in the periague, Bellamy stood still, not drawing his pistol, nor raising his sword in defense. Instead, he calmly said, "All of ye—hold your fire." As they strained their brains to process his command, Bellamy further confused them by sliding his sword into its scabbard, spreading his arms wide, and saying, "Xiang Yu, my old friend! Damn, it's been too long…"

*I*f the bees would just stop buzzing, I could enter the hive…
If the bees would just stop buzzing, I could enter the hive…

If the bees would just stop buzzing…
Then they did.
"Her response is not what I had hoped, Nurse Stiles. I suspect that my protocols were not—"
"I followed the protocols, doctor. Perhaps they are inappropriate for this particular subject. It has been weeks…"
"Nurse Stiles!" The doctor paused, collecting himself. "Forgive me. Passions run high. Reports are due to be filed… My dear Anita… you are invaluable to me. Your work with the CEO of— well, with our VIP subject of a year ago—was well beyond reproach. The data extracted made TRG's acquisition of his most valuable IP unimpeachable. I need not remind you that it is to TRG that we are answering now. Perhaps this patient is stronger than we thought."
Through a haze of pain, showing up as swirling reds and pulsing purples just behind her eyelids, Dr. Kirstine MacGregor strained to make sense of what she was hearing. Through her semi-conscious daze she fought for focus, desperate for clues to help her piece together just what it was that had taken place once she had left her fifth floor office at the Smithsonian's National Museum of American History after her confrontation with her boss, Director Flavian.
As a red-hot poker of pain stabbed the base of her brain, Kirstine forced her mind to focus.
Walking quickly down Constitution Avenue…
Was she being followed?
Those two men? Had they been in the lobby when she left?
Must get to the post office…
The post office!
The thumb drive. *Jake*…
It all came flooding back in split-second images cascading in a molten mental collage.
What had she been thinking, involving him?
"Jake!"
Had she said his name out loud?

"Doctor." It was the female. The nurse that he called Stiles. *Anita*... "Look at her eyelids. See the movement beneath them? She's awake. And in quite an agitated state. I'll prepare a sedative..."

Kirstine tried to raise her hand as one of her tormentors placed a cold clamp on the pointer finger of her right hand, but her wrists... her arms... her legs... her neck! were all held in place.

She was a prisoner in some sort of hospital nightmare.

Wake up, dammit! she willed herself.

Still she could not move.

"Look at the brain activity, Anita." The doctor sounded fascinated and beside himself with joy. "These areas here, in the temporal lobe. These are the ones I want to access. They are finally waking up."

Kirstine felt a firm hand on her shoulder. It was rough and cold, even through her hospital gown.

"Kirstine. Listen to me closely. It is all right. We are here to help you. You have been through a most traumatic series of experiences. Gently open your eyes and let us be of service."

Despite her internal warning systems all screaming at her not to, Kirstine was focusing on the quality of the doctor's voice. It was soft and soothing, with the faintest hint of a German accent.

So she opened her eyes.

"There's the girl. I am Doctor Friedrich Reinhardt. This is Nurse Anita Stiles. We have been very worried about you, dear."

Unable to shield her eyes from the blinding lights above, against which the doctor and nurse were dark, distorted shadow figures, because her hands were bound, Kirstine quickly closed her eyes again.

"That's fine, my girl. Keep them closed. All of this is easier with both eyes closed."

Although her dry throat made her words but a sandpaper whisper that set her throat aflame, Kirstine managed to say, "Tell me where I am."

"You are in my care." That was from the nurse.

"I need to speak to Jake. Jake—"

Why couldn't she remember his last name?

"Ah. Jake." The doctor again. "I am sorry to tell you this, my girl, but Jake is no longer with us. I am afraid the rigors of his resistance forced the men sent to undo your dire mistake and retrieve what was never yours to give away to do what they do in such a way that no one would be expected to survive it. Especially not one so ill-equipped and frail as the late, lamented Mister Givens…"

Kirstine began to weep.

Jake was dead, because of her.

She felt a pinch in her forearm. A needle.

I'll prepare a sedative…

"There, there. You must rest. This all can be made right, you know. Amends are what we need. What *Jake* needs. Just lie back and listen to the bees…"

As Kirstine's head began to swim in a chemically induced fog, she heard them. A massive swarm surrounding her.

If the bees would just keep buzzing, I could hide the hive…

If the bees would just keep buzzing, I could hide the hive…

If the bees would just keep buzzing…

The bees…

46 Princes of the World

Edward Thache watched in wonderment as Samuel Bellamy, fresh off his success in raiding the French merchantman *Marie Louise* without spilling a drop of blood, stood high in the ratlines of the mainmast of the sloop he had been captaining—a ship that he had quickly outgrown—addressing several sizable crews arrayed along the beach.

"I tell ye this, my brave and hearty men," Bellamy said, his voice full of thunder, "we are, each and every one of us, princes of the world! And we have as much right to make war upon a world that would deny us our natural rights as any king with two hundred thousand men in the field and two hundred ships upon the sea! These so-called noblemen in England and elsewhere, waging their wars for private gain with no thought to the lives that they destroy, for the hardships they inflict on young and old alike, dare to declare us *hostis humani generis*—enemies of all mankind! They vilify us, the scoundrels do, when the difference is only this: They rob the poor under cover of their laws while we rob the rich under cover of our courage! So let us move forward with all the resolve we can muster—to practice equality by redistributing wealth from those who have falsely earned it to those who are starving in the streets, to champion liberty wherever we find those who are imprisoned, and let us always remember our brotherhood—our oath to one another and to our noble cause!"

"Huzzah for Captain Bellamy!" someone from the now almost feverishly stirred-up crowd shouted, quickly joined by hundreds of others, all in one ferocious voice.

"Huzzah! Huzzah! Huzzah!"

If he gets any more popular with the crews, Edward thought, *he shall give our Commodore Hornigold a dangerous run for his money.*

Fifteen minutes later, after the crews had dispersed to the inns around the island to spend the bulk of their recent bounty, Edward entered the captain's quarters on Sam's modest sloop. Bellamy was studying a set of maps laid out before him on his desk.

With him was the Chinese warrior Sam had greeted upon and then taken with him from the *Marie Louise*.

Clapping his hands together to announce his presence, Edward said, standing in the doorway, "Apologies, I did not know ye were—"

Rolling the maps, which he handed to his companion, Sam said, "Just finishing. It has been a long time since I have seen my friend Xiang Yu. We were reminiscing about the past." Motioning with his head for the Chinese man to exit, Sam followed him around the desk, where he stood in the middle of the room to receive his latest visitor.

"To what do I owe the pleasure, Edward?"

Resisting the urge to watch the Chinese warrior exit, Edward instead smiled. "Do you actually believe half of what you say, Sam?"

"No, I do not, Edward," Sam said, his face looking grave. "I believe every word of it! As should ye. Ye will not be sailing master for long. Ye will soon have your own ship and crew. And your men will rely on ye to meet their moral and spiritual needs—not just their nautical ones. To remind them why it is we are out on the account. Now, my friend, what brings ye aboard my all too humble sloop?"

Trying to process all that Sam had said, Edward found himself unable to answer. In truth, he was regretting coming aboard.

"Moral and spiritual needs…" he began, trying not to let his lack of education in such matters betray him. "These are simple men, Sam. Many of them are like me—once the Royal Navy cut tens of thousands of us loose without so much as a 'thank ye for your service,' we had nowhere else to go. Those who carried a letter of marque, or served as crew on a successful privateer… well, I do not need to lay out the mathematics of it. Ye and Hornigold—your hopes for a fraternity, for a Republic. Perhaps, one far away day. But if ye push too far, too fast ye shall only succeed in making the men distrust ye."

Pouring them each a mug of rum, Sam motioned for Edward to sit. "I appreciate your honesty. Your concern. I do. But the cause for which we fight is greater than ye and I. And I know this, my friend—the men are hungry for meaning. For a cause. For moral and spiritual grass on which to graze. We simply need to shepherd them." Taking a long drink, he added, "While we are being so honest with each other, I am glad ye are here. I have been giving some thought to ye and your inevitable captaincy."

Edward raised a brow as he brought his mug to his lips. Downing the contents and wiping his mouth with his sleeve, he asked, "Have ye now?"

Sam nodded, moving closer to his comrade. "Ye have great potential, Edward. Ye are tall and strong like a mythic warrior of old, come down from Scandinavia to raid the fractured kingdoms of

England. The men fear ye simply for your size and strength. Ye should make full use of it. Could come in handy as we go after bigger prizes, helmed by prideful captains."

Leaning forward in his chair, Edward said, extending his mug for more rum, "Ye have my attention, Sam. Fully."

Pouring a generous draft for Edward, Sam stepped into the lantern light as though he were an actor readying for his monologue. "Excellent. First, ye should let your hair and beard grow long. It is working for Angus in his new persona as Conall... what is it? MacBlaquart. A bit much I think. Though his transformation is beginning to fit the role."

"Agreed. Grow my hair and beard. I will do that without question."

"Next, when your beard is long enough, ye should braid it."

"Braid it?"

Sam nodded. "And that is not the end of it. Once it is braided, tie bright red ribbons in it!"

Edward stood, once more regretting having come to Sam's cabin. "Ribbons in my beard? Rubbish! Will that not make me look insane?"

Again Sam nodded. "Exactly. Play their natural fear of ye as fully as you can." A mischievous grin spreading on his face, he added, "Speaking of things that look insane... all of the men are talking about the lit fuses ye put beneath your tricorne. I hear the Spanish have taken to calling you *El Diablo*. Tis damned brilliant. Keep doing it."

"Fine," Edward answered, shaking his head. "But I do not do it to look like the devil."

Sam pursued his lips. "Really? Then why *do* you do it? Looks rather painful."

Edward again wished he were elsewhere. "I would rather not say."

"Come now," Sam said, once more filling Edward's mug. "Whatever your secret may be, I promise it stays in this room."

"Very well, then," Edward answered, taking a long drink of rum. "Tis because I hate mosquitoes."

For a moment, Sam said nothing, thinking his friend was having him on. But the look on Edward's face—part embarrassment, part regret—convinced him otherwise. "Never mention that to anyone ever again. Now, there is one more thing: You must always wear at least two pistols across your chest, although a trio of braces would be ideal. Ye certainly have the long torso and broad shoulders for it."

Draining him mug, Edward smiled. "THAT I will happily do. Now Sam, if I agree to buy ye a fancy dinner worthy of such a tale as ye will no doubt tell, will ye share with me the story of how ye came to be as ye are? I have been around enough to know that deep convictions such as yours come at a price dearly paid."

"Gladly my friend. For your insights and assessment are true."

Twenty minutes later, at a back table in the least popular of the taverns on the island, as a rack of pig ribs launched their aromatic steam into the air between them, Sam began his tale.

I was born on a day, March 18, 1689, that would live on in the memories of my father and six sisters, not primarily as the day I entered this world but the black and desperate day that my mother, Elizabeth, or Libby as my father called her, departed it. Not that they were ever cruel to me about it. After all, I was the baby of the family, looked after by my eldest sisters as my father worked the fields and tended the livestock that kept us out of debt and protected the land that had been in our family for, as my father told it, as long as anyone had inhabited it. He told us tales by the fire each night of the Dumnonii tribe of Britons who had withstood the influence of the Romans and managed to remain in the violent times of the Anglo-Saxons and the Viking raiders. Our family allied with William the Conqueror and his barons and ultimately withstood the French when they came to try to take what we had always owned. My father never would speak, no matter how we begged him, of the time of Cromwell and whatever deals the Bellamys made with his agents to ensure that my grandfather kept the family lands, but we all do what we must. My father made that clear enough when pressed.

Not to skip too far ahead in my narrative, but I suppose that Devon men have always been strong and independent, especially when it comes to sailing the seas. We number Francis Drake, Walter Raleigh, and Henry Every amongst our greatest mariners and it was their stories that were told by the fire on the most special of occasions, especially to the boys from the surrounding farmsteads and myself.

I think my father always knew that I would take my place with the sailors who left Devon looking for something more. Perhaps it was something in my eyes or simply that he would be happier to not have to look upon my face, which so resembled my mother's, and wished to hide his loathing with well wishes for a more prosperous future than his.

Although, as I said, such cruel thoughts were never shared aloud. I grew up strong, never plagued by the ailments that took so many other children and other wives and mothers during childbirth and began working side by side with my father, who was popular amongst the other rural farmers. So much so that, when there were disputes concerning the common lands that the families used for grazing, it was my father who presided. They referred to him as the

Sword of Solomon for his intelligence and sense of fairness in settling disputes.

And so it was, when I had just passed my thirteenth birthday, that word was brought from Exeter that a powerful lord, an ally of the sixth earl, John Cecil, had instructed my father to leave immediately for the earl's castle.

Much to my surprise, as the sun rose, my father ordered me to prepare my things to travel the fourteen miles with him. "It's about time ye see what the world is truly like, Samuel," he said as we climbed atop our horses.

When we arrived, the earl's servants were readying the midday meal. I noticed with a growing pit in the center of my belly that no one would look at us. It was as though they were passing ghosts.

We were taken to a large room where a nobleman sat at the end of a long oaken table, his clothing and jewelry fancier and more gleaming and clean than any I had ever seen. Beside him stood a boy, not much older than myself. As the nobleman looked with disdain upon us while he devoured his meal, he threw lamb bones and bits of bread and fruit to a pair of mongrels at his feet.

We were offered nothing.

"Are you the Sword of Solomon I have heard so much about?" This was said through a mouthful of fowl he had torn from its bones with his teeth—grizzle, cartilage, and all.

My father bowed. "That is not a name I call myself, My Lord. I am Stephen Bellamy, humble servant of the earl. If I might speak to him…"

Dropping the picked-clean bones to the floor, the noble leaned back in his chair, expelling a belch with such force that it echoed off the walls.

"The earl has been called away. Which is why I have summoned you at this time. Since you are so wise as to claim comparison with one of the wisest kings who ever sat a throne, answer me this—who owns the common lands over which you are said to preside?"

Though I stood several feet away from him, I could feel my father's arms and torso tense. My being such a simple son of a farmer, his hesitation in replying to such a straightforward question confused me.

Until I heard the nobleman's answer to his silence.

"You are not so quick to speak when in the presence of your betters. I can see that well enough. Though I wonder… is this humility or its opposite? Think you too good to speak to me, to answer my questions when you have interrupted my meal by not coming with due urgency when called? Well, which is it?"

My father began to clench and unclench his hands, something I had never seen him do. His halting voice, also new to me, seemed a product of his throat opening and closing in time with his fists. "My Lord, uh… Sir, I apologize that I do not know to whom it is I am speaking… I spend little time in Exeter and—"

"Which is as it should be. You are nothing, you peasant. *Nothing*. Do you understand? To call you Solomon is to call these dogs Ramses and Charlemagne. And so," the nobleman now stood up, pushing against the table to move his chair to make room for his paunch, "I ask you again, and for the final time—who owns the common lands over which you falsely reign as arbiter in Hittisleigh?"

My father, who had been staring at the ground through the nobleman's tirade, now looked up. "No one, my lord."

When the nobleman laughed, I witnessed my father turn pale.

"Whoever refers to you as Solomon is as ignorant as dirt. Because you answer incorrectly. *I do*, you maggoty spot of vomit. As of yesterday morning, I, Lord Richard Colson, do own the former common lands of Hittisleigh. Is that clear?"

"Yes, Lord Colson, it is," my father whispered.

Turning to the boy beside him, who was watching the proceedings with a smile that, even as an innocent of barely thirteen years, I knew was one of utter superiority over others, Colson said, "Andrew, do you see with what I have to contend? These farmers are like the cattlemen in the unruly Highlands of Scotland. They forget themselves. Give them a little land, a little space, and they think they have control over their lives. We much teach them the truth. And teach them young at that, before the sickness of rebellion spreads and they stand before you claiming to be Solomon when they are no better than the louts who beg outside our home in London. And you must learn as well, my son. Learn that words are not the language of submission. That we must use other, stronger tools."

As the boy nodded, my father put up his hands, a premonition of some kind about what was readying to transpire. "My lord, I will do what you require of me… There is no need to—"

"Yes you will and yes there is," Colson replied, taking an ornate, silver-tipped walking stick from beside his chair and handing it to his son. "Teach the boy, Andrew. Teach him well, that you might never have to suffer the insults you have witnessed this oh so kingly pile of nothing thrust upon your father."

What happened next unfolded so quickly that neither my father nor I were able to move the slightest bit before Lord Colson whistled and four guards appeared from the shadowed corners of the room, taking my father and me by the arms. The two that held me, at a nod from their master, forced me to my knees.

As I struggled vainly against them, I heard my father say, "Be still, Samuel. It will be over quicker if you close your eyes and let it run its course. Do not let them break you. The bruises and cuts will heal. Do not let them take your dignity. For once removed, it cannot be replaced."

A moment later the boy was standing over me, the walking stick held high above his head. As the blows rained down upon me for what seemed the better part of an hour, although it lasted less than a minute, I took my father's advice and did not struggle nor let it break my spirit.

As for my eyes, I kept them open, that I might better burn the image of my tormentor into my mind.

For the next two weeks, my father did the bidding of Colson's agents. Worst of all was the initial announcement, which he was forced to make in his role of arbiter, calling to mind the sign tacked to the cross of Jesus Christ proclaiming him king of the Jews—a claim he never made himself.

All grazing livestock were removed from the commons to each individual farmstead to which they belonged—necessitating the re-designation of land once used for crops to provide acreage for them to graze, which meant a reduction in foodstuffs for family consumption and for barter and sale. Next, a fence was built around the perimeter and signs were posted threatening arrest to any man who crossed it and the seizure of any livestock that wandered into it.

As my father suffered humiliation upon humiliation as Colson's spokesman, my sisters nursed my wounds—mostly deep bruises and shallow cuts. The boy had not broken any bones and for some reason for which I found myself thankful, avoided blows to my face.

My father did not speak of it, a luxury I allowed him given the burdens he now bore.

With winter soon to be upon us and the common grazing area no longer available for sustaining livestock, my father was forced into a most unhappy choice. Abandoning his family's—*our* family's—lands, he would take us due east the one hundred and fifty miles to Portsmouth, where we would find work amongst the tradesmen rather than do the bastard Colson's bidding while we slowly but inevitably starved.

It was hard going from the start. We did not take well to the crowding, stench, and violence of the city after spending all of our lives in the country. It being winter, work was scarce. Nearly non-existent for those with only farming skills such as ours. My father retreated further and further into himself, developing a nightly ritual of drinking himself to sleep while my sisters worked piecemeal in the sewing and servant trades.

When I turned fourteen, I made a decision of my own. The stories of Sir Francis Drake and Henry Avery were always in my head, especially those of the feats of Avery, who had led a mutiny and then gone on to take the treasure ship of the grand moghul himself! And, as if this were not heroic enough, he claimed the moghul's daughter for a wife and was said to live a life of unimaginable wealth as a powerful pirate king, having made a trade agreement with Governor Trott here in the Bahamas when I was all of seven.

Avery's accomplishments foremost in my mind—for it would be many years until I was told the truth of Avery's poverty and obscurity at the time of his death—I was determined to turn to the sea as a means to changing my fate. I knew the life would be hard, but my appetite was putting a strain on the family's ability to feed itself and there were moments that I overheard my sisters lamenting the loss of our mother. Still, they pointed no fingers at their poor baby brother, but I knew by the way they looked at me whom they held to blame.

Having committed myself to the sea, it remained only to choose one of two routes—the Royal Navy or the merchant fleet. I had already seen plenty of the Royal Navy's atrocities in Portsmouth and heard tell of many more as I swept the floors and cleaned the tables in the local taverns. Vicious captains, poor rations, injury, sickness, and death all abounded on the decks and in the dark, dangerous holds of the ships of the Royal Navy.

And then there were the press gangs. Ruthless as Colson they were, pulling men out of their shops, or off the docks as they passed, or, worst of all, breaking down doors in the middle of the night, carrying away sons, brothers, and fathers who were never seen nor heard from again. Perhaps it was my lack of an applicable trade or just dumb luck that had thus far spared me, but my father and I agreed that it was only a matter of time. The war was ratcheting up and all of the families in Portsmouth lived in fear.

As winter began to ease, I bid farewell to my sisters while my father was sleeping off a two-night bout with the bottle in a drafty room upstairs. I was going to London. Two days earlier, I had signed on with a privateer whose owner had just received a letter of marque. It was a fine twelve-gun vessel, sleek and well captained by a kind man named Forster who took me under his protection. I had watched for a week as she was fitted out for the making of war and the taking of French and Spanish ships before I had approached him.

Taking on more men, munitions, and provisions in London, we went where the action was, scoring our victories and weathering our defeats. Forster was a fair and even-handed leader, and his crew was fiercely loyal. As for me, I was a fast learner and committed to bettering my prospects, so I continued to rise amongst the ranks for the next ten years, until I was able to handle myself below decks, in the rigging, manning the long guns, or working at the helm. I also learned the skills and experienced the horrors of fighting with men up close and what it meant to take a life, especially one in such close proximity that your opponent's last breath sat within your ear for hours.

Everything would change for me when we ran afoul of a pair of Spanish frigates near Tortuga as we ushered in the hard year 1713 and barely escaped with our lives. Captain Forster, by this time an exceedingly wealthy man, had no reason to continue to tempt fate and declared his intention to retire to a fine house he had ordered built near to the wharves in Boston.

Having no desire to serve under anyone else and with my pockets lined with enough coin to pick my prospects, at least for the coming months, I joined him.

How fateful that choice would be.

CAPE COD, MASSACHUSETTS COLONY, SUMMER 1713

As a man of twenty-four years, with little practical experience outside of farming and the maritime trades, I was determined to find a source of income and settle down. Although the years of war had opened my eyes to inequities and abuses that had forever made their mark upon me, I had a thought to practicing the law or another peaceful means of righting wrongs. Such a commitment would mean stability and setting down roots, which meant finding gainful employment on the land. My quest began at the Long Wharf in Boston, but little work was available, as the war was winding down and the navy and many of the privateers were already releasing thousands of men to the port cities and, as the summer months began, I took passage on a fishing vessel to Cape Cod.

There was something about Cape Cod—its sights and sounds, its tranquility and industry—that made me feel welcome, that made me feel at home, something I had not felt since our hasty departure from Hittisleigh a decade before.

I soon found employment mending fishing nets and sails and making rope. I also assisted in the scaling and gutting of the flounder, cod, and pollock when the boats returned near evening. Although these tasks were not easy, nor did the long hours pay a living wage, I found myself at peace and an increasingly accepted member of the community. I sent home what little I could to Portsmouth but heard little from my sisters, who rarely mentioned my father.

I had been on the Cape for barely two months when I met a girl in the marketplace that turned my mind and heart more solidly to the idea of settling down and taking a wife. Her name was Goody Hallett, and, although she was but seventeen, she had a strength of character and sharpness of mind that made her seem much older.

As the weeks of summer wound down, we spent an increasing amount of hours together sitting by the sea or beneath a pawpaw tree, sharing its odd fruit, which tasted to me like mango or pineapple, reminding me of my travels, of which I rarely spoke.

To her credit, Goody was content to focus on the present and the future. Although she knew—as did everyone in the small, closely connected community—that I had served on a privateer, she never asked for details. Details I was contented to forget.

As we grew closer, our evening talks turned more and more to the possibilities of forging a life together. I knew that my current mix of piecemeal jobs would not do for a man who wished to raise a proper family, so I decided to try my luck again in Boston, where competition was fierce but the opportunities to make something of oneself were plentiful and as ready for the picking as a ripened pawpaw on a low-hanging branch.

I had only been in Boston for a few days when I sought employment with a sailmaker named Maxwell whose grandfather had been exiled to North Carolina from Irongray, in southwestern Scotland, during the 1670s, at the height of the troubles with the Presbyterian Covenanters, who believed that Christ and not the king was the exalted head of the church. Not only did he hire me on after hearing the story of my own family's expulsion from Devonshire for much less treasonous reasons, he introduced me to members of other exiled families who had made their way north from the Carolinas and Caribbean during that turbulent time of religious unrest and obsessive, often unjust witch hunts.

There is nothing like the commonality of injustice to cement bonds between men. Maxwell's associates soon took me into their confidence, inviting me to a secret meeting of merchantmen, fishermen, and dock workers all crowded around a tall, self-assured man with a fiery voice, standing upon a makeshift platform of cobbled-together crates.

Paulsgrave Williams, who has since become a trusted companion and leader of the cause, was a silversmith and family man who spoke with fury about the atrocities visited on the Scottish by the British crown. The mystery of why such a man would risk his prosperity and the security of his family by agitating in Boston was answered when he spoke of the execution of his stepfather—an act of atrocity that he had been made to witness.

After the meeting and for reasons that Paulsgrave has never shared, he invited me to an out of the way tavern with him and a handful of others, where we sat at a back table where we could talk freely and undisturbed. These men, I have to tell ye, spoke not a word that night. Over mugs of ale and platters of roasted pork— much like this fine meal ye have provided this evening, Edward— Paulsgrave told me of a network of smugglers and black marketeers with whom he was working to raise funds to place the rightful king upon the throne of Britain. He was of course speaking of James Stuart, exiled in France but already plotting an offensive. He spoke of other important concerns as the ale flowed that night, such as something called the Star Quorum and its centuries-old struggle for power with another cabal, called the Mammon Lodge, over a group of ancient artifacts reputed to have a supernatural potential. Although I was a simple farmer and sailor who at the time dismissed such outlandish ideas, of these same cabals I have since heard plentiful whispers and rumors. One such rumor is that Andrew Colson, the boy who so badly beat me with his father's walking stick, is a primary member of the latter. I tell ye—if ye have any belief in God within your heart, the tales of their dark acts are enough to make a brave man's blood run cold. From the African slave trade to the troubles in the Highlands, these forces are at work. There is much more at stake than who shall ultimately prevail in the matter of ruling Britain.

The next morning, well before the sun rose, my head clanging like the inside of a ship's bell from too much meat and ale, I was awoken by Maxwell and asked if I wished to aid in the rescue of a prisoner recently whipped in the square and due to be hung later in the day. A man who had done no wrong but to place himself betwixt a devil's cat o' nine and a slave who had been transported from Africa to Barbados courtesy of the East India Company. His crime? The slave had made the unforgiveable error of sneezing in the presence of a high and mighty lord whilst being sold at auction.

Both the man and the slave had been due to be hung in Barbados, although they managed to escape and stow away on a ship bound for Boston. They had arrived a month earlier. The slave had succumbed to whatever ailment had caused the offending sneeze and his defender, after confiding his story to Maxwell, was given a room by Paulsgrave.

A few days later, he was apprehended by the local authorities and sentenced once more to hang.

Seizing upon the offer to aid in his second escape, I splashed cold water on my face, quickly dressed, and had no sooner stepped out into a brisk breeze and flesh-chilling drizzle when Paulsgrave and a half dozen others arrived. Smiling wide at my presence, my new benefactor supplied me with a pistol and a saber.

"I knew ye would join us," he said, squeezing my shoulder as he has done many times since as we have readied ourselves for a fight.

We made our way in the lingering darkness of almost dawn to the gaol that held the twice-condemned man. I soon learned that there was to be no fight, as Paulsgrave handed two hefty sacks of coin to the pair of jailers standing guard. "It is best if we make it look like you struggled," he said to them, motioning for two of our group to enact enough violence on the jailers to make their cover story hold.

Keys in hand, Paulsgrave led the way to the end of the hallway, where we stood before a cell that reeked of rotting hay and human waste. Sitting in the middle of the mess was Xiang Yu, whose warrior's queue identified him as being from Manchuria, in China—although I was not to learn that information, nor the story of his journey from that far away land to Barbados, which I unashamedly declare pales in comparison with mine—for some time to come.

It was clear that Boston would now burn far too hot to hold us, so Paulsgrave had arranged for passage to Cape Cod.

As we sailed out of port, the alarm bells started to sound.

Like the recently liberated Chinaman, we now were wanted men.

CAPE COD, MASSACHUSETTS, CHRISTMAS EVE, 1713

It was no small endeavor hiding a Chinaman in a community like Cape Cod, where he was the only one of his kind and judging eyes abound. It would merely be a way station while Paulsgrave secured safer arrangements. A week later, Paulsgrave booked passage for himself, Xiang Yu, and the rest of the conspirators to Virginia, where they would be out of reach of the Boston authorities.

Paulsgrave agreed that they would wait for me there, as I had some pressing business on the Cape, and it would take some time to complete it.

First, I needed to find gainful employment in some activity beyond reproach or suspicion. Maxwell, who had remained behind when we made our daring prison rescue, had given me a letter of introduction to an Irish fishmonger who agreed to take me on for the short time I planned to remain on the Cape.

By day I scaled, gutted, wrapped, and sold fish at Sullivan and Sons and in the evenings I renewed and strengthened my courting of Goody Hallett. Since my return we had given ourselves to each other fully, if ye understand me, and the matter of marriage was a constant subject over picnics and trysts in a kindly farmer's barn.

So, on Christmas Eve, when all the world is in a convivial, charitable mood, I was set to complete my most important task. Goody had convinced her father, the hard-nosed owner of the local livery, to have me as a guest for what promised, by her detailed descriptions, to be a right and proper feast. I washed and mended my clothes as best I could, combed my unruly hair and tied it back with a new length of ribbon, scrubbed the fish smell from my hands, and wished the Sullivans a good evening. As I departed, Mrs. Sullivan handed me a colorful bouquet of flowers from her carefully cultivated hot house. "Is bad manners ta go emptay-handed, ya know," she sang in her pleasant lilt.

"Right," I answered, gratefully accepted the fragrant bundle. "Goody shall be pleased."

Mr. Sullivan rapped me on the arm with a rolled up copy of the *Boston News-Letter* I had brought back with me from the city. He had taken to using it for training his dogs after initially muttering about stuck-up Bostonians when he had first noticed me with it.

"Dey be farr her mum, ya English dolt," he said as I walked, slump-shouldered, out the door. "Shay's the woon ya need ta be pleasin'!"

As I made my way down the decorated path, a light snow began to fall, its flakes turned to diamonds by a bright silver moon. It was the perfect evening to set in motion the grand plan for the rest of my days.

The Halletts' home, modest as it was, was crammed full with tables trimmed with holly and pine wreaths and piled high with piping hot food and heavily spiced drink. A large central room held a dozen of their relatives and employees of the livery and their families.

We spent the evening feasting and playing various games, Goody smiling and winking at me every chance she got. I watched my consumption of alcohol and made careful strategy to let Mister Hallett emerge the victor whenever we wound up head to head in various games of skill.

Near to midnight, as the last of the guests said their goodbyes and extended their hopeful Christmas wishes, I prepared myself for the most important moment of my life. As Goody's father exited to the porch to have one last pipe before retiring, I, nudged on by Goody and her mother—Mrs. Sullivan's flowers had done just as we had desired—took a few deep breaths and joined him. Although Goody tried to hide, my keen seaman's eye spied her, along with her younger sister, peeking behind a curtain.

"Mister Hallett, sir, might I have a word?" I began, willing my voice to keep an even keel.

"What is it, Bellamy? Not had your fill of the feast? Or is it opportunity you seek? I must admit, I have been waiting for your request. Long overdue."

This was exceedingly fortunate! He was not only receptive but waiting for me to ask!

Armed with newfound confidence and ready to walk head held high through the door he had just opened, I said, "Opportunity indeed, sir. I love your Goody more than life itself. I know my prospects are not impressive at present, but I am a diligent worker and skilled in many areas and I most respectfully ask ye to grant me her hand in marriage."

The ensuing silence was deafening. My utter miscalculation was apparent and I wished to be elsewhere—anywhere—as he exhaled a thick cloud of pungent grey smoke and turned to face me. "Marriage! Preposterous! I thought you had come to ask for employment at the livery. The smell of horse dung is preferable to fish guts any day of the month! You insult me, Bellamy, and worse— you cheapen my daughter's worth at the very suggestion of such a thing! I know the company you keep! Undesirables of every skin shade and stripe. *Chinamen*. There are disturbing rumors about associates of yours from Boston. I have a mind to run you off this porch at the end of my musket!"

Having faced worse from better, I refused to give ground to a bully no different from Lord Colson and his son. "I am sorry to hear that, sir, for I say again, I love Goody with all my heart."

"Say that again and you shall regret it all your days!" he replied. "I would rather my Goody—and you are right about that, *boy*... she is indeed *mine*!—die a dried up, lonely, forgotten spinster than marry the likes of you! Am I clear?"

Seeing Goody, her mother, and her two sisters all crowded around the porch door, one paler with fright and shock than the other, I got down on my knee and proclaimed to all of Cape Cod, "I am leaving tomorrow for Virginia, sir—and then the world! And I shall earn my place and make my fortune and my reputation. I promise ye that. And when I do, and only when I do, will I return and take Goody for my wife, whether ye deem it a fair and desirable match or not! Though I tell ye this—I will not have to ask, for as great as my fame and fortune shall be, ye shall *beg* me to marry your daughter! Good evening and a Happy Christmas to ye all!"

As I walked away, I felt four inches taller and stronger than I ever had before. For, ye see, I finally had a clear and present purpose and was fully determined to make good on my promise no matter the cost or length of time it took.

I am sure ye can imagine, Edward, how my hurt pride and ever-opening eyes to the inequities and atrocities at work in the world combined to spur me on. Within days I had joined Paulsgrave and the rest in Virginia. It was clear he had underestimated the seriousness of our jailbreak and agents were making inquiries about our whereabouts, making it clear that we needed to be at sea.

As that very course of action was best suited to my purposes, I was eager to make it happen and, having hard-earned knowledge of the different classes of ships and what type would best meet our needs, I was put to good use for the first time amongst my rebellious cohorts.

We hired a sloop of six guns, which Paulsgrave christened *Expedition*, and began to fit her out and stock her under the guise of being cloth merchants with anxious buyers in the Caribbean. Paulsgrave, whose access to funds seemed unlimited, would disappear for days at a time, always coming back with new recruits. As we amassed our provisions and put the sloop through its paces, we integrated more and more crew until we had the five or so dozen needed to properly sail and safeguard the ship.

Catching a break in the winter weather, we headed south, venturing steadily further from the coast as Paulsgrave and I slowly turned our disparate band of volunteers into a harmonious, hardworking crew. Xiang Yu, who had no skills in sailing, was a fierce fighter with the sword and axe. He drilled the crew for hours each day, under Paulsgrave's watchful eye. What his plan was, our leader would not reveal, although I had seen enough of captains prepping for battle to know that we would soon receive our opportunity as a crew in a trial by powder and sword.

I would welcome it with open arms and loaded pistols.

We soon after had that opportunity, as January became February off the Caicos Islands, taking several modest merchant ships, and in the process building a war chest, stockpiling supplies, and adding two more cannon to our complement.

I shall not bore ye with the details of our mounting successes. Paulsgrave and I proved a more than capable pair of officers, and the men, emboldened by their bulging seaman's bags, Xiang Yu's combat tutelage, and Paulsgrave's impassioned speeches—versions of which ye have heard from my own lips as of late—were quick on the guns—of which we now boasted a dozen—and appropriately brutal in boarding actions.

Yet Paulsgrave continued to keep secret his larger plans, although I knew our moving further east, to a location away from the richest hunting grounds, was not an arbitrary choice. Something significant was in the works.

In early March, I was proven correct.

As we sat anchored in a thick fog that had settled down around us and seemed intent on lingering, a watchman atop the main mast called the sighting of a ship. When Paulsgrave made no move to call the men to stations, I enquired as to why.

"Because, Sam, we are about to meet a friend."

Imagine my surprise when, an hour later, this "friend" came aboard in the full red regalia of a Catholic Cardinal.

"Cardinal de Fleury, Your Eminence," Paulsgrave said, bowing low before kissing the ring on the Cardinal's outstretched hand. "Welcome aboard the *Expedition*. I trust your journey from France was uneventful."

The Cardinal grunted. "Poor food and poorer quarters aboard this vessel, although she did make proper time. I congratulate you, Captain. Word of your fledging enterprise is positive and growing. Shall we go somewhere private? My absence from Paris may not be lamented but it certainly shall be questioned."

Indicating to the Cardinal that they would be going below decks and motioning for me to join, Paulsgrave said, "I will have our cook prepare a meal. I have some excellent Madeira in my cabin from a recent endeavor."

The Cardinal again grunted. "Things are looking up, Paulsgrave. I might extend my stay through the evening."

My introduction to the Cardinal was cursory, Paulsgrave making a quick statement about my promise as a contributor to the cause. Entering the cabin, he directed me to a spot on the far end of the room as the two men exchanged news.

"The Duke of Orleans is poisoning young Louis's mind," the Cardinal said. "His unsanctioned interest in an alliance with England and plans in the financial sector are counter to our purposes and those of the Star Quorum. It is time to up our efforts in the Caribbean, my son. I believe that conditions are right in New Providence. There are men there loyal to James and embittered by the Treaty and subsequent withdrawal of their letters of marque. We will need men capable of operating in the American colonies as well. I hear you have made a good start in Boston and Hampton."

"I appreciate Your Eminence's praise," Paulsgrave said, showing a level of pleasure at another man's favorable assessment of him that was new to my eyes and ears. "It will not be long before Mister Bellamy here will be able to act without direct supervision."

For the first time, the Cardinal looked me in the eyes. It was clear he was attempting to search my soul. "Come closer, my son. Yes. I see a passion within you. A sense of doing the Church's work for the betterment of your fellow man." Returning his attention to Paulsgrave, he said, "I am more than satisfied. All that remains is to give him a proper initiation. Then I will take my leave."

I felt my body tensing at the word "initiation." I had visions of personal bloodletting and animal sacrifices, though I knew not from whence they came. Seeing my apprehension, Paulsgrave smiled. "No harm shall come to ye, Sam. I promise. We merely ask ye to take a knee before His Eminence and pledge your allegiance to the Jacobite cause and the overthrow of tyranny."

So I was initiated. As I have promised my betters, I shall not divulge to thee the words of allegiance which I spoke—and which I have had many others speak since that life-defining night—until such a time as ye formally volunteer yourself to the cause of the King across the Water.

As we emerged onto the quarterdeck the following morning, the Cardinal anxious to depart, Paulsgrave summoned Xiang Yu to his side. "My friend," he said, a touch of sadness in his voice, "your service to the crew of the *Expedition* has put me in your debt, although, rather than repay it, I must add additional debits to the account. There are tasks awaiting ye in France. To that end, ye shall accompany His Eminence on his journey home."

Bowing low, and much to my surprise, Xiang Yu, who spoke, so I thought, very little English, flawlessly pronounced his fealty to the cause and allegiance to James Stuart in words only slightly modified from my own.

It then became clear that there were networks the size and reach of which I could barely fathom. Even now, two years later, I scarcely understand the power and substance of the forces, arrayed one against the other, in this fight within which we find ourselves.

"That is quite the hero's tale," Edward said, finishing off the last of the ale. "And the hour is exceedingly late."

Pushing his empty plate away and reaching for his tricorne, which hung from a nearby peg, Sam asked, "I trust payment for this memorable meal has been paid in full?"

"More than. Though there is one more bit I must request."

"Anything."

"Let me take the Oath to James and the House of Stuart."

Through the sweat of their backs and a firm resolve to remain independent and in command of what direction their communal life would take, the Flying Gang of New Providence was beginning to see tangible signs of the fruits of their labors.

Through the day and well into the night, crews worked to restore the fort to its former formidable state. They erected new ramparts on all four sides, with the most elaborate facing the sea and cannon captured by the crews of their steadily growing fleet of periagues, sloops, and brigantines put in place to repel any would-be invaders.

At the entrance to the harbor, they had sunk a newly captured Spanish frigate as a defensive measure and all around the island were earthworks manned by cannon crews and musketeers.

Within another few weeks, any captain fool enough to make an assault on Fort Nassau or its republic of pirates would be calling down the angels of Hell itself upon himself and his crew.

Commodore Benjamin Hornigold, as he packed his pipe and watched the blacksmiths fashioning heavy hinges for all of the fort's interior doors, half wished one would try.

As Grandpa puffed contentedly away, with visions of a repulsing line of fire pounding in his white-haired head, Samuel Bellamy, on the beach below him, saw his friend Xiang Yu working a saw quickly and efficiently through a stout piece of oak destined for one of the ramparts. As Sam approached him, he noticed an extensive crisscross of dull pink scars disrupting the elaborate scenes and symbols tattooed across the Chinaman's back, from his shoulders to his belt line.

"My God, Xiang Yu," Sam began, not wishing to embarrass him, but hungry to know what had happened, "your back…"

Reaching for his shirt, Xiang Yu answered, "It is nothing, Samuel. A foolish man with too much pride needed a place to put his frustration, and he found it on my back. I rarely think of it now."

Not one to be deterred, or suffer a mystery, Sam persisted. "Ye must tell me. Was it the Duke of Orleans? I have heard the French manners are but a mask for a vicious disposition… Because the next time we happen upon a French frigate…"

Xiang Yu shook his head. "It was not the French. It happened on Cape Cod, a little more than a year ago. I had returned on urgent business of the Cardinal's. The fault was mine. If

I had done my task unobserved I never would have run afoul of the man who did this."

Perhaps it was the years of honing his intuition on the sea under the conditions of combat, or a vague memory of the word *Chinamen* said with such malice and distaste that put the answer on the tip of Bellamy's tongue, begging to be spoken, no matter the pain it might cause.

"Abraham Hallett. That son of a bitch..."

Xiang Yu looked downward. Sam could see he was right.

"But why? Surely not to punish ye for *my* supposed indiscretion so many months later? I do not—"

"And I cannot," Xiang Yu whispered, picking up his saw where he had placed it and setting back to work. "Let it be, Samuel. Some things are best left unknown. As I say, I rarely remember they are there."

As his friend attacked the wood beneath the serrated blade with a brutal, exacting efficiency, Sam knew that nothing could be further from the truth.

JUNE 15, 1716

Having spent months at sea since narrowly escaping being murdered by his uncle's man, Duncan MacDonald, Angus—Conall MacBlaquart, he still had to remind himself each morning (the name henceforth used in the telling of this tale)—barely recognized the man he saw in the wash bowl's reflection as he readied for the day. His beard and hair were getting long enough to have braids worked into them by a friendly barmaid at his favorite tavern and the muscles beneath his shirt and in his neck were beginning to thicken. His voice, which had always had a higher pitch than those of his cousins, causing him ridicule at home, was beginning to deepen. As much as he worked on lessening his brogue, he could not shake the rhythms, vernacular, and idioms of the Highlands. It was no small source of frustration for Captain Bellamy, who continued to be his primary mentor.

"Again, Conall," he had said at their daily lesson just hours earlier. "'I do not understand.'"

Angus shrugged his shoulders. "I cannae ken." Captain Bellamy glared. "Tis troo," Conall answered. "I doan ken what ye want a' mae!"

Seeking a diversion as he awaited assignment with an outbound crew later in the day, Conall made his way down the beach to where the newly arrived—and completely intriguing—Chinaman was working, crouching behind a pile of fallen trees as Captain Bellamy, who was apparently the man's longtime friend, headed away from the target of Conall's attention.

He filled the time by gazing in wonder at the elaborate tattoos of dragons, landscapes, symbols, and Chinese characters visible on the Chinaman's muscled chest and arms.

When it was safe, Conall grabbed a waterskin hanging from a hook in a supply tent and approached the recent arrival. "Hallo thair, mate," he said, pulling the cork from the waterskin and thrusting it toward the tall, fit Chinaman. "Fancy a drink?"

Leaving his saw suspended in a half-cut tree trunk, Xiang Yu accepted the offer with a smile. Conall watched as the Chinaman took a long pull before refitting the plug and handing it back. "Appreciated."

Before Xiang Yu could put his hand around the handle of the saw, Conall said, "I am Conall MacBlaquart. I serve on the crew a' the *Marianne*. Boot I am also a fraend a' Capt'n Bellamy. I oonderstand yer fraends."

Conall had been sized up aplenty between his cousins, the clan leaders in Perthshire, and since arriving in New Providence, but never before had a set of eyes looked into him like Xiang Yu's.

It seemed an uncomfortable eternity before the man spoke. "Yes. Bellamy and I, through the teachings of Captain Williams, are allies in the cause. I understand that you, Conall MacBlaquart, have risked much, including your own kin's wrath and your given name, to aid the cause as well. So we are also friends."

"Look at zees! China *et* Scotland as friendly as zee pea an' zee pod! *Mon Dieu*, but zayr ees hope fur *du monde* yet!"

"Olivier. News travels fast. It is good to see you." Xiang Yu and the ornately dressed Frenchman who had approached unseen and unannounced wrapped each other in a firm and warm embrace.

"And who ees zees?"

"Conall MacBlaquart," Angus said, straightening his neck and spine to look the Frenchman squarely in the eye. "Boot I cannae ken who ye are, sir."

"Ah, I see we have a *gallo* on our hands, Xiang Yu! A most *extraordinaire* young cock of zee walk!" Pulling his large-brimmed, ostrich-feathered hat from his head, the Frenchman made an elaborate bow. Conall was surprised as he stood back up that there was not sand on the tip of his sharply angled nose. "I am Capitaine Olivier Levasseur of zee vessel *de guerre Oiseau de Proie*."

Xiang Yu laughed. "The *Bird of Prey*? The only bird of prey is you, La Buse."

Vigorously nodding his head, Levasseur once again bowed. "Zee buzzard! *Oui*. I am guilty as charged! And now my ship and I are one *magnifique* unit for the waging of zee true king's war. To zee king across *la mer*!"

As Conall opened his mouth to speak, Levasseur snapped his fingers and put up his hand in a stopping motion. "*Non*, Highlander. Now ees not zee time fur questions, eh? You must run an' fetch Capitaines Williams *et* Bellamy, fur I have come on zee most urgent of bizeeness. *Aller! Aller!*"

Although Conall spoke no French, he clearly understood what the hand waving him toward the fort was commanding. With a nod of understanding, he did as he was told.

Well… *almost*. Stopping on the far side of the tent to have a bit of a listen to what these two odd foreigners might say, he quickly found that he was not in the least bit disappointed.

"Eenteresting lad," Levasseur said, dropping his voice. "There is much to report, *mon ami*. And I have come a long way to do so. James's return to France in defeat has made zee members of zee Star Quorum *très* unsettled. Eel at ease, *comprendre*? Zee Cardinal ees rendered ineffective by zee *duc* and we must strengthen our reesolve and make a better action, eh?"

"I will obey any command and all directives from the Star Quorum," Xiang Yu answered. "For I am only alive because of their intervention during last year's failed operation in—."

"Ah, ah, ah. It ees best not to say too much, *mon ami*. Zayr are prying eyes *et* ears everywhere. Zee Ravenskalds have a broad network of spies and informants. But, *oui*, we all owe zem our lives. So let us do what we must."

Assured he would get nothing else of value from the conversation, Conall headed for the fort as Levasseur had instructed him to, his head abuzz with questions about what he had overheard.

PART THREE:

THOU CAMEST TO BITE THE WORLD

It had been several hours since Conall had delivered his message from the Frenchman to Bellamy and Williams, who reacted with the utmost urgency, slipping on their baldrics and indicating that Edward Thache should join them. Conall noticed that the sailing master was as surprised as he was that they did so. He watched as they headed to the beach and then into a waiting longboat with Levasseur and Xiang Yu to row out to *Oiseau de Proie*.

It had been a damned odd day and the early evening proved to be more of the same.

As most of the pirates of the republic enjoyed their evening meal, criers made their way through the streets, taverns, and workspaces, announcing a special performance by a newly arrived magician.

Curious as the rest of the men who made their way to the front of the fort, where a makeshift stage had been created from uninstalled lengths of rampart, Conall took a seat up front. Moments later, a man with a short, pointed beard and black velvet cap like those worn by alchemists and philosophers in the woodcuts of books he had found in a chest in the fort took center stage, pulling a length of sail from a table full of instruments and oddities. In the center of the table, a brightly colored macaw flapped its wings inside a bamboo cage.

"Welcome, fellow travelers," the man said, his voice crisp, clear, and melodious. "I am Abraxas Abriendo, newly arrived to you via the wondrous town of Messina in Sicily, where the oranges are as plump and sweet as the bosoms of the girls who pick them!" Pausing for the applause, grunts, and hollers he knew would come, Abriendo undid the clasp on his cape, which was heavily embroidered with golden stars and silver moons, which he whipped three times over his head like a mace before tossing it to the side of the stage, and proceeded to entertain them.

His tricks were the kinds of things Conall had often seen in the tavern and in the holds of ships. Sleight of hand, the disappearing and reappearing of various items—including the macaw—and simple feats of mind reading, which might have been no more than lucky guesses. After all, the men of New Providence were many things, but complex was not amongst them. It was more the melody of his voice, the piercing gaze of his eyes—not so different from that of Xiang Yu—and the speed of his hands that kept the audience mesmerized well into the night.

"For my last demonstration of the evening," Abriendo said, to scattered calls to say it was not so, "I need a volunteer. You. You there, lad. Would you be so kind as to assist me?" As Conall looked around him to see where the conjurer was pointing, he realized it was at him.

Heading for the stage with a broad smile on his face, Conall tipped his tricorne as members of the audience applauded.

"Very good, lad. Have a seat here," Abriendo instructed, pulling a red velvet cloth from a mass on the stage, revealing a chair with an oval mirror on a stand before it, the surface of which was highly polished obsidian. Delicately carved symbols, the likes of which Conall had never seen, were arrayed evenly around its gold-gilt frame.

"Now then… this demonstration is unlike any other that each of you has witnessed thus far. For the meagre donation of three silver pieces, which the lad no doubt has in his coin sack there on his belt—a mere fraction of the price paid to Judas in a time so long ago—I will speak an incantation over this mirror. A mirror which once belonged to the summoner and astrologer, advisor to two queens, John Dee—allowing its eye of darkness to clear, revealing to this brave lad… his future!"

Completely mesmerized by the proximity to the magician's eyes and voice, Conall opened his coin pouch and counted out three silver pieces, which he watched himself hand to Abriendo without willing his arm to do so.

"A smart choice indeed. I knew you were one of the wise ones, lad. Now close your eyes and concentrate on a moment, oh… thirty years in the future. The year is 1746. Where you choose to be is wholly up to you. Perhaps it is home. We all miss our homes. Use all of your senses. How does it look? Sound? What do you feel beneath your feet. What is the taste upon the air? Good…"

He placed his hands gently upon Conall's shoulders as he took a stance behind him. "Now I shall speak the spell to clear the mirror. *Sanco tupanché, tecco du mané, té-liggo, té-liggo nupanché. Sanco du mené, heelo du ché ché. Sanco tupanché, tecco du mané, du mané, du mané. Vibra sume ché ché. Sanco tupanché, tecco du mane…*"

Although Abriendo's voice rose in power and volume with each word he spoke, Conall's mind was less able to hear it. He heard a buzz as if a million honeybees were swarming inside his head. As he kept his eyes closed tight, concentrating on his beloved Scotland, he heard the sound of cannon fire and the screams of dying men. He smelled the powder, the metallic quality of blood, and the grasslands as they burned away. He could taste the awful paste of fear and fatigue on his tongue. And there, beside him was a man whose face resembled his own...

"Stop this! Immediately! Or feel the sting of my blade!"

In the few seconds it took Conall to open his eyes, all the world fell silent. Abriendo had stopped chanting. From the crowd came not a peep.

Blinking away the vision that had settle around him like an early morning fog, Conall saw Edward Thache coming up the makeshift stairs and onto the stage, sword drawn and fire in his eyes.

"Give the lad back his silver and let him return to his place in the audience," Edward said, moving close enough to throw the velvet cover back over the mirror. Though not before Conall got one last glimpse of a moor littered with hundreds of dying Highlanders.

Abriendo stood his ground. "I gave him what I promised. Why should I make a refund? I thought the pirates of New Providence adhered to certain principles of fairness. Of what is right. Isn't that correct, my lad?"

A quick, seething glare from Edward kept Conall's lips together.

"Ah... I see he is afraid of you," Abriendo said, shaking his head. "How unfortunate. Very well," he said, pulling Conall's fee from a pocket in his vest. "Take the coins and go. Tell no one what you saw. It is always wiser that way. Unless you wish it to come true."

As Conall sat back in the sand, and Edward sheathed his sword and motioned for Abriendo to bring the evening to an end, a request with which the magician enthusiastically complied, the young Highlander tried to put from his mind what he had seen.

Because now he was aware of just how long the Catholic king's rebellion would last and how close to his home in the Highlands and bloody it would be.

Opening the door of the yellow taxi in which he rode as it was coming to a stop in front of the nondescript federal building that was his destination, Jake Givens, who was fighting a searing white-hot headache that was making it almost impossible to see, handed some cash over the seat to the driver. Stumbling out of the cab, and leaning over a nearby garbage can, he fully expected to lose the lunch of fish sticks and steamed broccoli that was his final meal at the Johns Hopkins neurology lab, where he had been transferred after being visited by FBI Tech Specialist Tino Alvarado a few weeks earlier.

Despite the best efforts of one of the best teams in the world when it came to traumatic brain injury—all paid for by the US government—there was little they had done to mitigate the lingering effects of the brutal beating Jake had taken.

Letting a groan escape his lips as he waited for his stomach to decide whether it was going to release its contents, Jake heard a voice above him. "Sir, are you okay? Are you in need of assistance?"

Before he could answer, Jake heard another voice. One that was familiar. "I'll take it from here, Officer. Thank you. Mister Givens is a guest of the DTEAU for the day. He was injured in service to his country. Healing has been slow. Right, Mister Givens?"

Feeling the nausea and the worst of the headache begin to subside, Jake looked at Tino, and then at the cop beside him, and tried to smile. "That's right. Service to my country. Thanks for that. And thanks for your concern, Officer—"

The patrolman was already gone.

"Fairfax County coppers don't usually linger long in front of our building," Tino explained, positioning himself for a retina and hand scan at the tinted glass entrance. "You must have looked awfully suspicious leaning over that trash can."

As they crossed the lobby and headed for a bank of elevators with additional scanning equipment, Jake said, "How did you know I was here so quickly?"

Pulling his phone from his pocket, Tino said, "GPS tracking of the cab. I had the service tagged to alert me when a fare requested this address from Johns Hopkins. Pretty simple, really."

As they got off the elevator on the seventh floor and walked left for several feet before coming to yet another door with bio-scan technology, Tino smiled. "Welcome to the Domestic Threat Early Assessment Unit. Or, as we call it, DTEAU."

There isn't much to it, Jake thought as they entered the office. Several large-screen monitors mounted on the walls of the central workspace showed various maps of the United States, marked with symbols in a variety of shapes and colors. Spread out through the room were half a dozen workstations, their computer screens either full of data or on screen savers with the FBI logo in the center. Two rooms encased in glass (*most likely bulletproof*, Jake surmised) held similar workstations. In one was a pretty redhead in a dark blue pants suit talking on the phone while pages came spilling out of a hi-tech printer. In the other was a stereotypical FBI supervisor type smoking a Marlboro and leafing through a thick stack of files.

"Is this it?" Jake asked, not knowing what he had been expecting but feeling markedly underwhelmed. After all, the DTEAU had been at the forefront of thwarting a pair of terrorist attacks in San Diego and Atlanta as of late and had also prevented two school shootings in as many months.

"This is all it needs to be," Tino answered, leading Jake to a back corner cubical with half a dozen computer towers and three 20-inch screens. "This is my domain. Away from everyone else. They're okay, but I prefer to work alone."

"The redhead..." Jake said, not exactly sure why. Did he want an introduction? He looked like hell, having lost twenty-five pounds and still sporting yellow-purple bruises around his eye and mouth.

"Magdalena Sorrus. Maggie to her friends. She and another SA, Kevin Connor, who is on assignment in Chicago, coordinate all the fieldwork. They are both top notch. The guy behind the glass is my boss, SSA— "

"Haxx! Are you back? I thought I saw you skulking to your hole..."

It had to be Tino's supervisor, Jake surmised, judging from the direction from which it came and the authoritative—more like pissed off—tone.

"Yeah, boss," Tino said, taking the opportunity to hit a series of buttons on his keyboard and switch on two of his screens. "Back here hard at work." To Jake he whispered, "SSA Peter Vance. Call him that. He'll love it."

As Vance came around the corner, Tino put on his best apologetic face. "Sorry I didn't tell you I was leaving. I grabbed some lunch in the cafeteria and then headed for the lobby. This is Jake Givens. He was the one Doctor MacGregor sent the thumb drive to. He was just released from Johns Hopkins."

SSA Vance gave Jake a cursory glance and focused his attention on Tino. "I got a call not twenty minutes ago from Admiral Christopher Adler. I'm sure you know the name."

By the low whistle and widening of his eyes, Jake could tell that Tino knew exactly who he was and it was not good news that he had called.

"Head of DED 17, 27, and 37. Navy liaison to DARPA and RAND. If I'm not mistaken, he also oversees the Naval Research Lab. Or, certain sections of it. Sorry boss, I can pull his profile and brush up if you need me to. Is the admiral coming by?"

Sitting on the corner of Tino's desk, SSA Vance shook his head. "No, he's not 'coming by,' Haxx. And you are damned lucky that he's not. You told me you covered our ass after you tapped into their computers."

"I did. Wait… you mean they… because that's—"

Vance pulled a nearly empty pack of Marboros from his shirt pocket. "Jesus. Just bought this pack this morning… You see what you're driving me to? You're making me regret saving you from a life sentence writing code for the NSA. Or federal prison. You forgotten that?"

Tino looked past Vance at Jake, expecting him to look embarrassed.

He looked enrapt.

"Not at all, sir. I'm grateful every day. My mother's grateful. My entire family prays for you in church on Sunday, sir. But what happened to Kirstine…"

Vance, who had just put a lit cigarette to his lips, inhaled and exhaled hard. "Kirstine? You're referring to Doctor MacGregor? Her disappearance is not a DTEAU matter. If that's why you've brought this fella up here…"

Jake took a step back as Tino leaned forward in his seat. "How is it not a DTEAU matter? An employee of the Smithsonian has her computer hacked by the NRL—"

"The *government's* computer…"

"—she's threatened with termination, fears for her life, sends files related to one of her own ancestors to a friend and *he* gets beaten so bad by two hooded thugs—probably also from NRL or one of the admiral's other operations—and then she disappears.

Without a trace. Something foul is certainly afoot in our fifty states, sir. And our job is unquestionably to nip it in the bud."

Looking at the tip of his glowing, already three-quarters-smoked cigarette, the ashes of which he had been flicking into Tino's FBI coffee mug, Vance licked his lips and did his best not to lose his temper.

"I get it, Tino. I do. An old friend has gotten herself caught up in something big. Something she unwittingly dragged you into. Something that, I am sure if you had known what it was, whom it involved, you would have steered clear of. And I told the admiral as much. But his directive is clear. We are not to get involved."

"But, sir—"

Vance put his hand out and stood. "You stand the fuck down from this, Tech Specialist Alvarado, do you hear me? Or NSA won't be an option. You'll do your forty years as originally planned in the worst hole the Federal Bureau of Prisons can find for you." Heading out of the cubicle, Vance put his hand on Jake's shoulder. "The admiral asked me to convey his concern to you, Mister Givens. He regrets that you were caught up in this unfortunate incident. He knows your father well."

"Thank you, SSA Vance," Jake said, remembering Tino's advice. "And, um, sir... you should know, what is on that thumb drive is absolutely about threats to our domestic security."

Taking one last, long drag on his stub of a Marlboro, Vance raised a brow. "And how the hell would you know that, Mister Givens?"

"Because I had a look at the files before those two guys who beat me up broke into my recording studio and stole them."

After watching the last of the smoke from his now dead cigarette dissipate above the cubical, Vance said, "Okay, then. That's enough to go on. But we have to do this under the radar. Damned near impossible considering who's watching the screens, but so be it. I'll make some calls—call in some favors. You no doubt have a secondary setup somewhere, Haxx, mirroring this one?"

"I'm not sure how you know that, sir," Tino said, still processing Jake's revelation and Vance's change of stance, "but yeah. I'll start digging as soon as I get there."

"Keep Mister Givens with you while you do. If the people who have that thumb drive figure out he's looked at it—and they will—then... Well, let's keep him safe."

Once Vance had left the cubicle and was out of earshot, Jake leaned in toward Tino and said, "The admiral asked him… How the heck did he know I was going to be here?"

Waking up the pair of computer screens and running his fingers over his keyboard, Tino replied, "Because they know *everything*, Jake. And it kinda makes me sick." As a logo of a brain wired to a machine appeared on the screen with the text "DED 47" overlaid on it, Haxx added, "Why didn't you tell me you had time to look at the thumb drive?"

Leaning in close to Tino's ear, Jake whispered, "Because that would have been a lie."

Capitan Amaro Rodriguez Felipe y Tejera Marchado, known by many as simply Amaro Pargo, had been pacing like a caged, wounded beast on the quarterdeck of his ship, *Ave María y Las Ánimas*, for the better part of an hour. Every few moments he would still himself long enough to look through his spyglass at the Spanish ship being relieved of its goods and stores of silver and gold within the harbor of Port Royal, Jamaica.

"*Cerdos!*" he yelled, collapsing the glass with a furious slap of his palm. "Piratical pig swine! I have suffered yet another grave defeat at their pig-oiled, slime-stained hands!"

Lieutenant Renaldo de Recalde's pronounced limp, suffered during an encounter with an English pirate ship the previous November, served as a constant reminder of just the kind of defeat his captain was lamenting. The closest thing Amaro Pargo had to a friend, Renaldo stayed where he was, several feet away, rather than move closer to comfort the man who had saved his life as his thigh wound was emptying him of life.

"You are not to blame, Capitan," he said. "The *San Miguel* was already in distress and to the point of surrender when we happened upon her. You did all that you could. The fact that dozens of her crew members are now in our care rather than suffering at the hands of the *cerdos* is victory enough."

"My friend, my friend," Pargo replied, stopping his pacing and leaving his spyglass for the moment at his side, "you do me no great honor by lying to my face. Defeat is defeat. It is absolute. She is a poxied whore without mercy who will not suffer being painted and dressed like a *pedazo de mierda cerdo*! Those two *bastardos*, Jennings and Vane, are no doubt drinking wine with their traitor governor Hamilton, celebrating a great victory in his pig-swine palace—at our expense! What am I to tell the king and queen, Renaldo? They rely on me for victories and I do nothing for them but fail!"

Seeing the fire in his captain's eyes and the white of his knuckles as he gripped the spyglass, Renaldo knew full well that the next few moments would decide if he and the crew would be ordered to do something brave but foolish or set a course to fight another foe on a strategically wiser day.

"*Mi Capitan*," he began, choosing his words with care, "I know what you are thinking. You are thinking to move the *Ave María* within range so that our cannon can deny them their prize. But that would mean being in range of *their* cannon. And we cannot match them on our own. You must first seek reinforcements from His Majesty. He will no doubt comply. You will have your vengeance on Jennings, Vane, Hamilton, and all those who dare to be their allies."

"Renaldo," Amaro Pargo said, moving to stand beside him. "Do you know why *Dios* answered my prayers to save your life that horrible day last year? So that I would not end many others pursing a foolish quest! We make sail for the Windward Passage. We must take several worthy prizes to atone for recent losses. We shall put these rescued men to good use as boarding parties. Until these *cerdos* can pay, we shall have to find abundant proxies. Let us go, my friend!"

In a back room of a Covent Garden tavern, as beer and spirits flowed and showgirls danced and sang beyond the barred and guarded door, Andrew Colson, Henry Bolingbroke, and dozens of men from their own and three other Masonic lodges around the city knelt before the man they had just elected Grand Master of their new endeavor, the Free Masonic Grand Lodge. Although it would be a year before the unification was official, the members of the four lodges knew the bulk of the work was behind them. Now was the time for the renewal of their oath and the taking of the reins of power from other organizations in the city.

One in particular, Andrew Colson thought with a smile. *The era of Mammon will now come to a close.*

As his new master, Anthony Sayer, donned his robes of office, Colson whispered to Bolingbroke, "There is no turning back now, Henry. Are you ready?"

The former lord and earl, who had risked much and lost it all for James Stuart's thus far abysmal campaign to take his rightful throne, who had now become an informer for King George's amoral band of enforcers, nodded. "With all my heart, Andrew. My spies are gathering new information every day. We will dismantle the rebellion man by man until there is nothing but corpses hanging from the scaffolds."

Such eloquence in the safety and comfort of non-action, Colson thought, knowing full well that Bolingbroke had proven himself a poor bet and even worse collaborator. Anyone who took his coin would not be worth a damn and might ultimately betray them. They had produced little of value thus far and Colson did not expect it to change.

Taking position in front of the group, Grand Master Sayer opened his book of rites and had the men before him repeat the following oath:

I solemnly promise to be as the Sphinx. That I will not write nor share these, our sacred secrets. Nor print, carve, nor engrave, nor otherwise delineate them. Nor cause or suffer them to be so done by others, if in my power to prevent it. Not on any item moveable or immoveable under the canopy of heaven, whereby or whereon any letter, character, or figure, or the least trace of a letter, character, or figure, may become legible or intelligible to myself, or to anyone in the world. I swear this to prevent our secrets, arts, and hidden mysteries from becoming known through my unworthiness. These several points I solemnly swear to observe, without evasion, equivocation, or mental reservation. I do so freely, under no less a penalty, on the violation of any of them, than to have my throat cut across, my tongue torn out by the root and buried in the sand of the sea at low water mark, or a cable's length from the shore, where the tides regularly ebb and flow twice in twenty-four hours.

"A bit dramatic, would you not say?" Bolingbroke whispered to Colson as the group stood and began to break up into smaller knots around the room. "My God... tongue torn out by the root! It is positively barbaric."

"Then I would suggest you do not break your oath, Henry," Colson answered. "Although, by comparison with the rites and rituals of the Lodge of Mammon, this is all no more than a children's bedtime story."

"Then you are in grave danger indeed, my friend," Henry said. "Should word of your defection to the Masons get back to Carteret and his latest protégé."

Turning to Bolingbroke with a sneer, Colson whispered, "Should word get out, and should I even think for a moment that it was you, Henry, who did so, I promise you this—the punishments you heard of today will be nothing compared to the revenge I personally exact upon every inch of your ashen, flabby flesh."

Seeing a look on Bolingbroke's face that clearly indicated he understood the message, the mask of fury on Colson's own dissolved as quickly as it had formed. Grasping Bolingbroke's shoulders, he said, in a full and cheerful voice, "Now let us celebrate with ale and meat our new, united lodge!"

PORT ROYAL, JAMAICA, JULY 1716

"This was not the reception we was 'opin' fer, Guv'nah, I 'ave ta tell ye."

Charles Vane sat back in his chair in the office of the governor of Jamaica, Archibald Hamilton, so he could show the red-faced man that he had at the ready his pistol, knife, and sword.

Vane and his partner Henry Jennings had arrived in Port Royal earlier in the day with a stout French merchant ship named the *St. Marie*. At this very moment, Jennings was making deals with the local merchants on the sugar, rum, and fine cloth in her ample, half-filled holds. Their ship's carpenter was already drawing up plans to outfit her as part of their growing armada.

Vane wished he were with him, rather than having to hear the governor's tirade.

"You must understand, Captain Vane... Charles—may I be so familiar? I should think so considering our long-term and admittedly fruitful relationship—I am in a delicate position. It is not that I do not appreciate the fine prizes you are securing—they are contributing to the well-being of Jamaica, and especially Port Royal, in immeasurable ways..."

Vane leaned forward, pouring himself a mug full of ale from the governor's desk but not drinking as of yet. "This 'delicate position' a yers... which led ye ta talk ta me as tho' I's no betta than a slave set before ye not ten minutes passed... ye'd best enlighten me on the particl'ahs while I am still somewhat sober an' calm."

Sitting behind his desk for a moment before rising up again and coming around the desk to sit in a chair beside his agitated visitor, Governor Hamilton patted the sweat on his upper lip with a lacy monogrammed handkerchief.

"Of course, of course... I should have done so from the start. The difficulty stems—through no fault of your own—from the unfortunate coincidence that my brother and I—who is, as you may know, the royal governor of Virginia colony and of Edinburgh Castle—is the same as that of Lieutenant General Richard Hamilton—the foremost advisor to the agitator and rebel, James Stuart."

Lifting the mug to his lips but still not drinking, Vane said, "So fah I don' see the problem, 'cept fer an over-concernin' streak on yer part wit' *last names*."

As Vane finally drank, pouring more ale down his throat than made Hamilton comfortable—he had heard stories from the local taverns about Vane's inclinations when he had had too much—the governor surreptitiously moved the pitcher of ale out of reach. "The problem is, Charles, that my brother is thoroughly committed to George of Hanover, who, I need not remind you, *sits on the throne of Britain*. And, for all appearances, I must be as well. Tell me you understand."

"I do," Vane answered, reaching for the pitcher across the desk. "I understand that yer a coward, 'Amilton, too afraid a' the consequences ta stand up fer what ye know is right. Yer too worried some fatter, falser man that ye will come in an' take this little empire a' yers away. See there, Guv'nah? I understand yer worries perfectly."

Afraid though he was of the man who sat before him, Hamilton would not deign to be called a fool.

"You miss the mark, Captain Vane. It is far more complicated than you know. My brother is close with the deputy governor of Virginia, Alexander Spotswood, who is popular and powerful. He has aligned himself with a group of Carolinian merchants and soldiers known as The Family. This so-called Family is in the partial employ of Lord Carteret and other lords from the Royal African Company, which means they control a sizable portion of the trade in sugar, tobacco, and slaves. When you openly use the term 'Jacobite' and 'in the employ of Governor Hamilton of Jamaica' in the same sentence, as you seem oh so regularly want to do, you draw attention to us all. And that is *not* the kind of attention that any of us want. The Family is not likely to have infinite patience in the matter."

Vane's silence indicated that he was finally beginning to understand.

A moment later, he confirmed it. "Aw right, then, Guv'nah. We will be more circumspect in announcin' our loyalties an' motivations in the fut'cha. In the meantime, what can Cap'n Jennin's an' meself do ta aid ye all in yer vast an' no doubt lucrative entahprises?"

Filling Vane's mug to the rim with ale, Hamilton pulled a map from a shelf behind him, unrolling it on the desk and securing the corners with chunks of ornate stone. "I am glad you have asked. See this island here? This, my friend, is a prime piece of a very, shall we say, elaborate undertaking. One in which your particular skills could prove to be, shall we say, undeniably valuable…"

Checking the charge in his pistol before hiding it beneath his frock coat, Edward Thache entered the tent of Abraxas Abriendo. The magician, surrounded by candles, exotic statuary, and burning sticks of incense, was wrapping his black mirror carefully in burlap, his eyelids fluttering and his breathing shallow as if he were in a trance.

"I wondered when you come," Abraxas whispered, putting out the candles one by one with his fingers without looking at them. "Turns out you are right on time, Edward."

Edward shook his head. "Ye shall address me as Mister Thache, as befits my station on this island. And I do not give any credence at all to yer hocus-pocus, so save the false prophecy for the gullible rabble."

Abraxas laughed. "False? The Scottish lad no doubt saw *something* in the mirror and, whatever it was, it was not pleasant. Did you not ask him about it?"

"Why would I?" Edward answered, looking around the tent with disgust at the skulls, bones, feathers, furs, antlers, and feet of dozens of animals strung all around. His eyes came to rest on a small iron pot surrounded by various dried herbs and corked bottles of odd-colored liquids and powders. "Ye obviously put him into some manner of trance, convincin' the lad he saw what he possibly could not. And to make matters worse, ye told him not to tell or what he saw would come to pass. Clever bit of mind-work on a lad who is still an innocent. Do not forget, Abraxas—I know ye from our boyhood in Jamaica, when ye were nothin' but a gutter snipe and pickpocket. And not an able one at that."

Laughing once again, but this time more warmly, Abraxas stood and stretched his legs, his spine making a sharp cracking sound that made Edward wince. "You are no doubt referring to your father catching me *in flagrante delicto*, yes? Most unfortunate—I recall his coin pouch as being particularly bulging that day—but I was distracted by your stepsister. Such a pretty little thing. No doubt still is... Yes? Or would it be indelicate to say? Do you even know? I suppose it is no matter... She has most likely grown fat and prosperous from your unanticipated generosity. The spoiled boy who bullied all the rest of us suddenly given to charity... To give away your father's plantation in Spanish Town to his second wife's offspring... To then enlist in the Royal Navy... What were you thinking? I have heard whispers, of course, but I have never been much for gossip. Although I do wonder what your fellow pirates must think… Or have you not enlightened them?"

Resisting the impulse to pull the pistol from its hiding place or a dagger from his boot, Edward willed himself to remain calm. "No man here has need to talk of his past. My decisions before and after I left Jamaica are none of your concern, nor are the affairs and impressionable minds of this island. Ye may think ye know why I left Jamaica, but ye do not. Ye are a poisonous snake in an Eden of yer own makin', Abraxas. And I shall not allow it. I have come here to tell ye to leave."

Abraxas raised his eyebrows and gestured to the mirror, which he had placed in an oval case of polished wood crafted perfectly for the purpose. "You accused me of putting the boy in a trance. Of magically making him see some kind of vision. There is no need, Edw—Mister Thache… such an absurd request… No need because, you see, the mirror's power is real. And it could be the key to your halfcocked rebellion actually succeeding."

"I will not listen for a moment more to yer nonsense, Abriendo. That is quite a name ye have given yerself. So authentic-soundin'. Exotic an' mysterious—the traveler to a thousand foreign lands. But remember—I know the truth."

"No, my old friend," Abraxas answered. "You only think you do. Allow me a demonstration. What harm would it do?"

Edward shook his head. "I will not subject myself to yer sorcery. Ye have no doubt learned well yer despicable charlatan's trade. Yer audience was enrapt. All the more reason to insist that ye leave. On tomorrow's tide. Or—"

Now it was Abraxas who shook his head. "Not possible. My host, Olivier Lavasseur—"

Edward's eyes and voice turned harder. "Ye came here with a Frenchman?"

"Oh, that is right… How could I forget… We do not like the French, do we?" Abraxas closed the mirror's case, locking it with a key from around his neck. "More pieces of your secret past… Really, Mister Thache, you should live more in the present, or," he patted the case, "in the future. Your past is full of things best not remembered—or shared with those with whom you live and work… Ah, yes. I have paid attention to the exploits of Edward Thache. Indeed, indeed I have…"

Before Edward could react—and, hours later, when he had a chance to reflect, he honestly did not know how he would have, although it certainly would have meant some degree of bloodletting—Benjamin Hornigold was at the entrance to the tent, summoning him outside.

"What is it, sir?" Edward asked, trying to hide the tremble in his voice.

Lighting his pipe and motioning Edward to walk with him a dozen feet away from the bustling clot of tents, Hornigold said, "Tis all the new faces. Tis getting damned near impossible to keep track of everyone. That tent you were in... belongs to some sort of self-styled magician or something, is that right?"

Edward nodded. "Self-styled is wholly accurate, Captain. Not the sort of mountebank conducive to strengthenin' our fledglin' republic. And I just learned he arrived with a Frenchman. Olivier Lavasseur..."

"That certainly stirs the intrigue," Hornigold replied. "This Lavasseur has become increasingly friendly with Bellamy and Williams. They are apparently mutually acquainted with the Chinese fellow as well. Damned complex and all too unsettling, all this new blood. I need ye to keep a careful eye for me, Edward."

"I already have, sir. I was just tellin' the mountebank to leave. I will have a chat with Lavasseur to see that it happens sooner rather than later."

Patting his lieutenant on his shoulder, although he had to stretch his arm to do so, Hornigold nodded. "Excellent. Little things become big ones if we let them develop without watch."

*A*m I now to be destined to be daily bathed in deer's blood, pig shit, and goat's urine, My Lord? If that is my penance for my wrongdoings, my indiscretions in this Earthly realm, then I shall accept it and thank you for your Grace.

Cardinal Giulio Alberoni, newly arrived from Spain and sitting amidst the pigs and sheep in a dilapidated barn whose rotting thatch roof was struggling to keep out the rain, looked at his two red-robed companions, who looked equally pained and supplicated before the judgment of a God that none of them thought for a moment to be able to understand.

"Tell us of King Philip, Giulio. We hear unsettling things about his wife. Can you manage her, my friend?"

Cardinal Alberoni looked with tempered amusement at Cardinal Filippo Antonio Gualterio. Ironic that he would be concerned about Alberoni's handling of royalty when his own charge, James Francis Edward Stuart, had left Scotland in abject defeat to scuttle back to France, where his once-warm welcome was now beginning to cool.

Leave it to the French to be so predictably fickle.

"The wife of which you speak, Elisabeth—or, as she prefers to be called, Isobel—Farnese, is exceedingly intelligent and gives Philip exactly what he needs to keep him focused on what is best for Spain—and for us. She and I are working to bring a better brand of counselors and attendants to the Royal Court, so we may better dilute Philip's misguided claim that he belongs as well on the throne of France. And she fully supports James's claim, being utterly devoted to the His Excellency, Pope Clement."

Cardinal André-Hercule de Fleury, who was finding himself kept further and further from young Louis, thanks to the growing power of the Duke of Orleans, pulled his raiment tighter against the large drops of rain falling on his shoulders and cursed the stink of dung wafting up from the goat that lay at his feet. "Meaning no offense, *Filippo*, may God deliver us from all those named Philippe and Philip! *Phili*stines, all. Louis must be protected, Giulio. I am relieved to hear you agree."

Perhaps if they were sitting somewhere far more pleasant the others would have laughed. Met with only their silence, de Fleury continued. The smell was somehow less pungent when he talked. "I know I am of little use here, so I have taken the liberty of making contact with the order to which we all swore our allegiance as priests."

Cardinal Alberoni's eyes grew wide. "You have spoken with those who lead the Scarlet Knights of Grotth? I thought the order was all but dead. We have heard nothing in decades... All those rituals and oaths. All of the training and sacrifice in addition to that required by the Church... All for naught."

De Fleury patted his friend on the knee. "Far from dead, Giulio. And not all for naught. The order thrives. It suits their purpose—*our* purpose—to seem as if they have fallen into legend. A page taken from Satan himself. But the royal families of France, Britain, and Spain have perpetrated evils through their unholy alliances that have necessitated a new level of involvement, such as in the earliest days of the Church, when pagans and blasphemers sought to eradicate Christ's Holy Servants. And it has been decreed that we three here assembled are now to lead the way."

Putting his hands together in prayer, Cardinal Gualterio lifted his face toward a patch in the rotting roof where a beam of sunshine had found its way through, the rainclouds having dissipated a moment before at the mention of St. Grotth.

"It is an omen, my friends," he said, making the sign of the cross and grasping his companions by the hands. "We must not lose faith. I will strengthen James's resolve. He has fight in him yet. His advisors, led by Lieutenant General Hamilton, have learned from their mistakes upon the battlefields of Scotland. Their pride will not again allow them to fail. And you, Giulio—continue to cultivate, to guide as you thus far have, Philip's queen, this Isobel Farnese. Spain must be ready to raise its swords in alliance with our cause when the time comes for James and his armies to once more enter Britain, and without design upon the throne in France. André-Hercule, you have given us the precious gift of hope. Little Louis will no doubt see the error of the regent's ways and come back to you in time."

As steam began to rise from the animals' coats and the hay stacked all around them, so strong had the rays of the sun become, the trio of Cardinals went their separate ways, although more united than they had been for many a month.

Devon Ross, known to his victims and a growing number of whispering traitors on his list of targets as *Faccia del Diavolo* because of the horrific scars inflicted upon his face by a conjured spirit-dog in Africa, watched with amusement as Joseph Stanton pummeled another young pirate to near oblivion during one of Captain Jennings's daily boarding-party drills. The enigmatic teenager had quite the reputation, having slit a merchant captain's throat against Captain Charles Vane's orders and nearly killing one of Hornigold's own promising pets during a tense interaction between their crews.

As a pair of ashen-faced deck hands carried the bloodied man away, carefully averting their eyes from his ruthless assailant, Stanton moved from his position in the chalk-outlined fighting circle and approached Ross, who realized the only reason the young tough did so was because he stood beside a barrel of water.

The lad had hardly broken a sweat.

"Ye aughta be careful," Ross said, stepping aside as Joseph dipped a wooden ladle into the barrel, splashing Ross's arm. "Ye might kill one a' them fellas one a' these days."

"Maybe so," Joseph answered, wiping a smear of blood from his face with a thick-veined forearm sporting a freshly made tattoo of a leering skull with angel's wings inked in green and black. "They ought to fight with more ferocity. Half the crew is a damned disgrace. The other half is only slightly better. Why do the captains put up with it?"

Inviting Joseph to sit, Ross washed his mouth out with some water and sat beside him. "Look 'ere, lad. See whattit says?" Ross had pulled the volume of Shakespeare's plays they had taken from the dead merchant captain's ship off the coast of Jamaica the previous February and, finding the place he wanted, which he had marked with a length of crimson hair ribbon normally tied around his wrist, laid it open in front of the boy. "Tis from Henry the Sixth, part three. 'Teeth hadst thou in thy head when thou wast born, To signify thou camest to bite the world.' Tis what ole 'Enry says ta Glousta' just before that schemin' clubfoot hunchback kills 'im and takes the throne. I trust ye unnerstand why I am showin' this ta ya now?"

If Joseph did, he was not saying.

"Fine, then," Ross said after a moment, slamming the book shut with enough force to ruffle Stanton's bangs. "Act like ye don' need no one. Like yer teeth are enuff ta bite every man on yer list an' then some. But believe me, *boy*—they ain't. Ya keep disobeyin' orders an' beatin' yer shipmates like ya been an' yer more likely ta see Davey Jones's locker afore ya satisfy yer cravin' fer revenge."

Staring into Ross with a look that might shrink a lesser man, Joseph whispered, "What is it to you, anyway? With a face like that you are lucky any captain will have you on his crew. They all say it—'*Faccia del Diavolo* will be the undoing of us all.' Some even doubt on whose side of the line you stand. So save the fucking lectures for the rabble."

Grabbing Joseph hard on the still tender tattoo as the teen made a motion to stand, Ross leaned in close, making him wince with the foulness of his breath. "Ya wanna take a look beneath me mask, boy? Get a reminder a' the things I 'ave seen an' survived? Trust me—yer teeth are nothin' but nibs compared ta what done this ta me."

Turning away as Ross started to lift his mask to reveal the mess of a visage beneath it, Joseph saw Captain Vane standing against the mast not four feet away.

"Learnin' our Shakespeare, are we?" Vane asked, though it was clear he was not interested in an answer. "I've 'ad a bit a' disturbin' news, Mista Ross, an' I seek yer perticulah brand a' counsel."

Shooting Joseph a look to confirm the lad was aware what Vane's request meant in terms of pecking order and leverage, Ross stood and tipped his tricorne to his captain. "Always ready ta serve ya, suh."

Looking thoroughly unimpressed, because he expected no less, Vane answered, "Our landfall at Port Royal 'as been aborted. Guv'nah Hamilton 'as been arrested by the Royal Navy. 'E's bein' taken ta London ta stand trial fer encouragin' acts a' piracy. They 'ave chosen an ignorant plantah ta replace 'im, no doubt loyal ta the German, meanin' 'eel be no friend ta us. We are now on our own, meanin' we can no longer ignore the growin' strength of 'Ornigold's lackeys on New Providence. I been 'earin' they 'ave made some new alliances. See me in my cabin at the next bells an' bring ideas aplenty."

Before Ross could finish saying, "I, suh, that I will," Vane was gone. Squatting beside Joseph, Ross said, "There will no longer be any leniency, Stanton. Ye can count on that. So when I am done wit' the cap'n, I will come back. Ye need ta learn the art a' subterfuge an' I am jus' the one ta teach ye."

As Ross walked away, Joseph felt himself smiling for the first time in months. If anyone had seen it, they would wish upon his face his usual dark-eyed scowl, so terrible was the sight, so sinister the smile's secret, searing intentions.

When Angus MacGregor was living out his final years on Earth—at a ripe old age it would be imprudent to disclose at this particular point in what shall be a narrative spanning decades—he often wondered what might have been if the pirates of New Providence had banned together in a lasting, common cause rather than splintering off into ever-greater and more malicious factions. He thought the same of the Highland clans. What if Benjamin Hornigold and Angus's uncle, Rob Roy, had been able to identify enough common ground to unite those beneath them to mount a sustained and multifront rebellion against those who would continue to oppress them for decades still to come?

Such were his thoughts as he arrived aboard the *Marianne* with Mister Thache and Commodore Hornigold at the scene of a recent battle at sea. As the tired crews of the recently battling ships swabbed their decks of blood and cleaned and secured their cannons, he heard the reports made by captains Bellamy and Williams. With the aid of Olivier Levasseur, in command of his new flagship the *Postillion* and the recently appointed captain of his former one, the *Oiseau de Proie,* the enigmatic Xiang Yu—who was learning to handle a ship from a carefully chosen sailing master and quartermaster—they had taken Jennings and Vane's new flagship the *St. Marie* and its considerable store of treasure in a brutal exchange that saw many wounded and damage to all of the ships.

"And that is not all, Conall," Bellamy had whispered when they were alone in his cabin later that night. "Your friend the conjurer used his black mirror to somehow call up an ill wind that brought the *St. Marie* so beautifully to us I could have cried."

"Hae is nae fraind a' mine," Conall answered. "Thair is nay nicety lost between hae an' Maister Thache. An' thair's nae doubt whose side I am on."

"That's wise of ye, indeed. Rumor has it Mister Thache will soon be *Captain* Thache. And his good fortune will no doubt be yours. Still in all, it was a sight to see."

"How did hae doo it?"

Pulling a piece of parchment from his pocket, Sam sat beside Conall, bringing a candle close so he could read it. "Through a chant. I wrote it down, more out of curiosity than a wish to ever speak it. It went: *Sanco tupanché, tecco du mané, té-liggo, té-liggo nupanché. Sanco du mené, heelo du ché ché. Sanco tupanché, tecco du mané, du mané, du mané. Vibra sume ché ché.* This he repeated thrice, before chanting some other foreign mumblings I could not begin to remember, and the wind began to bring the ship toward our guns. You should have seen the faces of Jennings and Vane!"

"Tis how hae clairs the mirror!" Conall said, feeling a little swell of pride at having himself been involved with the black, mystical mirror, despite the terrible visions it had shown him.

Bellamy shrugged. "It is well beyond my range of understanding, but I am grateful for it all the same. Captain Levasseur has brought us the means to get rid of Jennings and Vane once and for all so we can concentrate on building the Republic and sitting James on the throne."

Conall shook his head. "I cannae ken how ye think those two weel doo anythin' 'cept dooble thair efforts tae bring it all doon."

Folding the paper containing the mysterious words and putting it in a drawer of his desk, which he then locked, Sam smiled. "I surely do not. Although their ability to disrupt our operations has now been seriously hampered. We have taken their best ship—one with which Levasseur was well familiar and in which he has a keen interest—and much of their war chest and their chief benefactor, the former governor of Jamaica, Archibald Hamilton, is on his way to London to stand trial for enlisting the aid of pirates. Why, Jennings is so angry that, as they sailed away on the inferior ship we permitted them to keep, he swore at the top of his voice to burn the next several ships they come upon who sport crews loyal to Commodore Hornigold."

"An' this nae concerns ye?"

Sam patted Conall's shoulder, unknowingly taking the tone Rob Roy always had when he was imparting a lesson. "Those who are truly capable of terrible things such as that do not shout out their intentions to do so. They simply do them."

Less than a year later, Conall would have reason to question Samuel Bellamy's words under circumstances that would shake his faith and strength to their core. But, on this pleasant midsummer night, with the sounds of victory increasing with each pass of the bottle above them, Conall trusted that things were going the way of the good and true, the vision of carnage he had seen in the mirror for the moment gone from his mind.

THE ALBEMARLE, CAROLINA COLONY, JULY 1716

The last of the patrons and the barkeep himself had just exited the Constant Companion, the always filled to bursting tavern where The Family conducted almost all of its business, when Edward Moseley and Jeremiah Vail opened the well-hidden hatch in the floor that led to a portion of the basement walled off from the rest of the storage room.

Sitting at a table, making marks on a map by a weak candle specially crafted to burn without making any smoke, was the man they had been answering to and doing the bidding of since they had first made his acquaintance while searching the lieutenant governor of North Carolina's office five months earlier. Although taking orders was against their nature, their association with this man—and by extension his powerful and mostly unidentified network of aristocrats, spies, and well-placed allies in the Vatican and major European halls of power—had put considerable coin in their pockets and, more importantly, supplied them with a new legitimacy and reach beyond the machinations of The Family. For this alone they were more than willing to keep things going as they were.

"Good evening, Absalom," Edward said with a slight bow, a gesture that Jeremiah would no doubt berate him for when they were alone. "We come with news of the utmost import."

Not bothering to look up from his map, nor to cease his marking of it, Absalom Ravenskald responded, "You say this as though you are giving me a gift, Colonel. You must make no mistake—when your nightly reports are no longer of interest to me, you are no longer of interest to me, and The Family will no longer be of consequence here or elsewhere."

Placing his hand surreptitiously on Jeremiah's to preempt even the slightest grimace or other telling indicator from his partner, Edward said, "We have had a communication from our agents in South Carolina. One recently returned from the Caribbean. We finally have reliable information on the Jacobite pirates of interest to Lord Carteret... and Baron Craven." The latter's growing prominence in their dealings with the Royal African Company was still something to which he was getting used. "Bellamy and Williams continue to strengthen their influence in New Providence."

Putting aside his map, Absalom asked, "And the two upstarts they took from Boston?"

Edward felt himself relax. Ravenskald's question was one he was able to answer. "The one named Stanton is making a name for himself as rather ruthless and unpredictable. As for MacKinnon... there is no word of his whereabouts. We do know that the Scots have continued their infighting and there is talk that an emissary of Rob Roy Campbell's murdered another Scottish spy in the stronghold in New Providence."

"I see. How about you, Vail—have you anything to add?"

Taking a step closer, Jeremiah said, "Vane and Jennings, once thought to be the strongest of the Jacobite knot in the Caribbean, are all but undone. Our agents... Pardon me, sir—*your* agents—have installed a friend in Port Royal to replace the traitor Hamilton. We have it on good authority that Williams is making Vane and company's life difficult in a growing play for power."

"Excellent," Absalom answered. "Although we must never underestimate Vane. In many ways, he is like the both of you. Did you know he sails with the one called *Faccia del Diablo*? And with this throat-slitting rascal Stanton?"

Such demonstrations of his keen knowledge of the things Moseley and Vail were reporting were a nightly occurrence. Edward always tensed a little, positive that, one night, perhaps after a rum or ale too many, Jeremiah would finally lose his patience over it. "We had some indication...," he said, hoping it was enough of a stance to keep his partner calm for another night.

"Listen to me, both of you. There are forces long dormant that are as of late waking up to join the fight. I have been working on deciphering the missives Benjamin Hornigold had sent to Lieutenant Governor Eden. Have either of you heard of the Star Quorum?"

Cursing their ignorance, the leaders of The Family shook their heads.

In response, Absalom mumbled something derisive. Raising his voice, he continued, "Then you only need know that they are as ancient as the Ravenskalds and nearly as capable. They stand to benefit both materially and spiritually by having a Stuart again on the throne. I hear your associate in South Carolina has brought to an end the Yamasee annoyance. I will be pleased when he is able to return. You would do well to learn from him and emulate his actions."

Edward could feel the muscles in Jeremiah's body tensing, although there was a good three feet between them. With any luck, this meeting would soon be drawn to a close.

"Colonel Moore has our full respect," Edward replied. "His return will be welcomed by us all."

Returning his attention to the map, Absalom motioned the two men to come closer. "Look here. This is Fish Town." He pointed to a spot on the map roughly one hundred and sixty miles south. "It would be less than nothing were it not for its inlet."

Glancing at the spot on the map, Jeremiah said, "We know it, of course. It is now called Beaufort, named for the hereditary title of a recently deceased proprietor, Henry Somerset. It was The Family's engineering of the Tuscarora War that made its resurrection possible... as I am sure you are aware."

Careful, Jeremiah, Edward thought.

"I am," Absalom answered, not showing any sign that he took Vail's utterance as an affront. "Hornigold's letter references it as the last known location of an artifact of great interest to our cause. An artifact that, in the hands of our enemies, would strengthen their position to an intolerable degree. Ergo, someone needs to retrieve it. Bellamy and Williams are working with new associates. Ones that must not be allowed to have this artifact, which is referred to in the letter by its proper ancient name—the Tiber Vial."

Anxious to be done with the meeting, Edward bowed again. "We shall do your bidding, Master Ravenskald, rest assured."

Putting out the candle and speaking from the darkness, Absalom whispered. "Yes you will. And with all possible haste."

The Bahamian pirates' ambitious republic was starting to look to Edward Thache as though it might succeed.

Scanning the harbor with a practiced eye, where myriad ships were offloading and onloading goods, crews, and supplies, Hornigold's lieutenant recognized signs of true community, similar to those he grew up with on the plantations of Jamaica. The work on the fort was continuing daily, progressing to the point where it would take a great many ships with dozens of cannon to put the stronghold in jeopardy. The sunken ship at the harbor's entrance would slow or halt an assailing fleet's progress and the growing number of cannon arrayed in redoubts on the beach and along the walls of the fort would answer fast and fierce should anyone be foolish enough to mount such an ill-considered assault.

For the time being, it appeared as though the Royal Navy would continue to tolerate their persistent but relatively minor acts of piracy. With tensions always high between Europe's handful of empires, they had no other choice—the downsizing Britain's Admiralty administrated after the signing of the Treaty of Utrecht had left their ranks stretched thin and tasked with prioritizing the protection of the busiest sea-lanes and most lucrative merchant companies.

It was not the Royal Navy that most concerned Edward Thache, however. Years of service had taught him their tactics, tempers, and levels of tolerance. In addition, the pirates' fast-moving, more maneuverable sloops and brigantines could easily evade the Navy's heavy frigates and ships of the line. It was a poor pirate indeed who found himself in range of the Navy's formidable guns with no method of escape. Especially if they kept their operations close to the shallower offshore waters and plentiful inlets and bays of the Caribbean and the colony of North Carolina, places where they could quickly, cheaply sell their goods to the countless poor who would be that much closer to starving without them.

Nor was it Vane and Jennings, who were no doubt off somewhere scrambling to recruit more undisciplined cutthroats and find a new sponsor to replace Governor Hamilton. The taking of the *St. Marie* from their grasp had been a strategic and well-executed blow. Edward glanced her way, where she sat in the water for further refit before Hornigold assigned her a crew. The fact that she was a French ship brought him no small amount of satisfaction, but he put aside such personal thoughts for now.

His mind returned to Jennings and Vane. They had no safe port, no system of resupply, and it was a hard sell to a sailor to have him leave the security of New Providence to take a chance with a pair of independent raiders.

No. The greatest danger to the Flying Gang was the members of the fledging republic themselves. They and their new allies.

Beside the *St. Marie* were the two ships under the command of Olivier Levasseur, the *Postillion* and *Oiseau de Proie*, not far from which sat Samuel Bellamy's latest command.

It was their growing partnership that was causing Edward a considerable amount of concern.

Events as of late, including the rumors that Abraxas Abriendo had conjured a storm during the attack on the *St. Marie* using his mysterious mirror, were signaling to the veteran sailor that once foundational sands were now beginning to shift. The professed wizard's assistance had put him in good stead with Benjamin Hornigold and Edward now had no choice but to work with him. The window of opportunity for having the commodore's support in banishing the conjurer was for the moment closed.

Now, Edward thought, *I must sway Abraxas to my side*. Somehow he had to convince the magician that his position would be further strengthened by distancing himself from the cocky Frenchman Levasseur and aligning himself closely with Edward. There was growing talk of a captaincy—it awaited only the right ship, the right situation—and it would serve Edward's purpose to keep the untrustworthy but admittedly powerful Abriendo close by his side.

He had to convince him to realign his loyalties.

That meant shifting Bellamy back to his side. And there the man was, having just exited a longboat from his ship and making his way up the beach. It was rare for him to be alone. Edward had to take advantage of it.

"Sam!" he called, using his long legs to cover quickly the distance between he and his target before someone else caught the popular captain's attention. "Have ye a moment for a friend?"

Opening his arms for an embrace and flashing an enthusiastic smile, Sam replied, "Of course I do. I do not dare say no… look at ye—the beard, the hair—ye have even begun on your braids! And the ribbons?"

Stepping back from their embrace, Edward said, "I am havin' trouble findin' just the right shade of red. Too bright an' I shall look... Well, dammit, Sam—ye know very well how I shall look! I cannot have it!"

Sam let loose a warm, lingering laugh. "I understand. Two braces of pistols I hear ye wear when the time is at hand for action. Excellent. Glad my suggestions have helped. Now that ye are fully invested in the cause, ye shall need to be at your best. We need every able man we can muster."

Grateful for an entry into the desired conversation, Edward asked, "Even a boisterous, egotistical Frenchman and his wine-stink rabble?"

Continuing to smile, although its width and energy diminished, Sam shook his head. "Really, Edward. This resistance to new allies is the last thing we need..."

Keeping his voice low so as not to draw attention, Edward said, "Ye know how I feel about the French. Especially Levasseur. He is dangerous, Sam. He does not belong in the Flying Gang. He is not one of us."

Sam shook his head again, his smile diminishing further. "Who is qualified to say who 'us' should be? Is that not the kind of small-minded tyranny against which we raise our blades? Besides, I know that ye are mistaken. He does belong. He perfectly suits my purposes. I am more than capable of handling him."

Electing to bypass comment for the moment on the insinuation that he was being small-minded, although it was against his nature to suffer such an insult in silence, Edward decided to press harder. "His nicknames are *La Buse* and *La Bouche* for a reason."

Letting loose another laugh, Sam answered, "The Vulture and The Mouth! He has earned those due to his fierceness! Which *also* serves my purpose. As a matter of fact, Edward, ye could learn some things from him."

Oh, my friend, Edward thought, his hands becoming fists at his sides. That *is a remark I cannot overlook*. Stepping in closer but keeping his hands at his sides, even as Sam's found the butt of his pistol and pommel of his sword, Edward said, "I shall *never* learn anything from a Frenchman! Do ye not know how I feel about them? Really, Sam. I think a lot of ye, but there has to be limits."

Removing his right hand from his sword—while keeping the left on his pistol—Sam again smiled. "We must not think of this one as French, this one as English, that one there as a Spaniard or a

Chinamen... Either they pledge to this republic and support the Jacobite cause, or they shall be our enemies. Levasseur has done both of the former. Therefore he stays, and I humbly but firmly ask that ye respect my wishes and accept him as our comrade."

Taking a moment to consider his answer, Edward replied, "I shall respect yer wishes, but ask me not to see him as my comrade. At least not at present."

"Fair enough, my friend. I am sure your mind shall change."

It would take Sam some considerable time to figure out how right—and wrong—he was.

PART FOUR:

DARK DREAMS AND DARKER MIRRORS

Abraxas Abriendo was never one to turn down a deal.

After all, patrons for those who practiced the occult arts and alchemy were few and far between, and Hornigold, who had been a gracious host for Abraxas's stay on New Providence, had in no way opened his purse or otherwise indicated that anything beyond verbal hospitality lay beyond the horizon.

Ergo, Abraxas needed to seek other options. Although he had received an extra share of the take from the *St. Marie* after his wind-conjuring trick with the mirror, neither Levasseur nor Bellamy had shown any interest in keeping him on with a handsome retainer and that was what he needed to keep his operations afloat.

A considerable length of the whole cloth of his frustrations was the fact that those who had sent him to the Caribbean in the first place were not filling his pockets with gold. At least, not at present. Promises of future wealth and power and a place at court had been the initial lure and now remained the sole reason he remained in this miserable stretch of nothingness week after week. He, a wizard and philosopher trained through a truly remarkable lineage, had been reduced to fighting against flies, pirates, and the cravings for creature comforts he had known little of in his life but had learned to value and desire in the brief periods he had managed to acquire them.

So here he was, crouched in the dark in the captain's quarters of the *Postillion*, working for Edward Thache.

Despite his dislike of Abraxas and some hot-blooded actions in his youth, Thache was a man almost wholly beyond reproach. His gift of his father's plantation to his stepsiblings, his loyalty and skill with ship and weapon, and his willingness to keep the magician around despite the bad memories of their very different childhoods in Jamaica went a long way toward Abraxas saying yes to Edward's offer.

That and a fat sack of coin.

Moving in the dark to Levasseur's locked sea chest, Abraxas pulled a pair of lock-picking tools from a pouch, making quick work of the simplistic mechanism. Rummaging through the typical sailor's effects, Abraxas smiled as his hand found a journal with a soft leather cover. It too was locked. Confident he had located the object of his operation, he returned the items he had moved back to their places as best as he could remember (and he had an excellent memory) and closed and relocked the chest.

Making his way to the deck, confidently nodding to the crew members hard at work on the sheets and cordage before another venture out on the account, Abraxas lowered himself over the side of the ship to a waiting longboat to make his return to the fort. He had planned his arrival and departure carefully, taking passage with a merchant and his sons delivering dry goods for the voyage while he knew Levasseur and his officers were in parley with the other pirate crews in Nassau.

"Jus' in time, sir," the merchant said, pushing them away from the *Postillion* with an oar. "We was about ta leave without ye."

Not bothering with a reply, Abraxas resisted the urge to unlock the journal and read what was inside.

An hour later, sitting at Edward's desk in his quarters in the fort, the journal's lock easily picked and its abundant contents scanned, the answer was not what either had expected.

"The damned bloody text is in code!" Edward bellowed, slamming his fist on the desk perilously close to Abraxas's open hand.

Pulling himself free of danger, Abraxas said, "I might have known. It explains the lack of ingenuity in the design of the lock. Levasseur is no ordinary pirate. He has connections in Europe… ancient connections. His patron in the Catholic Church was until recently the tutor of the next king of France."

Pacing the room like an agitated bear, Edward said, "You might have told me. Can ye not divine what it means? What if ye reflected it back from that damned mirror of yours? Would that reveal the message?"

Unprepared for this reversal in Edward's attitude toward the occult, Abraxas took a moment before realizing why. "You heard about the wind I stirred during the attack on the *St. Marie.*"

Edward nodded. "Men I respect much more than ye swear that it was legitimate. One of them, Samuel Bellamy, said that there was a blue flame ringed around the sea, from which the wind rose up and returned. Is this true?"

"It is indeed. It is essential to working with the elements. If you give me some of that ale over there and a share of your evening meal, I shall tell you more." Knowing full well the answer, he added, "If you are interested, that is…"

As Edward portioned out the food and drink, Abraxas began his lesson. "The alchemist's greatest art is *not* turning lead into gold.

Nor is it the pursuit of the philosopher's stone—the myth of eternal life. It is the cohabitation of fire and water. You are familiar with the pentacle?"

Tearing a hunk of bread from a long, fragrant loaf, Edward said, "The symbol of witches and warlocks… Evil thing it is."

Helping himself to a slighter larger piece of the loaf than his host's, Abraxas laughed. "That is what the churches in England and Rome want you to believe. But it is not malevolent in the least. Oh, I suppose some misdirected miscreants turn it upside down and pray to some dark devil, but the pentacle is nothing more than the alchemist's symbols for fire and water combined. This unity from duality is the greatest power there is. King Solomon the Wise knew this, and used it to his advantage."

"And where did a poor pickpocket and gutter snipe learn such mystical things?" Edward asked, no sign of sarcasm in his voice.

"I met a man just before I left Jamaica. A man whose name I cannot tell you, because I do not know it. He looked the part of the hermit—long grey beard, matted hair that fell well past his shoulders, tattered and poor-patched robe, complete with face-hiding hood. I was due to be whipped one morning for nicking some silver from the governor's and this wizard took me away. Taught me what he had learned in a lineage that went back to John Dee and further still to the Phoenicians, Sumerians, and Egyptians."

"Dee! Another occult conjurer!" Edward said, his eyes glowing fiercely in the candlelight.

"A genius and a most powerful wizard," Abraxas corrected. "He was instrumental in the defeat of the Spanish Armada in 1588, conjuring storms of unimaginable energy and consequence. And he did so using the very same mirror that I used in my much humbler effort. Dee was advisor to Mary of Scots and Queen Elizabeth, although that proved to be at times a life-threatening circumstance. The Star Chamber acquitted him in 1555 for calculating horoscopes for those two catlike rivals by the slimmest of margins. Female rulers can be fickle…"

"Ye sound as though ye know of this firsthand. But I ask ye… kings are not?"

"Fairly said. Now—before you get bored or lose your patience for my lesson in secret history, let me say that Dee's skills, which have been passed down to me through my unnamed mentor, can help us with our current dilemma of the coded journal. You see,

Dee was the author of the *Monas Hieroglyphica*, which was inspired by Johannes Trithemius's *Stenographia* and *Polygraphiae*."

"Which means… what?"

"Ciphers. The very same that I am sure are used by Levasseur, which are based on fundamental ideas of substitution and key codes. Here—hand me that parchment and quill and I shall give you your first lesson."

Edward did as asked, after which Abraxas neatly wrote out a series of letters:

ETAOINSHRDLU

"These are, in order, the most common letters in the English alphabet. Most ciphers are simple substitution—one letter exchanged for another. Being that 'the' is the most frequently used three-letter word, you see how one could apply these few bits of knowledge to unraveling a code?"

"I do," Edward said, genuinely interested. "But the cipher in Levasseur's journal is not based on letters… at least, not any with which I am familiar."

"Correct," Abraxas said, putting the parchment aside and cutting into a perfectly roasted piece of chicken. "As I said, this is only a simple, initial lesson. Once I have time to study the Frenchman's cipher, I can tell you more. In the meantime, there is more you need to know about the venerable Doctor Dee. There is great power in the natural world, Edward—I mean, Mister Thache—if one is willing to use it, and Dee most certainly was."

"It is fine to call me Edward… but only for tonight."

Abraxas hid a smile. Best not to press his luck. "I am sure you have heard tell of the Rosicrucians? Francis Bacon? Excellent. Dee was instrumental to the former and, when Bacon was selected to head their organization at the age of nine, Dee became his tutor. Be wary of pirates reciting Shakespeare, Edward. Bacon may have been the true scribe, though it is more likely he simply encoded Rosicrucian principles and secrets into one of William Shakespeare's early folios… but that is a story for another time. As to how Dee acquired the mirror and to what uses he put it, I do not believe you are quite ready for those revelations."

Refreshing their mugs with ale, Edward nodded. "I trust ye are right. Is the lesson over?"

Taking a long pull from his mug, Abraxas said, "Not just yet. The year Dee died, 1608, there were great occurrences—dismissed by even fellow practitioners of alchemy and the occult as coincidences, though they were not. For instance, John Milton was born in Cheapside. Perhaps he was the very genius himself, come in a new vessel to continue his work. Thematically, it is sensible... but, as I said, you are not yet ready for those revelations... Also that year, a great battle of sky-ships was seen over the harbor in Genoa. And the *Compendium Maleficarum*, the Italian manual against witchcraft, was published. Again, a sensible occurrence given the facts of Dee's pursuits."

Shaking his head and pursing his lips, Edward said, "Sky-ships? Manuals against witchcraft... Ye have about exhausted my understanding, Abraxas. What has this to do with the path that lies ahead?"

Abraxas leaned in. "Everything. Scarcely six weeks ago, the Masonic Lodges in England made an agreement to unite. They have even elected a leader, a grand master, just like the Scots. This is no accident. The Masons have their roots in both Rosicrucianism and the remnants of *la vecchia religione*, the old religion of the Stregheria in Italy. These in turn owe their power and structure to an ancient order called the Star Quorum. Even the rats in the Vatican have their skills and uses when it comes to this powerful group of seven. Make no mistake, Edward—what we are all involved in is no less than the age-old battle of good versus evil. Light versus dark. The mirror is one of a dozen relics, of which I am certain of the locations of only half at present. These sacred objects are the real reason for these eruptions over ascension, power, alliance, and boundaries. We are not fighting for the destiny of James or George—they are merely straw-stuffed puppets—but for humankind itself."

Edward sat in silence for several moments, stroking his beard, fingering its braids, and considering all Abraxas had said. Placing his hands on one of the now three braces of pistols strapped across his chest, he said, "These are where true power lies, Abraxas—not in supposed relics and mythical brotherhoods. Put your faith in these and abandon your mystical path. Ye shant live longer, but ye shall be a damned sight happier." Raising his mug as if to put the final punctuation on the evening, Edward smiled as Abraxas followed suit.

K irstine had not heard the bees in weeks.

Why had they abandoned her?

Punishment for Jake. Poor, pummeled, pulverized, perished *Jake. All her fault. All hers…*

Then there came the daily dose of blinding light, showing her the bright red of her closed, heavy eyelids, the rivulets of veins running through them, calling to mind the inlet behind her great-grandmother's house in the southern Outer Banks of North Carolina. The backdrop of her treasure hunts…

"Look here now, Doctor MacGregor. Here into this mirror. It is time to open your eyes. At least for a little while."

There was something about the faintly accented voice of Dr. Reinhardt that easily made her do whatever he asked of her, regardless of her will. Not so with the Nurse… Anita Stiles… She was given to force. A psychotic Nurse Ratched come to life from Kesey's novel…

"Open now, Kirstine. Nice and wide this time."

Doing as she was told, Kirstine scolded herself for the surprise she felt at seeing the machine into which she was strapped—with its cameras, computers, monitors, and apparatuses she could only make a guess at the use of, although many were needled into or otherwise attached to her—although she had seen it so many (*How many?*) times before.

"Why I am I…" she started to say, again remembering that she was heavily drugged. She struggled to remember the last time she had managed a thought not colored or shaped by drugs and found the task exhausting.

"The mirror, Kirstine. See it there in front of you? Look inside of it. Deep, deep inside of it… Therein lie the answers which you seek…"

Managing to focus her will, to keep her eyelids open (nightmare thoughts of Malcolm McDowell's clamped-open eyes in *A Clockwork Orange* flooded in as a possible punishment for failure), Kirstine looked at the ornately framed oval mirror suspended from its own alien-abduction-movie clamps less than a foot from her face.

Expecting a reflection, she saw instead an almost impenetrable polished obsidian surface.

"I don't see myself," she said, doubting that the doctor could be comprehending her words.

"You will," Reinhardt answered. "And much, much more. You will see your past, as you did yesterday. A family farm by the water…"

The inlet! The estuaries! She felt as though she had finally figured out a difficult math theorem, the last in the class to do so but once again back in the club. The achievers.

Kirstine had always been an achiever.

"Look into the center of the mirror, Kirstine… And listen to the words in your earbuds. Let them pull you into the center. There are so many people you love awaiting you there, waiting to whisper revelatory words…"

Unaware of the earbuds until the syllables began to slip from them like yards and yards of silk, Kirstine did as instructed, submitting to the words gently guiding her in.

Sanco tupanché, tecco du mané, té-liggo, té-liggo nupanché. Sanco du mené, heelo du ché ché.

They were so much better than the bees. So much kinder. And then she saw her cousin, Callum—named for a famous ancestor who had fought at Drumossie Moor against the false king's forces in the Highlands of Scotland in 1746—also staying for the week that long ago July. He had found something in the barn, where they were not supposed to be.

Sanco tupanché, tecco du mané, du mané, du mané. Vibra sume ché ché.

"If great-grandma were to find out," Kirstine mouthed along with the vision, eyes focused on a half-rotted box held in her cousin's hands. Held in his hands in the mirror. Deep inside the mirror…

"Wanna see what's inside?" Callum asked, simultaneously with Reinhardt's "You wish to see what's inside."

"Please," she whispered, her throat, naval, and groin all warming simultaneously as the mirror began to brighten so she could see cousin Callum prying open the box with a rust-spotted screwdriver and lifting out a brooch.

An acorn and oak leaf brooch. And papers. Old, old papers… ships' logs, and latitudes/longitudes on maps of secret places… Fortresses and temples, islands, castles, and deep, forgotten forests…

Papers she wanted to read. That Reinhardt *wanted* her to read.

That was the point of this. If she succeeded, she could get back to the bees, dangerous though they were.

Sanco tupanché, tecco du mané, té-liggo, té-liggo nupanché. Sanco du mené, heelo du ché ché.

Grasping the topmost of the papers through the ever-expanding mirror, she focused her eyes to read.

"1716. The Coast of St. Croix. Christiansted Harbor. Logs of Captain Olivier—"

Hiya, Kirstine. No need to be afraid. I'm a friend. I wouldn't read that text to the nice old Nazi doctor. I really, really wouldn't.

"Who are—

Uh-uh. Don't give the game away. Not like that. Tell him the mirror's darkening. After all, it always does.

Reinhardt in the earbuds, replacing the lovely silk. "Whom are you speaking to? Is it Captain Olivier? Tell him he can trust me. I am an ally to the cause."

You can't kiddo. And he isn't. Trust PF on this.

"I… the mirror is closing. I cannot read the writing any more. The inlet's drying up. That's what's chased away the bees…"

Kirstine knew what was coming next, as it always did. The pinch of a needle in the big vein in her arm and some soothing words whose contradictory tone betrayed their subtext of threat: "An excellent effort. Closer than ever… Such a good subject. Not to worry. We shall try again this evening…"

As Kirstine drifted off, her eyelids like lead, she willed herself to remember. Because she knew the brooch. And the last name of Captain Olivier.

But who this PF was, she hadn't the slightest idea.

"I will not have it, Isobel! I will *not*! No! No! No! No! NO!"

With each uttered syllable, King Philip the Fifth slammed his knife into the face of the freshly fallen wild boar that his wife had brought down with an expert arrow shot from the golden bow her father had gifted her when her marriage to the king of Spain had been arranged by Cardinal Alberoni.

Prior to this incident, their expedition had been going rather well. For three days they had hunted four-legged creatures and beautifully feathered fowl all across the Castilian countryside, their prizes field-dressed by a retinue of skilled attendants and piled into a fast-filling trio of carts.

Like Camilla, the huntress warrior of Vergil's *Aeneid*, Isobel had been dedicated to the service of Diana and Minerva when she was a child. On the trips to Florence she took with her father, Isobel would stand for hours in front of Botticelli's *Pallas and the Centaur*, seeing glimpses of herself in the armored beauty with the poleaxe.

Now, like the subject of the painting, she must help the centaur—the mythic symbol of the untamed beast within the striving man—restrain his wild ways.

Placing her hand over Philip's as his blade pierced the boar's one remaining eye, Isobel stopped him from removing it by placing her other hand on his shoulder. "Enough now, My King. You are scaring those who must have confidence in your resilience enough to respect you. Leave the poor beast be."

Pulling a thick black bear pelt around her as she lay down to sleep beneath the stars that evening—a gift she had received from a mysterious traveler when she was a child in Parma—Isobel scolded herself for not seeing the early signs of what the court physicians termed as one of Philip's "spells." A growing number of the Court—appointments made by she and her collaborator and confidante, Cardinal Alberoni—referred to them less kindly as his "mounting madness." In response, Queen Elisabeth (Isobel—although she much preferred it, as it more closely associated her with Isabel *la Católica*, the power behind Ferdinand and the unification of their country—was still reserved for those she kept closest) had taken an increasingly larger role in the running of Spain.

Happily, she thought, *but these incidents must be managed*.

After all, Philip was no Ferdinand.

Training her eye on the cloudless evening sky, Isobel looked to another queen, the constellation Cassiopeia, for guidance and commiseration. Given Philip's earlier actions and accusations, she needed comfort that only the banished braggart who had so angered Poseidon by boasting of her and her daughter Andromeda's beauty surpassing that of the Nereids could give.

Cassiopeia, whose stars encoded abundant secrets Isobel had been nurtured on like the milk from her mother's breast. Shifting her eyes, she saw Mary Magdalene and Solomon's mother Bathsheba. It was whispered that, were you to gaze upon them using a certain oval mirror with a polished obsidian surface, they would reveal the location of the balm contained in the Magdalene's alabaster box and a honeycomb brought to the wise wizard-king Solomon from far-off Ethiopia by a queen called Makeda (also known as Bilqis of Sheba), the properties of which were vague but valued.

Then there was the hand of henna—the Fatima Hand.

Cassiopeia held many, many secrets—as did Isobel herself.

So why did she fail to anticipate Philip's latest spell before it was upon her?

Pulling the bear fur tighter around her although the night was pleasantly warm, Isobel thought back to her hand upon her husband's boar-bloodied own.

The red hand. The henna hand. The Fatima Hand.

That was where her thoughts had gone.

Cassiopeia had sent a sign.

Her trusted friend, Cardinal Alberoni, had scoffed when she told him of these things, but she knew it was a ruse. Alberoni had not initially taken her under his majestic, godly wing only because she had succeeded in satisfying the king's conjugal urges after she had so enthusiastically accepted the marriage the Cardinal had arranged. He held no grudge at her insistence on the best of Spanish jewels—God himself knew Philip would be demanding and special compensation was something that the Roman Catholic leaders in Spain and elsewhere clearly understood. Indeed, the Cardinal had been abundantly forgiving and accommodating.

Alberoni knew her value, which means he knew that she knew.

He had no idea how much.

How could he have guessed that she had used the bulk of the jewels to purchase a precious relic known as the Jeshua Cask, which held the blood of the crucified Christ? It was something she had done on her own and the cask was now well hidden.

"What troubles you, My King?" she had whispered to Philip, simultaneously motioning with a subtle flick of her head to the encircled attendants to drag the desecrated boar away, the knife still standing upright from what used to be an eye.

Placing his head upon Isobel's bosom, the king began to weep, as he so often did after a manic expenditure of energy such as the repeated violation of the boar. Sometimes it was furniture or royal portraits. Once, after tearing apart their bedsheets and pillows, he had made a move for the ornate box containing what remained of the jewels that had cost Spain her plate fleet in the hurricane of 1715.

She stopped his hand then as deftly as she had done earlier during the hunt.

"I do not know a growing number of faces in my very own court," Philip whispered, thick strands of mucus running down his lips and chin onto Isobel's hunting clothes. "That scoundrel Alberoni conspires against me, as do you. The throne of France belongs to me. I shall see it claimed."

Stroking his hair to settle him down—one of her maidens was already approaching with a cup of Madeira laced with a dose of belladonna supplied by her personal apothecary—Isobel assured him that their working against him was the furthest thing from the truth. "The Cardinal loves you, My King, as do I. All courts have changing faces. As our empire grows, our need for allies and administrators increases. Do not let it worry you." Taking the cup from her maiden, Isobel lifted the king's head. "Drink now. You need your strength for later tonight. There is one more beast you must conqueror with a thrust of your mighty sword."

Watching as Philip drank the contents and let his head loll back, Isobel knew, for this night at least, she would not have to perform that particular marital duty.

Instead, she lay gazing at the stars of Cassiopeia until she drifted off to sleep, praying the celestial queen and her consorts would whisper to her in her dreams of the mystical secrets they held.

Breathing in the musky odor of fear and a foreign, feral diet emanating from the recent arrival from the Congo chained to a wall in a dimly lit cell between he and Lord Carteret, Baron William Craven resisted the urge to gather the sweat on the lithe girl's neck and lick it from his fingers.

Though not so long ago he had been thoroughly repulsed by the sights, sounds, and yes—the odors—hanging in the air like a blanket of putrid misery in Carteret's secret corridor of horrors, Craven was now fully indoctrinated in the sense and surety of such places and the acts that they contained.

Mammon demanded delectable feasts of sex and sacrifice to be satiated, to pass on his copious favors to his disciples in the Temple not far from where they stood and fear was the only suitable appetizer to ready them all to receive.

"I must have her, John," Baron Craven whispered, flicking his tongue at her collarbone as a viper might a mouse.

Such familiarity, Carteret thought, running a single unclipped nail, filed to a subtle point, along the slave girl's arm. Before accepting Mammon's dark embrace at the turn of the year, his once sniveling associate would never have dared to speak his given name.

Change was part of power. Carteret knew that well enough. Although it was coming in such torrents at present that he questioned—albeit only briefly—Mammon's will. Lifting Craven's chin as it headed for their entertainment's flat and shining belly, he said, "This morsel is for Mammon. You know that."

"He always gets pick of the herd."

Ignoring Craven's rarer but still recurrent petulance, a trait Carteret could not suffer even in women and children, he reached into his coat, pulling forth a knife. As he watched the savage's eyes go wide at its polished, pointed blade, Carteret smiled.

"Is that the blade?" Craven asked, his tongue again emerging from his mouth as though he was prepping to lick its length.

"It is," Carteret answered, pulling its point along the top curves of the slave girl's breasts, where it drew a thin line of blood. "Care to do the honors? Mammon must not be kept waiting. Her lovely neck awaits."

Taking the blade in his sweaty, shaking hand, Baron Craven squared his shoulders and tightened his grip on its exquisite carved bone handle. Since he had been denied the penetration he desired, this would have to do. As he brought the blade close to the savage's pulsing jugular, Craven paused at the sound of an entry door opening at the far end of the corridor. "Lord Carteret! My Lord Carteret! Are you in here?"

Snatching the blade from William's hand and hiding it behind his back, Lord Carteret motioned for him to exit the cell. Snuffing the handful of candles that illuminated their captive, leaving the cell in darkness, the target of the summons joined Craven in the hallway, slamming the cell door behind him.

Two other members of the Mammon Lodge were approaching. Baron Craven had never before seen another of their number in the dungeon.

"What is so urgent?" Carteret asked them, his tone and facial expression insisting that it had better be nothing less.

The taller of the two men, whom Craven recognized as also being a member of the Royal African Company, took a step closer. "George Seton has escaped the Tower of London, apparently by sawing through the bars of his window with a smuggled-in file, and is on a ship to the Caribbean."

Surreptitiously passing the knife to Craven, who was standing just behind him, Lord Carteret brought his hands together in a clap of anger and frustration that echoed off the chamber walls, eliciting a childlike cry from one of the darkened cells behind the messengers.

"You have had this information for how long?" Not allowing them to answer, he added, "I shall tell you. Long enough to let him on a ship! Utter incompetence!"

Coming forward to stand in solidarity with his companion, the shorter of the two men, whom Craven knew only by his nickname, said, "With all due respect, this was an inside operation. How else could he have gotten hold of a file? It was only my skill with the tools of the trade of persuasion that compelled the guards to speak. But such extractions require time."

God save me from ever having to have this savage between me and anyone who wants to know my secrets, William thought. Any man who went by the nom de guerre Scream-Bringer was best to be avoided.

"Leave us," Carteret commanded. "I shall join you shortly in the Tower to make an inspection of the Jacobite traitor's cell."

As the messengers departed, Carteret gripped the bars of the slave girl's cell with such force it would not have surprised William had he bent them. "Seton is important. Damned important. What do you know of him?"

"That he is Fifth Earl of Winton and a Scotsman, jailed earlier this year for his participation in last autumn's Jacobite uprising."

Carteret, still gripping the bars as though to break them, nodded. "Yes, William. And plenty more. He is a damnable Mason, most likely central to the recent joining of their London lodges, and his holdings are extensive. Holdings of which I was set to take possession. Not for myself, you see, but for another. A family of great power and importance to our plans. This betrayal from one of our own must not go unpunished."

He appears to be afraid, William observed. The thought was damned upsetting.

What family could be so powerful as to make Lord John Carteret, Second Baronet, MP, and head of the Royal African Company and Mammon Lodge of London, afraid?

Gathering himself together, Carteret turned and motioned to the knife he had handed his associate minutes before. "Mammon must not be kept waiting. You will slit her throat quickly and cleanly as you have seen me do on countless occasions with no further indulgence, am I understood?"

Glancing down at the shining blade and sensing its hunger and also that of Mammon, which was now beginning to permeate the walls around them, William nodded, asking, "What are you going to do?"

"I am going to send word to our man in the Bahamas to chase the dog Seton down, retrieve from him the estate papers and bank ledgers he most assuredly now has back in his possession, and make of him an example."

William raised a brow. "There is talk, Lord Carteret, of Devon Ross joining the other side."

Carteret's laugh in response to his query made William regret making it. "That is what we wish for there to be! He has thwarted the Jacobite cause through assassination, subtle sabotage of the ships on which he sails, and Hamilton's recent arrest in Jamaica was in no small part due to his subterfuge. You must be wiser than the rabble, William. Truly."

Nodding his head in embarrassment, grateful Colson was not there to bear witness, Craven asked Carteret to continue with his plan.

All too happy to accommodate, Carteret said, "I am then going to make up for the loss of the one by netting the spoils of two. Radclyffe and Gordon were also in the Tower before their executions on the hill. Someone must know their secrets besides Seton. It is just a matter of searching their cells. These Jacobite bastards have their symbols and codes, just like the Masons. I shall soon uncover them.

"And then, my friend, I will unmask the traitor at the center of this plot and his weeks-long despair in my playhouse shall give me immeasurable joy."

TOWER OF LONDON, AUGUST 1716

Lord Andrew Colson, standing in a cell in the innermost keep that gave the iconic complex of various-use buildings its name, looked at the stinking bed of straw on a low-legged frame in the corner and, giving a sigh of resignation for what he was about to do, removed his coat and lit a brand new candle.

Since secretly joining the Masons, Colson had become an apt pupil, reading the texts that Grand Master Anthony Sayer supplied him, learning the symbol systems that dated back to the time of the Knights Templar and Rosicrucians. Codes and practices that had their origins in the priestly orders and architects in the time of the pharaohs and pyramids of Egypt.

The more he read, the more he knew he was exactly where he needed to be.

Positioning himself on his stomach on the dirty, urine and feces stained floor of the cell so he was parallel with the bed, he moved the candle slowly forward, careful not to ignite what passed as bedding, to the spot where the outer wall met the floor by the head of the bed.

There it was, exactly as Sayer said it would be.

The cell where he lay had been inhabited by the Jacobite leaders James Radclyffe, Third Earl of Derwentwater and William Gordon, Sixth Viscount of Kenmure after they had been betrayed by Rob Roy Campbell as an offering to the Duke of Montrose to protect the outlaw's family.

Since their hangings on Tower Hill, the cell had remained empty and hopefully unsearched.

It was by comparing his own recent behavior and betrayal to the distasteful actions on the part of the uncultured, at times savage, leaders of the infighting Scottish clans that Colson found himself so sharply at odds with himself. It was not outflanking Carteret and Craven, nor abandoning the Mammon Lodge, nor even the man who sat on the throne and dared to proclaim himself king. No. These were minor actions given the immensity of the cause to which he had now pledged his life.

What truly made him cringe as he looked into the mirror in his bedroom each morning was the simple notion that, if the only way the Scottish clans could have survived the hammer of Edward Longshanks and his son was by being so incredibly savage, so unapologetically ruthless, then what lengths would he go to now that he had, at least indirectly, aligned himself with them?

George Seton, whom Colson had conspired with Bolingbroke to free, was on his way to France and then Italy—although they had taken the precaution of having the guards overhear that he was going to the Caribbean—where he would work on the Freemasons' behalf to restore some semblance of order in the Highlands. He had turned over the deeds to his lands and his accounts in payment for the privilege of escaping the fate of his compatriots, Radclyffe and Gordon, whose own records of holdings and other information vital to the operations of which Colson was now a part were hidden in a place revealed by the Masonic symbols they had carved beneath the bed, as was the practice for the captured.

Committing the symbols to memory and not paper, in case he was detained, Colson did his best to obliterate them from the wall beneath the bed before blowing out the candle and exiting the cell.

As he rounded the corner at the end of hall at the head of the stairs he paused, hearing the protestations of the newly installed and properly paid-off guards as someone approached and opened the cell he had just left.

He knew the voice quite well.

"Tear this damned room apart! Disassemble the bedding! There are papers here—important papers—and they must be found!"

Although it was imprudent—reckless, actually—Colson stood in the stairwell, listening with contentment as the guards did Carteret's bidding. It took but a few moments and the racket of forcefully moved items before Carteret again began to yell.

"Nothing? How can that be! Damned useless, the lot of you! What the Scream-Bringer did to your incompetent compatriots will be a lavender bath with bon-bons compared to what I shall do to you two fools!"

He then was in the hall. Colson moved further down the stairs, until he was standing fully in the shadows.

"If any of you bastards rotting in the cells of this tower are involved in any way with the fugitive Seton, know this and mark it well—you have well and truly earned not only my wrath but that of Athelstan Ravenskald and those whose blood runs hotly in his veins!"

As his adversary exited the way he had come, Colson moved slowly down the stairs on his own end of the keep. Carteret must be undone indeed to have spoken such a name.

He was signing his death warrant if things continued to go poorly for him and the London sect of the Mammon Lodge.

Colson, slipping unseen into the night, made a renewed pledge to make certain that they did.

"It is damned irregular, and I shall not abide it!" Captain George Gordon of the HMS *Pearl*, a Royal Navy 42-gun Fourth-Rate, was crushing the communiqué Lieutenant Robert Maynard, his executive officer, had just handed him, as if to visually demonstrate how serious he was about what he was saying.

Although they rarely agreed on even the smallest of matters, in this instance, Maynard understood his superior's position. It had been nearly a year since the Admiralty had assigned them to the frigid waters of the Baltic and North seas, chasing the phantoms of Jacobite ships rumored to be bringing guns and men to Scotland to aid the Old Pretender's cause. Although they detained and searched ships when they found them in any way suspicious, there was never anything nor anyone aboard worth their time and effort.

Adding to their difficulties was the fact that they had encountered, when one bothered to make a tally, precious few that met their rigid criteria, and their inability to intercept James Stuart's ships as they fled Scotland the previous February had caused Gordon and his fellow captains no small amount of embarrassment and ridicule.

Their orders therefore had been to continue in this half-frozen hell even longer.

Maynard had only recently returned from dinner on the HMS *Garland*, a 32-gun Fifth-Rate Ship of the Line commanded by the much more agreeable Captain Ellis Brand, when Gordon had waved the communiqué in his face and begun his latest rant.

"He would rather keep me as his slave, doing the lion's share of the work aboard the *Pearl* than have me be in a position to get my promotion to captain," he had complained to Brand during dinner. That was the only possible explanation for the difficulties Maynard had encountered while angling for transfer to Brand's command staff in the early months of summer.

Gordon, the senior officer, simply refused to relinquish him.

Removing a communiqué from his coat (an exact copy of the one Gordon would later wave in Maynard's face) Brand had smiled. "Perhaps this will ease your pains. We are closer than ever to a choice reassignment to the Port of Virginia. Which means we shall soon be chasing pirates! That is where the true glory lies, Robert! So be patient, I beg of thee."

Taking the communiqué, Maynard read it with enthusiasm. Lord John Carteret, governor of the Royal African Company and a growing force in London, was personally instructing the *Pearl* and *Garland* to detain and *interrogate with all necessary force* the crews of any ship suspected of aiding the Jacobite cause. Of most interest was the much broader criteria for what they could now consider suspicious.

Handing the paper back to Brand, Maynard asked, "And who is this Seton he is so interested in acquiring information on?"

"An excellent question," Brand said, filling their glasses with a sweet, heavy port. "A traitorous bastard recently escaped from the Tower of London. Although he sails for the Caribbean, he has surely sent word of his plans to the savages in Scotland. You see what this means, Robert, do ye not? What it allows us to do?"

Although Maynard had indeed seen it, Gordon had as well.

"We are the Royal Navy, for God's sake!" the agitated captain continued from the deck of the *Pearl*. "We do not do the private work of lords, even those as powerful as John Carteret. And this is very much a case of private work. Seton's holdings are substantial. They would place Carteret and his gang of miscreants in an even stronger position. What are the standards of suspicion that would call for interrogation with 'all necessary force'? The man seems to say there are none! Ridiculous! Our standards, forged by the Admiralty over hundreds of years, are what make us who we are! This communiqué sets us on a perilous and most slippery slope indeed."

Maynard resisted the urge to roll his eyes. The warm feeling from Brand's generous pourings of port was beginning to diminish, replaced by the damned North Sea chill he was beginning to doubt he would ever get out of his bones. Even now, in August, the nights were damp and cold.

"It seems to me, Captain, that if we succeed in getting the information the lord is requesting, and he is of benefit, then we shall also be of benefit."

"Ah... so we come to it again." Gordon looked to the sky, his chapped lips curled in disappointment. "Always seeking unearned promotion, Maynard. No doubt Brand has told you that he is angling for command of the *Lyme*, which is now being refitted in Portsmouth. I am sure he is relying on Lord Carteret to see it done, despite the reservations of myself and others as to his ability to command such a formidable vessel."

Knowing it would not be prudent to argue Brand's merits to his supposed superior, Maynard answered, "I must prepare for the change of watch, Captain. No doubt your good sense and sounder judgment will keep us all on the straight and narrow."

As he walked away, he silently added, *You prim and proper and utterly useless git.*

BALQUHIDDER, PERTHSHIRE, SCOTTISH HIGHLANDS,

AUGUST 1716

In the months since his return, Duncan MacDonald had not been able to look Ailish in the eye. Being they were both of clan Donald, their lives intersected far more than what made Duncan comfortable, and his avoidance of her was beginning to be noticed.

It had been easy at first to make excuses for his continued somber mood—having to see Angus's corpse and bear the news of his death back home would cause anyone untold despair, even a rough and tumble Highlander. But things had only gotten worse. Duncan's hope that Ailish's guilt and pain would diminish over time was beginning to fade, seeing how Ailish blamed herself for making Angus's life a hardship through the angry letter she had sent the previous December and how she broke down so completely at the memorial Rob had held in his honor.

Duncan could not let things continue as they were—especially not with James MacGregor pretending at every meeting he could orchestrate between them that he was sympathetic to Ailish's loss. The spoiled lad's machinations against his cousin were unforgivable enough—to be capitalizing on what Rob should have punished him for was more than Duncan could stand.

Not that he had any options. Telling Ailish the truth was out of the question. Angus's best hope for the foreseeable future was to be thought to be dead. It was the only way to keep him safe. James Stuart had been grateful for the list of traitors Duncan had supplied through the pirates of New Providence and seemed satisfied that justice had been served. Making matters worse, Duncan could not see his way to telling either Ailish or Rob what the clan leader's eldest son had orchestrated—though he sensed that, deep down, Ailish knew well enough that the withholding of Angus's letter was not completely free of malice.

And so it was, as he rode by Loch Voil one afternoon, as he had taken to doing several times a week, where the deep, reflective water flanked by gently rising hills and stands of oak, birch, and spruce as the two enemies, the eagles and ospreys, eyed each other overhead, soothed his tired, tortured soul, that he happened upon Ailish casting stones into the water.

"Mae I join thee fer a spael, lass?" he asked, part of him hoping that she would decline.

Holding out a handful of stones, Ailish turned to him, tears in her eyes. "Aye, coosin, ye may, if ye caen teach mae tae make one a' these numpty stones ta skip."

Getting down from his horse, Duncan nodded. "Aye, lass, tha' I caen. Boot these woont doo." Motioning her to cast away what she held, he stooped and chose two flat stones, his shoulder aching as he did so.

"Ye naed a stone flat like a plate fer it tae doo as ye ask."

Ailish nodded, taking one of the stones in her hand. "Are ye weel, Dooncan? Mae da an oothers hae noticed ye favoorin' yer shoolder since ye raeturned."

"I am weel enoof, lass," Duncan answered. "'Twas a haird journey hoom. Ye donnae naed worry, ken? Noo—grip yer stone like sooch an' snap yer wrist as ye let it fly." His stone skipped five times before sinking into the water. "Five. Raespectable. Noo ye doo it, lass, like I shooed ye."

Ailish nodded, took a calming breath, and let her stone go. It hit the water at a beautiful angle, launching up and skipping six times before it lost its momentum.

Duncan clapped. "Six skips, lass! Yer a natural!"

The flood of tears that ran down her face left him breathless.

"Lass… I donnae ken what mae bae the—"

In answer, Ailish turned and ran away. Duncan knew the last thing she wanted was for him to chase her down.

Taking the saddle, Duncan placed his hand on the hilt of his claymore, praying that James MacGregor would appear before him for just a moment, that he might cleave his head from his neck.

In answer, a cluster of dark, angry clouds began to form over Duncan's head, confirming what he had known since the moment he raised his pistol at Angus.

His actions were unforgivable and God had cursed him to Hell.

A MONASTERY OUTSIDE MADRID, LATE AUGUST 1716

The Franciscan community of the Monastery of San Francisco had just concluded their evening prayers after supping with their unexpected guests of honor, Cardinal Alberoni and Queen Elisabeth Farnese, when Friar Paulo, the order's minister general, summoned to the library Guillermo Vincolaré, a seventeen-year-old post-novitiate who had just received his trio of knots.

Guillermo had been in the care of the Franciscans for nearly nine years. Friar Paulo had visited his home one early winter evening after receiving a report of the strange dreams he was having from a Jesuit priest who had taken shelter with the family during a violent autumn storm. For many hours, the minister general had sat and talked with Guillermo's mother and his older brother, who had broken his confidence and told his mother all that Guillermo had told him about his nightly visions.

Although the abrupt decision to separate him from his family had been at first unsettling, Guillermo had taken to monastery life with uncommon ease. He had been a devoted personal servant to the minister general, a passionate novitiate, and now promised to be a friar of note if his studies continued as Paulo was confident they would.

Entering the library where he worked at transcription for several hours each day, Guillermo paused in surprise before genuflecting before the waiting personages of Cardinal Alberoni and the radiant queen of Spain.

Careful, Guillermo cautioned himself, feeling his cheeks begin to flush. *You have not worked so hard and been given such rare opportunities to be so easily taken by this rare specimen of a woman.*

"Forgive me, Your Eminence. Your Majesty. I must have misunderstood. I thought I was to meet with Friar Paulo."

Cardinal Alberoni motioned for the gray-robed post-novitiate to take a chair near to where they sat by a blazing brazier.

"You have misunderstood nothing, my son. Queen Elisabeth wishes to hear of your dreams."

His cheeks feeling suddenly aflame, Guillermo eased into the chair, choosing to look at the fire instead of the Cardinal and the queen. "They were many years ago, in what seems another lifetime. A call from God that has long since served its purpose."

Placing her pale, exquisite hand beneath his chin and raising it so he was looking her in the eyes, Elisabeth whispered, "Friar Paulo believes your dreams never ceased. That perhaps you still have them, even nightly. I wish to know what it is that you see."

As though he were suddenly drunk on ale, Guillermo felt his head lighten and reluctance to share abruptly fade away. "It is always the same, as it was that initial night in my youth. I am being led, blindfolded, into what I know to be a secret room in the Papal Basilica of Saint Peter in the Vatican. My knowing is confirmed when the cloth is pulled from my eyes and I am standing before the pope, who is flanked by six others, a combination of men and women—Cardinals, nuns, soldiers, and scholars—sitting upon ornate chairs in a semi-circle. Sitting apart from the rest is one in the robes of an order not familiar to me."

Guillermo paused as Cardinal Alberoni patted the queen's knee, to which the queen returned a nod. "Continue, Guillermo," she whispered, so softly he had to strain to hear it.

"They are discussing matters of a most pressing nature. The unleashing of a dark-winged demon, enslaver of powerful men with riches, navies, and nations at their disposal. There are maps of the Spanish Main and of Egypt and Jerusalem."

Cardinal Alberoni flicked a finger at him, adorned with a dark red ruby ring, to continue.

"I do not always remember," Guillermo lied, for this was the part of the dream that had removed him from his home and set him on his path. "But there is a long, oaken table and upon it are biblical treasures…"

"Go on," the queen commanded softly, leaning forward even more.

Exhaling a shallow breath, Guillermo, incapable of denying anything the queen might ask, began to list them. "A coin, a cask, a blade, a bowl, a staff, a vial, a scroll, a four-faced wheel, and a mirror, although it was darkened…"

Had he seen her eyes open a little wider when he said "cask"? Isobel had to be careful.

"And a balm," she whispered. "And comb. Is this not correct?"

When Guillermo hesitated, so great was his surprise that the queen could know the substance of his dreams, Alberoni took him by the shoulder, in the same manner his mother had the night Paulo had arrived on a donkey to take him away. "Answer the queen,

Guillermo. The hour grows late, and there is still so much to discuss."

"Yes, Majesty. Exactly as you say."

The queen smiled. It was kind but also mischievous. She had woven a heady spell with her gaze and whispered words. "And a hand. The hand of the Fatima, fashioned in the days of Potiphar."

"As you say."

And then the spell was broken.

"Pack whatever few items you are permitted, Guillermo Vincolaré," the Cardinal commanded in a voice not half as kind as the queen's. "You shall return with us to the palace in the morning and from there we travel to the Caribbean. We have need of you, my son. For the things you have dreamed are real and the time of the Second Gathering is at hand."

Standing in the bow of the *St. Marie*, where it sat at anchor facing five other cannon-laden ships, Benjamin Hornigold looked every bit the true commodore that he was fast becoming. Tugging the sleeve of a brand new frockcoat dyed a deep, regal blue, trimmed with gold buttons and piping and sporting black cuffs and collar that he had commandeered from the merchant captain of one of their latest conquests, Hornigold placed his newly polished boot upon a stool and leaned in to address the gathered crews.

"We are prospering as promised, my men of the pirate republic," he began, his voice deep and full of confidence. "Our numbers grow and those who would see us weakened and undone are themselves now weak and nursing their wounds. Wounds that we all pray shall not heal."

Although the overwhelming response was that of happy shouts and Huzzahs!, one accented voice among the crews, from the deck of the *Postillion*, sliced through the crowd to linger in the air.

"But what of English sheeps?" its source, Olivier Levasseur, inquired. "Or those of zee hated Dutch? Eh? Zees ban of yours, 'Ornigold, ties our hands. I say eet eez time to take what we must!"

Standing beside his captain and commodore, Edward Thache stepped forward. "We cannot risk fightin' all the world. Not at present. Captain Hornigold's restrictions are wise. For the good of our republic, ye must respect and obey them."

"Thank ye, Edward," Hornigold said, holding up both of his hands to stem any further comments. "I do understand your concerns, Captain Levasseur, and those of others who have chosen to come to me in private. And we shall continue to assess our laws, as any true republic must. But today is not the day for such an examination. No. I have asked ye all to gather here so that a man may be rewarded who has earned such a large measure of our trust and gratitude that to not see him lifted in stature would be a most egregious crime." Turning his eyes to the captain of the sloop anchored directly across from his own, Hornigold said, "Samuel Bellamy, from today shall ye be the captain of the *Marianne*, as my own crew formally take charge of the *St. Marie*—a ship in our possession because of your strength and wisdom."

As the crews around him began to hoot and holler, most loudly of all his own, led by Paulsgrave Williams, a few even firing their pistols into the air, Bellamy bowed low. "This is most appreciated, Commodore Hornigold. I shall endeavor to continue her tradition of honesty, fairness, and success—traits ye have taught us all."

Hornigold tipped his tricorne in salute. "I have the utmost faith in ye. Both ye and Mister Williams have undone Vane and Jennings while carrying forth our cause with unwavering determination."

As the celebrations continued, Hornigold heard Edward Thache grunt in frustration beside him. "What is it, Edward?" he asked his sailing master. "I thought I had your full approval?"

Shaking his head, Edward replied, "Ye do, sir. Samuel Bellamy is a fine choice for captain. He shall no doubt put the *Marianne* and her cannon to best use. No, sir. It is not your decision. Look at Levasseur, leading his men in such an overblown manner... Do ye see him there, spread-legged, hands on his hips like some romantic's portrait done in oil from a hundred years past, flanked by Abraxas Abriendo and Xiang Yu? Something needs to be done to trim that peacock's feathers."

"Again on Levasseur?" Hornigold asked, amused.

"He should not have called ye out."

"Agreed. Nor should ye have answered in my stead. Although, however prudently and subtly, I know I made it clear for all here gathered that there are proper ways to express one's concerns. And concerns must be allowed to be expressed, do ye not agree?"

Edward nodded. "Of course." And then an idea struck him with such immediacy and force, his mood was spun from anger into joy. "Captain—I want to do something, something that cannot wait for counsel. Only this moment shall do, as though it were preplanned. Do I have your trust and permission to act?"

Without hesitation, Hornigold agreed. "Please men!" he shouted. "If ye will quiet down, there is one last bit of business I have asked Mister Thache to conduct."

Impressed by Hornigold's facility with aiding his ruse and how quickly the crews acquiesced to his request, Edward turned to the rear of the ship. "Conall MacBlaquart! Front and center now, quick as ye can!"

With a look of surprise at hearing his name in the midst of the ceremonies, Conall made his way to the bow of the *St. Marie*, men moving out of his way with questioning looks that mirrored his own.

"Aye, Maester Thache," he said as he reached the sailing master's side. "At yer sairvice."

Placing his hand on Conall's shoulder, Edward turned his head and winked in such a way that no one but the Scotsman could see. He then turned back to address Samuel Bellamy. "As fine a ship as the *Marianne* is, God knows she has her quirks. And no one knows them better than this man here, Conall MacBlaquart. Who, as ye and everyone gathered here knows, has proven himself a knowledgeable seaman and able fighter, against all early prognostication..."

Letting the crowd, including Bellamy, have a laugh, Edward continued. "And so, if ye shall have him, Conall MacBlaquart shall continue with the *Marianne*, that he may ease your transition as her master. What say ye?"

Raising his arm in the air, Bellamy yelled, "I say yes—and thank ye for it as well!"

As the crews began again to holler and huzzah, Edward took the opportunity to lean into Conall, whispering in his ear, "I need ye to be my eyes an' ears, for the good of this republic. Can ye do that, lad?"

With a tone of surety that hid his conflicted hesitation, Conall answered, "Aye, sair. That I caen."

Samuel Bellamy's new flagship, the *Marianne*, was a sloop of eight guns that required a crew of seventy for optimum operation. A shallow-draft vessel, sleek and fast, featuring a large bowsprit that allowed a trio of jib sails to give her great maneuverability, she was of the type fast becoming the preferred vessel for pirates on the prowl.

It was a vast fleet of Caribbean-built sloops like Sam's that were now playing increasing havoc with the merchant vessels in and around the islands and along the Atlantic coast, where they were able to hide from Royal Navy ships and other heavy-draft vessels and offload their stolen goods to the poor fishermen and craftsmen who so sorely need them in colonies like the Carolinas.

Colonies that now required the "protection" of men like Colonel William Rhett, whose philosophy had always been simple but effective: If you want to best a successful enemy, do at first what he is doing, exactly as he does it.

Then do it all the better.

With this golden maxim in mind, Rhett, upon his commission, had ordered two sloops—of eight guns each—to be employed for dealing with the pirates, whose ways he knew well, having once been one himself.

Not that he ever made the mistake of calling himself as such.

His flagship, the *Henry*, had a crew of seventy sailors, while the *Sea Nymph* boasted sixty. Their captains, young firebrands named Masters and Hall, were the colonel's carefully groomed protégés. No matter what he asked, they would do his will.

Watching closely as the stevedores directed the loading of provisions onto the sloops and into their holds, including crates full of swords, pistols, and muskets and ample ammunition to do their coming work, Colonel Rhett tensed against the approaching interruption in the form of four legs walking toward him.

He could not wait to be once more at sea.

"Good afternoon, gentlemen," he said, not taking his eyes from the careful dance of his well-trained crews. "As you can see, I am very much engaged."

"And a spectacular engagement it is, Colonel." This from Robert Daniell, the deputy but de facto governor of the colony of South Carolina. "A finer pair of pirate hunters I have never seen."

Ignoring the remark—Rhett would be surprised if Daniell had seen *any* prior to these—he instead turned to the governor's companion.

"And what do you say, Colonel Moore? Last we met, you were wondering if I could be of practical help to the military cause. What do you think of my proud pair of avenging angels?"

Impressed by his counterpart's audacity, Moore smiled. "I have been known to be mistaken on occasion, Colonel Rhett. I meant nothing by my remark. As I also said that day, I am well acquainted with your skills. You did a brisk trade in elephant teeth and tusks and African savages out of Cape Corso and into Antiqua and home here to Charles Town. And in a ship named, I am certain most fittingly, *Defiance*. I am sure a man who overcame what must be tremendous obstacles in such a hazardous trade is more than a match for these Stuart outlaws and vagabonds of the sea lanes."

Offering a shallow nod to indicate his shallow gratitude, Rhett asked, "And what of you, Colonel Moore? With the Yamasee now yoked, will you be leaving the *prosperous* Carolina for the one you and your *family* wish to see become its eventual equal?"

Moore's visage darkened. "It shall, sir, and sooner than one might think. And from there, who knows what heights our humble colony may achieve with a push and proper guidance?"

Annoyed at the interruption and posturing these men were forcing him to endure, Rhett step closer to Colonel Moore. "I do not see how. You have no deep-water ports and the north is little more than a refuge for freebooters, runaway slaves, the abjectly Godless who clamor for religious freedom, and skill-less fisher folk who offer succor to the very scoundrels whom I am tasked with destroying."

Placing a hand between the two men out of instinct and not a conscious desire to intervene physically, (Deputy) Governor Daniell said, "I see sparks like off of flint stone as two great men collide. Careful you do not set both of our colonies aflame. After all—north or south, we are all Carolinians, am I right?"

The silence with which they met him spoke volumes of what might come.

Conall MacBlaquart, who had been drilling with one of the *Marianne*'s cannon crews for most of the afternoon, looked out across the calm, crystal seas toward the still far-off tip of the Lesser Antilles, through which they were passing in a gentle, windward arc. On his lap was a journal he had started keeping a few weeks before in an attempt to make sense of all that had happened since Ailish had culled him from her life and Duncan had traveled to the Bahamas at the instruction of Rob Roy to murder him.

The words coming hard, from thought to pen to paper, as they so often did, Conall lay down his quill and looked to his left and right, where their traveling companions, Olivier Levasseur's *Postillion* and Xiang Yu's *Oiseau de Proie,* along with Paulsgrave Williams's lesser support and supply ship, sailed in an almost perfect line with the *Marianne.*

Within days, their flotilla of four would rendezvous near Curaçao with two Spanish smugglers, named de Saavedra and Luzardo, based out of Maracaibo in northwestern Venezuela on the Spanish Main.

Conall would not normally have known even this much regarding their plans. But Edward Thache had made it abundantly clear before his departure as a new crew member on the *Marianne* that, if he wanted to repay Samuel Bellamy for the kindnesses he had done Conall since rescuing him from the authorities in Boston eighteen months earlier—how much longer now it seemed!—then he needed to protect him from La Buse, which meant keeping Edward apprised of their dealings.

As he had placed himself strategically behind some barrels to hear Bellamy and Williams converse several days before, Conall's heart had begun to race when he heard them speak of the Spanish Main. Like most boys his age, his elders had raised him on stories of Sir Henry Morgan, who had plundered Portobelo before moving on to the villages around Lake Maracaibo. Hero to some, villain to others, Morgan had become the means by which Conall had measured the pirates with whom he had sailed and those against whom they fought. Bellamy, Williams, Hornigold, and Thache were heroes. Men like Vane and Jennings—and his former friend Joseph—were unquestionably the villains.

He did not yet know how he truly felt about Olivier Levasseur and Xiang Yu, although he knew he liked the latter better than the former.

"And what is zees I find?" Levasseur had silently emerged from the hatchway as Conall was in his reverie and now hovered above him. Conall reflexively closed his journal and stood.

"*Oui... Très bien!* Keeping your journal, your private thoughts, private ees very wise, *mon ami*. I salute you!"

And, Levasseur being Levasseur, he actually did so, his peacock-plumed hat with its oversized brim making a wide arc before returning to his head.

"I must tell you zees... eet ees *le plus dangereux* to be writing openly such as you were with such treacherous people about. If you weesh to visit me on the *Postillion* some evening—with zee permission of *Capitaine* Bellamy of course—I shall teach you a simple cipher so that you may write in code and keep yourself safe. Do you agree to take my offer?"

Conall had barely nodded in agreement when the men of the watch had rung the *Marianne*'s bells and a voice from atop the mainmast called down, "A three-masted ship flying the French flag is making its way toward us off our starboard bow!"

In a flash, Captain Bellamy was beside them, both he and Levasseur raising spyglasses to their eyes. His voice tense, Sam asked, "Olivier—what do ye make of her? Coincidence, or should we call our crews to the cannons?"

"I know zees ship, *Capitaine*, and, *mon Dieu*, she ees no friend. How she knew of our meeting with de Saavedra and Luzardo, I cannot say. But she must not be allowed to interfere with our arrangement. The object zat we have come to collect ees most important to zee Star Quorum. Abriendo cannot truly be of service to us without eet. Eet ees essential zat we procure eet as planned. She must be delayed by you while Xiang Yu and I proceed to zee rendevous, *oui*? Three or four hours ees all zat we require."

Putting away his spyglass, Bellamy nodded. "It shall be so." Before turning away to return to the *Postillion*, Levasseur addressed Conall. "Our lesson in ciphers may have to wait, *mon ami*, but I will make good on my offer. *Adieu*."

Gesturing for Conall to join him at the helm, Sam said, "It looks as though ye have made a friend in Captain Levasseur. I am not sure Mister Thache would approve."

As Sam barked orders for the delaying action, the chief gunner of the cannon crew to which he was now assigned ordered

Conall to rejoin them. As he took up his position near the powder box, he felt his head begin to buzz with the mounting layers of intrigue and unsure loyalties Mister Thache was continually asking him to manage.

And worse—to keep a secret.

At times like these, tending to the cows in Perthshire seemed to Conall like it had been a dream come true.

PART FIVE:

ALLIANCES, FORGED AND BROKEN

Matters between them had been coming to a boil for quite some time.

Charles Vane, standing over his bloodied former friend, Henry Jennings, told himself he had been well within his rights to strike him.

He hoped that the two crews arrayed around them felt the same.

"Ye damnable madman!" Jennings cried, wiping blood from his mouth and nose, which was almost certainly broken. "Any man that follows ye is settin' his course fer Hell!"

The losses have mounted as of late, Vane thought—there was no doubt of that at all. Samuel Bellamy, whom he had taken for a flea, had grown into a dragon, aided by the Frenchman La Buse, whom none of Vane's contacts could tell him was friend or foe to the pirates' fractured rebellion.

Extending his hand—which Jennings thankfully took—Vane helped the battered man to his feet, offering him a goatskin full of ale. "It were not wise ta pull yer knife on me, 'Enry," he said, loud enough that Jennings's crew would be sure to hear. "Ya left me no choice but ta defend meself. We may no longer agree on the proppa path fer our endeavors but ye will always be a mate a' mine. I mean that."

Running his eyes along the arc of men standing behind Vane—Devon Ross, Joseph Stanton, and the rest of his dog-loyal ruffians—Jennings knew that his best chance to see the morning was to agree. "We have taken a grand beatin', Charles," he said, not willing to part ways without having a chance to state his thoughts before the men. "Hamilton is undone, Bellamy took the *St. Marie* from us and now is assuredly second only in strength and allies to Hornigold himself, and the Jacobite cause in which ye so deeply believe is gaspin' its final breaths…"

Before he could continue, Vane closed the distance between them so they were standing nose to nose. "See… now there ya go again… speakin' ill a' the cause. I shall not suffer it, 'Enry, even if it does come from the mouth a' tha closest thing I 'ave ever 'ad to a brutha. Ye best be on yer way before I change me thoughts on given ya an' any man set on goin' with ye a periague an' a week's worth a' supplies."

Handing back the goatskin, Jennings growled, "Ye profess to have some secret knowledge, Charles, handed down to ye from Hamilton. I pray fer yer sake he has not duped ye, or ye and the rest of yer crew will find yerself at the end of the hangman's noose."

Thinking it best to keep silent, Charles watched as Jennings and some twenty others climbed into the offered periague, which he had already ordered his quartermaster to outfit for a planned excursion. As they rowed away, Vane turned to address the remaining crew. "Pay 'im no mind, mates. The information I 'ave is good. An' once we reach our destination an' take what's rightfully ours, we will make Bellamy an' the Frenchman pay fer the 'urts they 'ave put upon us, I swear ta ye all!"

Devon Ross, knowing this would mean a higher station as second in command, raised his fist in the air. "A loud huzzah fer our captain, lads!"

Once the men had heartily followed Ross's command, Vane called out, his voice full of enough authority to bolster even the few among them loyal enough to Jennings that they still harbored some doubt about the soundness of the choice they had made to stay, "Set a course fer St. Croix an' our destiny!"

OUTSIDE THE HARMONY DINER, PLEASANT ACRES, OHIO,

THE PRESENT

No one walking past the five-year-old white Ford Transit van with GRIDIRON CLEANERS emblazoned on the side as they walked down the tree-lined sidewalks of this stuck-in-time town on the Ohio River would ever have guessed what was going on inside.

Halfway out of a pair of seafoam green hospital scrubs, Jake Givens paused to take in the aroma of burgers grilling inside the diner Haxx had parked beside.

"It's a double cheeseburger with extra bacon and an order of well-done fries for me," Jake said, wishing Haxx would hurry up. Clicking away intently at a fancy laptop, Haxx had not even taken off his sneakers. The photo ID from Quarry Peak Psychiatric Hospital—which he had printed off this morning from inside the van—flapped impatiently from the end of the lanyard around his neck as he typed.

"Time to call it a day, Haxx," Jake said, slipping into his jeans. "You having a burger too? They smell beyond amazing."

Closing the lid on the laptop and putting it into a lockbox, Haxx pulled off the top of his scrubs, not bothering to first remove the lanyard, which momentarily tangled itself on his chin before slipping free. "You were impressively cool today, Jake. I guess you know your way around hospitals pretty well by now, huh?"

Jake waited a second before nodding, savoring the compliment. Having an FBI agent tell him he was cool during an undercover—technically an *infiltration*—operation almost made the beating he had suffered weeks earlier at the hands of the two thugs worth it.

Most importantly, they had found out exactly where the soulless bastards the pair no doubt worked for were keeping Kirstine. Inside the facility, that is. Because Haxx had identified the facility itself after two days of very little sleep and a deep hack into the databases of the Division of Eugenic Design (DED) 37, and its main campus, Quarry Peak Psychiatric Hospital—a high-security, privately run nightmare of sci-fi meets horror movie projects under the supervision of a man named Xavier Hearst.

"How'd you know where to look?" Jake had asked, remembering the logo that had come up on Haxx's DTEAU computer screen right after their meeting with SSA Vance nearly a week before.

"Intuition," Haxx had answered. "If Admiral Adler was that upset, I knew it had to be a DED facility. And most of them are so black op and super-secret they certainly deal with war tech. Anyway, if you want to get information from someone who doesn't want to give it—or might not even know exactly what it is they know—a psych hospital with military contracts is the logical place to look."

When Haxx had gotten clearance to do reconnaissance at the hospital, Jake had volunteered to go with him, never expecting Vance to agree.

The whole situation was utterly surreal.

Deep in reverie about the past six days, Jake tilted his head and looked at Haxx as he pulled on a Baltimore Orioles sweatshirt in the back of the van, his mouth ceasing to move and Jake totally lost about what he had just said.

"I said, hell yeah, burgers," Haxx answered, reading Jake's expression. "Why I chose this place. The lady who runs it, Connie Paulson, is apparently right out of the fifties, complete with beehive hairdo and horn-rimmed rhinestone glasses, and about the nicest lady ever."

"You get that from some kind of database you hacked?" Jake asked, only partly joking. Over the past six days he had learned just how networked the world had become and, if you possessed the right set of keys, nothing—not bank accounts, GPS, smartphone records, your home thermostat, or the past month's grocery bills were safe. And he had had no idea just how many security cameras—set up by police and local governments, businesses, and private residences—there were, just watching.

All the time. Watching, recording, and reporting. Everything you did.

Hell, there was probably a camera or two watching their van.

Pulling on a pair of dark red Sketchers, Haxx laughed. "Some of our intel we still gather the old fashioned way. What the dinosaurs at CIA refer to as human intelligence, or humint. The SA on assignment in Chicago—Kevin Connor—has spent a lot of time here. There's an airbase nearby and his dad, an ace Navy pilot during Vietnam, consulted for them when he retired. I'm about ready, dude. Just gotta do the conversion."

Having seen the collapsible panels that turned a hi-tech command center into a Mom and Pop corporate office cleaning operation emerge from the false walls of the van several times over the last seventy-two hours, Jake did not bother to watch as they locked into place.

Opening the rear door of the van, Jake stepped into the street and straight into a pair of husky men dressed in black hooded sweatshirts. The hoods were up and pulled tight, obscuring their faces.

"Well, well, well... If it isn't our old friend *Jake*," one of them said.

"Hi there, *Jakey*," said the other.

Holy shit, he thought. *They found me*.

Before Jake could vocalize a warning to Haxx, the two thugs had shoved him back into the van and closed the door behind them.

Having been thrown into a metal shelf as Jake was pushed into him, Haxx craned his neck around Jake's shoulder to get a visual on their assailants. "What the hell, guys?" he said, trying to play it cool. "We just got done doing all six floors of the hotel up the street—including a bathroom where a bachelorette party must have simultaneously lost a night's worth of lime and tequila Jell-O shots—and all we want are some burgers. All payments are electronic. We don't carry cash."

"Cut the shit, Julio," thug one said, pulling a nine-millimeter pistol from his hoodie pocket and aiming it at Haxx's face. "We know who you are."

Seemingly unphased by the new threat, Haxx said, "Julio? That is very racist, Cornelius. Like I said—we have no cash."

As thug two pulled a pistol of his own, Jake's breath caught in his throat as, in about as much time as it took to blink, the back door of the van was wrenched open and the two thugs were disarmed and on their knees, a very serious-looking automatic rifle trained on them by a man in a black jumpsuit and logo-less ball cap.

"You two going for burgers?" he asked, not lifting his hyper-alert eyes from the two thugs.

"That was the plan," Haxx replied. Whatever bravado he had mustered to try and outwit the thugs was gone. He was clearly as scared as Jake was.

"No time like the present," their mysterious savior said. "Leave the keys by those bottles of glass cleaner. I'll take care of these two and have the van back to you before you order dessert. The chocolate eclairs are highly recommended. Tell Connie that Abel sends regards."

Ten minutes later, as Connie was bringing them water and menus, Jake had gathered it together enough to ask Haxx about their rescuer.

"I haven't a clue, dude. I'm just glad he was tracking our trackers."

Edward Thache was not one for losing his temper. He had first learned its dangers as a young man with responsibilities on his father's plantation in Jamaica. He had come to control it through hard-earned experience as a Royal Navy man, privateer, and now as a pirate out on the account. Even as a budding revolutionary who had taken yet another oath—one in which he believed more than any other—Edward had learned one thing well enough—raising your voice was a sign of weakness, not of strength.

But as he watched dozens of men swarm like colony ants and worker bees in and around the gaping wounds of the *Marianne*—fresh home from a disastrous mission about which Bellamy was offering naught in the way of explanation—he also knew that on the rare occasion when rational arguments had been ignored, extensions of alliance and friendship had been rejected, and the greater good was being placed in jeopardy by a select few whose greed and pursuit of power were their only occupation, a show of force was not only the one remaining option…

It was to be expected.

Edward's resolve had only strengthened as he inspected the torn shrouds, damaged mast, cracked bowsprit, and decks awash in debris and puddles of blood of the ship on which he had recently spent so many of his days.

And so it was that he had rowed out to the *Postillion*, which had returned a day after the *Marianne*, prepared for any and all outcomes to make his feelings known to the French son of a whore enjoying a glass of sherry in his cabin with one of his officers as Edward barged into the room.

"Ah, Édouard Thache," Levasseur said with a smile, raising his glass. "I do not suppose you wish to join us in celeebration, eh?"

"Celebration?" Edward answered, storming up to the table at which Levasseur sat. "I want to talk to you in private, La Bouche. Are ye man enough to grant me my request?"

Waving the officer away with a nod—the man seemed reluctant to go but knew better than to question his captain—Levasseur stood and locked the door behind him. Turning to Edward, he said, still smiling, "Zees ees regarding the unfortunate incident with *La Marianne, ai-je raison*?

"Unfortunate incident?" Aware that his constant repeating of Levasseur's words was weakening his position, a situation he could ill afford, Edward quickly added, "Only in your world of selfishness and greed would such damage to a newly bestowed ship and the death of one man and wounding of three others be remarked upon so dismissively. Worse yet, bragging about your exploits over fancy wines! Another statement like that and I will not hesitate to fight ye."

Keeping the table between them for the moment, Levasseur shook his head. "Please, Édouard. Zees ees most unneceessary. We are not so deefferent, *toi et moi*. I too was born eento wealth. I too served in zee navy and procured a letter of marque to fight in zee war between our nations. And, when zat war was brought to an end, most uncereemoniously considering the great sacreefice on both sides, I defied orders to return home and joined zee cause in zee Caribbean!"

Edward pressed himself against the table. "Not for the cause! Only for personal gain. I have watched ye, La Bouche, strutting around New Providence like a rooster and smelling twice as bad!"

Remaining calm and further weakening Edward's position, of which the Englishman was well aware, Levasseur answered, "Ah, my poor Édouard... I hear from many zat you are jealous of my mounting conquests. So ignorant to call me a *gallo* when you go about with zees *rubans rouges* in your braided beard! And zees smell you accuse me of? It ees the smell of *la victoire*! Have you come to whine? Save your tears. Let me offer you some of zees... how do you say? Fancy wine—zees wonderful sherry—instead."

Before Levasseur could uncork the bottle, Edward said, "Save the false hospitality, Lavasseur. Or is it the Mouth? Or perhaps it is best to call ye the Vulture—ye are certainly no stranger to picking at the carcasses of other's honest kills!"

Pouring two glasses, Levasseur made a dismissive *tsk-tsk* sound with his tongue. "Such odd displays of passion you Engleeshmen display. But never when eet counts..."

"So I see it truly *is* right to call ye the Mouth."

Draining his glass, Levasseur slammed his fist upon the desk. "They call me so because I speak my truth! Do you? Or are you merely a shill for *Gran-Pere* Hornigold? I think I hear him calling hees errand-boy. So run along, Errand-Boy... I am sure zee repairs to *La Marianne* weel be quickly finished and Bellamy and I weel soon be sailing again. Ah... zees ees why you have come. Did you see yourself as hees good friend? Hees *matey*, as you say? Is zat what he told you? You should hear the things he says about you and *Gran-Pere* when you are— "

Before La Bouche could finish, Edward was up and over the table, sword unsheathed. Retreating to the corner behind him after evading by mere inches a swing of the blade aimed with deadly force at his neck, Levasseur pulled his own sword from its sheath.

"Come zen, Errand-Boy, and let us see what Engleeshmen can do weeth a blade beyond hacking away clumsily at an unarmed man!"

Their engagement lasted no more than a handful of minutes, each proving the equal of the other. When it was clear that only death would dictate a victor, they retreated from one another, both winded from full exertion.

Sheathing his sword, Edward said, backing toward the door, "Consider yourself warned, Vulture... If ye betray Sam Bellamy, even in the slightest measure, our next meeting shall end in a river of your blood."

Laying his sword on the table and applauding, Levasseur answered, "Bravo! Bravo! Finally, I see some passion from zees cold, hard Engleeshman! Keep eet up, Édouard, and you might prove useful yet. For now, I bid you *adieu!*"

Edward unlocked the door, pushing through the knot of men, among them Abraxas Abriendo, without saying a word or looking anyone square in the eye.

As he rowed back to shore, he began to second-guess all he had said and done in Levasseur's cabin. It was clear that he would one day face his proud French foe again, and he would have to do better, verbally *and* with his blade, or the outcome might very well be his severed head upon the deck of the bastard's ship.

Absalom Ravenskald looked around the meeting room where the Council of Trade and Plantations was having its annual meeting and wished he were somewhere else.

Anywhere, truly, would do.

Wincing in discomfort, he shifted his backside in an attempt to settle into one of the hard-backed oaken pews that sat in rows in the meetinghouse. *The pious rigidity of these Virginians will be their undoing*, he thought, before letting his mind drift back to the evening his father, Athelstan, had called him into the central hall of the Ravenskald estate in Zurich, in the Swiss Confederacy, a year earlier.

Athelstan was sending him on a mission to Britain's colonies in America.

It had felt like a punishment then, and more so now, having suffered the posturing and incompetency of Moseley and Vail and the rest of their thuggish cohorts in The Family. The North Carolinians were anything but pious—they were an undisciplined assemblage of rogues, freebooters, runaway slaves, and the ugly dregs of humanity. And the insufferable game-playing of Alexander Spotswood, who was more interested in the fool's endeavor of trying to annex North Carolina and build a mansion more suitable for a king than a lieutenant governor in the Colonies rather than look after the larger interests of those loyal to the Mammon Lodge, only added to his misery.

Sitting Absalom and his twin brother, Adonijah, beside the great fireplace in the drawing room, Athelstan had poured himself a glass of Madeira, taking his accustomed spot at the mantle. Then, for hours, he had droned on about the family legacy, pointing out for the who-knew-how-manyeth time how the Ravenskalds, led by a Viking named Jórkell, had ascended through the inter-warring ranks of the Danish jarls by supplying weapons, mercenaries, and advice to those such as Sigurd and Sigurd the Mighty in the Orkneys. After a few early victories bought with hard, bloody lessons and personal losses, they began mediating services behind the scenes instead of getting directly involved in the centuries of warfare amongst and between the Danes, English, and French. While others bled, they made strategic alliances and provided personal security for Saxon kings the likes of Egbert and all of the Aethels, Rollo in Normandy, and William the Conqueror before expanding their influence further into the ripe-for-the-raping European continent.

In 1042, at the behest of Edward the Confessor, whom they much preferred to reign as king of England while Magnus the Good took the throne in Denmark, they poisoned Hardicanute, who had held both thrones, at the wedding of one of his thanes.

They had worked to secure the release of Richard the Lionheart from the Duke of Austria in 1194 while at the same time building support for his brother, Prince John. This was not the first time they had worked both with and counter to Richard—they had supported both he *and* Saladin during their conflicts in the Holy Land during the Third Crusade and then brokered the lucrative peace between them.

They had been simultaneously working closely with Philip August of France.

Prior to that, they had outfitted and oversaw the training of the Knights Templar after Hugh de Payens had founded the Order in 1119, in order to gain access to the secrets and substance of Solomon's Temple and other riches of the Holy Land, such as the Shroud of Turin, acquired by the Templars during the sack of Constantinople in 1209.

When that particular Holy Order had become too wealthy and powerful for comfort a little less than two centuries later, the Ravenskalds had engineered their undoing with the eagerly given aid of King Philip the Fourth of France and Pope Clement the Fifth. It was one of the Ravenskalds' own artifacts—the converted-to-a-bowl skull of John the Baptist—that was the foremost piece of evidence to damn the Templars as devil-worshippers.

Allowing one of Templar Grand Master Jacques de Molay's lieutenants to make off with the skull was an unfortunate mistake for which Philip and Clement paid with their lives. This world-shaking act of double assassination less than a year after the purging of the Templars was conveniently blamed on the Ravenskald-manufactured claim that de Molay—at the time of his arrest on 13 October 1307 (the thirteenth falling on a Friday being an important occult decision) and again as the purifying flames feasted on his flesh after his conviction for heresy—had cursed the king and pope.

The year before that momentous coup, on 10 February in Dumfries, Scotland, they provoked the argument that resulted in the death of Red John Comyn, paving the way for Robert the Bruce to claim—in due time—the contested Scottish crown.

A time the Ravenskalds decided.

The extent of the Ravenskalds' role in the arrest, torture, and death of too-much-freedom-craving William Wallace in 1305 was a closely guarded family secret Absalom's father refused to share.

They then aided the Medicis in holding Florence against the jealous Albizzi and Pazzi families while also holding influence in Milan and Venice, parlaying their services to the Italian city-states into connections in the Vatican, culminating in the 1570s when they made a formal—but secret—agreement with Pope Pius the Fifth to uphold the Catholic faith when needed.

And it was always needed.

They made sure of that.

By the start of the seventeenth century, wherever there was an uprising, border dispute, or war, Ravenskald weaponry and hired armies were involved. It was their cunning and position as advisors that allowed the Thirty Years' War to last as long as it had, and on its heels the family had positioned itself well enough to support Charles the First and Oliver Cromwell simultaneously during the English Civil War and Charles the Second at the start of the Reformation and after. Their involvement in and influence on the War of Spanish Succession was again only known fully to Athelstan, who seemed content to take the details to his grave.

More recently, they had made an even stronger alliance with the Holy Father in Rome through a series of evolving business deals with France, whose current favoring of the Catholics after years of Protestant favoritism in the Swiss Confederacy had made them the most powerful family in their adopted homeland.

All while worshipping a winged, blood-feasting demon and undermining the Church's secret council, the Star Quorum, every chance they had.

Absalom had learned not to take his father's arrogance and dismissiveness personally. Athelstan had certainly earned it, having done as much or more than his predecessors to further the Ravenskald mission of global domination. Besides, if Absalom could cobble together a coalition amongst the supposed leaders of the Colonies—and here he had to admit that meant The Family in the Carolinas and Spotswood in Virginia—he could do in America what his ancestors had done everywhere else in the world.

What his twin brother, Adonijah, had been doing as head of the Mammon Lodge in Dublin.

Such grand names we have, he thought. The Ravenskalds and their rivals had mostly chosen Biblical and kingly names for their offspring, with zero piety but plenty of hubris.

Shifting yet again in the pew—how long would this damned meeting go on?—Absalom wished that his brother was dealing with at least as many dimwits and fools as was he.

That would be only fair.

Resisting the urge to break wind as one of the Council patsies introduced *Governor* Spotswood—none of these colony representatives bothered with the qualifier of "lieutenant"—Absalom reminded himself that diplomacy with one hand whilst one dipped his dagger in poison with the other was the surest way to inherit the family mantle.

Those were lessons well learned from both the Medicis and the Borgias.

The Borgias… what an alliance that had been.

Taking his place at the podium, Spotswood welcomed the crowd and got immediately down to business. "The pirate threat in the Bahamas is a pestilence we can no longer afford to ignore," he began, his voice full of confidence and just a hint of arrogance. "I am working with the Royal Navy to see that our shores continue to be protected." Expertly pausing for applause, he changed his tone and tack. "Thanks to our close confederates in the Carolinas—Moseley and Vail, who are here with us today—stand gentlemen, thank you—and Colonel Moore, recently triumphant again against the savages in the south—we are in a position to show those stuck up peacocks in Massachusetts what true wealth, power, and influence can be!"

Absalom was impressed—the wave of applause that washed over the room and lingered longer than was comfortable was proof that Spotswood was the man of the moment.

Yet there was more.

Spotswood had recently returned from an expedition up the Rappahannock River Valley that had yielded abundant information about Virginia's richly resourced interior. Along with four dozen other intrepid explorers, including Indian scouts and other veterans of rugged terrain, he reached the Blue Ridge Mountains before arriving at the headwaters of the Rappahannock. Having crossed the mountains they had descended into the Shenandoah Valley and reached another river they christened the Euphrates (Spotswood was nothing if not grandiose). That evening they reveled, indulging in good wines and naming the two nearby peaks after their king and their expedition's leader.

After claiming the lands in the name of George through the mechanism of a paper declaring them as such stuffed into a bottle and buried, they returned home to Williamsburg to such shouts of heroism that Spotswood bestowed upon all of the expedition's officers a small golden horseshoe. Inscribed in Latin upon each were the words: *Sic juvat transcendere montes.*

"Thus he swears to cross the mountains," Spotswood translated for the crowd, holding his own miniature horseshoe aloft for all to see from where it hung from his lapel. "May the men who wear these—whom we call our Knights of the Golden Horseshoe—serve as a reminder and inspiration for all gathered here today that courage, fortitude, and faith in our destiny will make us the architects of a powerful and prosperous future!"

As the applause swelled and died and the men in attendance began to rise and go about their business—which, for most, meant lining up to shake Spotswood's hand and get a closer look at the heady new emblem of his modern-day knights—Absalom cornered Moseley and Vail as they attempted a hasty retreat.

"Gentlemen. I am sure it is an oversight, so elevated is everyone's blood by *Lieutenant* Governor Spotswood's rousing speech, that you were leaving without making a report on the retrieval of the Tiber Vial."

Stepping forward to speak before his rash associate said something offensive, Edward Moseley tried his best to sound reassuring. "An oversight indeed. The future is bright, is it not? And as to the matter of the artifact—we are working daily to pinpoint its location."

"Is it no longer in Beaufort? Is that why you are standing here with me in Virginia, hundreds of miles away?"

Knowing the answer, Absalom turned and exited before either of The Family's foremost representatives could answer.

OFF OF HISPANIOLA, LATE SEPTEMBER 1716

It had not taken long for Captain Samuel Bellamy to puzzle out what had occurred between Edward Thache and Olivier Levasseur after he had returned to New Providence with the damaged *Marianne*. Neither would share the full narrative, but each begrudgingly offered enough that Sam knew it had come to drawn swords and ended a hair's breadth from bloodshed.

With the surety that he could not negotiate a truce between his two stubborn, hot-tempered friends, Sam stepped up efforts to have his ship repaired well enough to be seaworthy. Within days, the flotilla of four, of which Levasseur was nominally the commander—at least in Bellamy's mind—had set sail southeast for Hispaniola, where they knew the pickings would be easy and lush. A bit of quick success—meaning heaping treasure chests and holds full of sellable goods—was their best course of action to keep Hornigold on their side and out of the way of their affairs.

If they could manage that, Edward Thache—still not made a captain—would be powerless to break up their alliance short of murder, and Sam knew him well enough to know he would not let it come to that.

Not for now.

They had been sailing for less than three days when they tracked and captured an English ship near Santiago de la Buena Esperanza, a bay named by Alvaro de Saavedra nearly two centuries before.

After undergoing the normal procedures for offering of options and eventual boarding—despite protests by Paulsgrave Williams that this was the worst possible time to be taking an English ship—Levasseur had forcefully removed a packet of letters and directives on the person of an emissary from Vane and Jennings, written in the probable hand of Devon Ross. It was, they guessed, his signature scrawled like the claw-tracks of a tortured tiger at the bottom of each page.

They had then proceeded to lock the ship's captain and crew in the hold before attending to the most unexpected and concerning matter of the emissary.

Vane's operation was seeking volunteers from and spies in New Providence and Ross claimed to have the gold to pay excellent rates for services rendered. The letters mentioned Lord John Carteret offering his support and resources in several places, though that was not the total of it. "Although such generosity from one so closely aligned with the king is of aid, he is not our sole source of resources. For we have secured a sizable store of same from a virgin saint whose prayers were learned to us by a now departed friend," Sam read, his eyes going wide in surprise before narrowing in anger at their apex as Levasseur ripped the letter from his hands.

"*Non, non, non!*" Levasseur yelled, reading the offending passage to himself before striking the emissary, whom he had lashed to a chair, with enough force to shatter his nose and send the chair flying backward, where the (perhaps fortunate) man felt the back of his skull crush like an ostrich egg as it met an errant block and tackle before quickly bleeding out.

"My God, Levasseur!" Williams shouted. "Now we are guilty of killing an Englishman! This makes ye no different than Ross's dog Joseph."

Seeing Le Buse's face redden as he absorbed Williams's heated words, Sam stepped between them. "Enough! I must agree with Paulsgrave on this," he said, trying to keep any tone of threat from his voice. "To attack an English ship is one matter, but to kill this man for carrying a letter…"

Levasseur stood his ground. "Zees ees thinly veiled code to a man such as *moi*," he began. "I know of zees virgin saint as well as zee deeparted friend. Our eentire mission—our very purpose Sámuel—shall be compromised eef zees letter indicates what I believe eet does. We must deespose of zees corpse before releasing *le capitaine* and hees crew. First, we must transfer our supplies from Williams's ship so zey can be placed upon eet. We then return to New Providence to properly outfit zees vessel and find Vane quickly and dispose of him once and for all. Agreed?"

Seeing the fire in Paulsgrave's eyes, Sam took him by the shoulders. "This is a fine ship, Paulsgrave. It has great promise as a vessel of war. And ye are the one who has prompted me these years to stay committed above all else to the cause. We cannot allow that villainous Carteret to undo us."

Rubbing his cheek in thought before nodding his head, Williams replied, "I agree… for now. But I must have proof that this is not some scheme to take further control, Levasseur. For I am far from convinced that we are indeed fighting for the same cause, despite our common enemies."

"Ah, you Eenglish!" Levasseur said with a laugh, knowing he was once again getting his way, "so senseetive! We must act weeth haste. Every moment we linger ees a moment of advantage for Vane and Carteret."

As this conspiratorial scene unfolded, Conall MacBlaquart sat on a barrel on the deck of the *Marianne*, taking careful notes about all that was transpiring, using a simple substitution cipher that Levasseur had taught him the week before.

Making his notations, Conall knew that he was now part of something so large in scope and importance that he must increasingly be the keeper of its record. If he were diligent and careful, his writings would one day make known the true details of this strange, violent time in the history of humankind, serving as an alternative to the lie-laden narratives the illegitimate gatekeepers in their walled cities and corrupted castles and mansions preferred their sheep to eat.

Captains Bellamy, Levasseur, and Williams watched in disbelief as unforeseen events unfolded in the harbor of New Providence.

This, Bellamy thought, *should have been foreseen. And my ignorance shall cost me dear if I am not shrewd in how I react.*

They had no sooner returned to port with their new prize and violently acquired intelligence concerning Vane than the bells were ringing in the fort's tower, calling an assembly of the crews.

The focus of the meeting was a newly won six-gun sloop, on the deck of which stood Benjamin Hornigold and Edward Thache.

"Another successful raid," Hornigold was saying as the three men ran their small boat to shore and took their place amongst the curious crowd, "made possible by the courage and action of Mister Thache. Therefore, it is my duty and honor as leader of the pirate republic of New Providence to bestow upon him the rank of captain and offer this worthy vessel, appropriately named *Marauder*, as his long-due first command."

Applauding along with the rest and urging Levasseur, who stood, arms folded, to do the same, Sam praised Hornigold's brilliant maneuver and again cursed his ignorance that he had failed to see it coming.

This simple action—which Edward undoubtedly had earned, although the timing could be questioned—would potentially change the balance of power on the island at the worst possible moment. As capable and motivated as he was, Edward would surely work quickly to take a larger ship, allowing himself the opportunity to recruit more men to his cause.

And his cause, of course, was first and foremost Hornigold's.

"Look at how he gloats," Levasseur said, spitting into the sand. "He weel be most eensufferable weeth hees silly beard of *rubans rouges* and zee six pistols on hees chest. We must move against them, and soon."

Sam turned to face him. "What are ye saying? We may not agree on a number of points, but we are all brothers, Olivier. I shall not make war on my own without proper provocation."

Before the Frenchman could answer, Conall was standing before them, out of breath and grinning like a poor man on payday. "What ees eet you weesh?" Levasseur asked, although it was not his place to do so—a breach of protocol noted by Williams and Bellamy by their mutually tensing expressions.

"Cap'n Bellamy's permission tae bae excused froom mae dooties tae congratulate Cap'n Thache on his noo command!"

This cow-herder's devotion to his enemy could become a problem, Levasseur thought, though he dared not say so aloud.

"Of course ye can," Bellamy answered. "And please give him our regards until we can do so in person." Then, as Angus turned to go, he added, "I need a favor, Conall. There is no need to mention that the ship we took is English. I will of course apprise Captain Hornigold—and Captain Thache—of the facts at the appropriate time. For now, it is best kept quiet, yes?"

"Aye, sair," Conall replied. "I caen see yer position. I weel nay say a waird."

As Conall walked away, Bellamy returned his attention to Levasseur. "I have given ye the lead for quite some time now, Olivier, and we have prospered, but I ask ye for your patience while I sort this out. There is much to be done and a war amongst us will not aid the cause. I need ye to agree. To give me your word that ye will not do anything rash."

Rolling his eyes toward the sky, Levasseur nodded. "*Oui, mon ami.* Abriendo needs time to feegure out zee true value of zee object we procured at such a dear price to zee men of *La Marianne.* Zerefore, I shall grant you zees request. Until such a time zat I no longer can."

If Sam would have known at that moment that "such a time" was only a few weeks away, he might have done something differently than shake Levasseur's hand and take him at his word.

It was yet another mistake he would come sorely to regret.

For the next two weeks, the pirates of New Providence, no matter beneath which captain's flag they served, reveled in the increasing prosperity of their endeavors. Commodore Hornigold ordered additional improvements to the fort. Merchant ships were captured and outfitted for increased operations, and the taverns spilled over with men with hearty appetites, thirsty throats, lust for the growing number of women employed by the tavern keepers, and sacks full of coin with which to pay their hefty tabs.

Of all the pirates basking in their prosperity, none was more successful than Samuel Bellamy. Following Edward Thache's promotion to captain and Levasseur's political impatience—which was causing a strain between Sam and Paulsgrave Williams, something he could neither afford nor abide—Sam had been sailing the shipping lanes in consort with Paulsgrave, leaving Levasseur and Xiang Yu to ply separate waters well away from them.

And so it was, with utter surprise and a feeling in his body and thoughts as though he was once again the boy from long ago being beaten with Lord Colson's stick by his son Andrew in Exeter, that Samuel Bellamy found himself put in an unwinnable position in a situation not of his making.

He was sitting in front of the fort, regaling an assembled crowd with the details of the taking of his latest prize. "So I told the captain, a fat scoundrel and an enemy to our cause, 'Ye sir are a sneaking puppy, as are any supposed men who will submit to be governed by laws which rich men have made for their own security, for the cowardly whelps—ye foremost amongst them—have not the courage—'"

"Samuel Bellamy! A word with ye, sir, if ye please!"

Coming through the crowd was Commodore Hornigold, flanked by Edward Thache and Paulsgrave Williams, looking as though their larder had just been plundered and Sam was sitting with the contents spilling from his pockets and dribbling from his mouth.

"To what do I owe this most unceremonious interruption?" Sam asked, getting to his feet. "If I have offended ye in any way—"

Hornigold, red in the face and as angry as Sam had ever seen him, waved his hand as if to sweep his words away. "It is not me ye have offended, but the contract to which ye and your men have agreed. And, far worse, the very foundations of what we have committed to build here."

"How have I done so?" Sam asked, his hand finding its way instinctively to the hilt of his sword. "By capturing more ships and treasure than any other captain under your command?"

As Hornigold made to answer, Sam noticed a large crowd gathering around them, its members slowly pushing in, to not only better hear the exchange but to have a clear view should the heated discussion descend into blows.

"By taking English ships!" Hornigold hissed, as if he were accusing Sam of laying with his sister. "Ye thought ye could hide it, but ye have been undone in your dissembling. I will not have it, sir— do ye understand me?"

In the seconds it took for Sam to formulate a response— further dissembling was out—Olivier Levasseur had appeared beside him, sword and pistol drawn, flanked by dozens of his crew. "Stand down, Horneegold!" he shouted, not being so bold as to point his weapons in the commodore's direction. "Zees policies of yours are no longer ours... We weel not be shackled by your inane loyalty to zee horrid Breeteesh crown! *Non*... Zees ees how eet shall be... in two weeks' time—zee first of November—we shall have a vote for who shall be commodore of zees *republique*! The articles you yourself created allow for eet and as a signing member, I demand eet!"

Sam felt his torso tense as his knees went weak. Levasseur's methods were unreasonable, though his demand was not.

Perhaps the time had come.

As those in the crowd began to raise a din of varied opinions and shouted names of candidates—of which his was shouted loudest and most often, Sam said, "I shall stand against ye, Commodore Hornigold. What say ye to my words?"

By nodding his agreement and heading into the fort, Hornigold had prevented a bloodbath. Surely that simple action would win many to his side. As the crowd, including Levasseur, dispersed, Sam approached Paulsgrave, who had strategically remained behind.

"Was it ye who told the commodore about the English ship?"

"Does it matter, Samuel? Levasseur is right—the time has come for a vote. I am relieved that ye have volunteered to stand against Grandpa Hornigold, rather than leaving it to a more ambitious candidate. It matters not which of ye wins, for both can be trusted—though ye know where my loyalties lie. And all shall know and abide by the future policies of the pirates of New Providence." Paulsgrave's tone was well aligned with the look of sadness on his face. "Circumstances cannot continue any longer as they are. And I am sure ye know it."

Looking toward the fort, Sam took stock of the events of the last few moments.

In his heart, he knew there was nothing for him to do but commit to the course set in motion against his will and hope to ride out the storm that was looming on the not so distant horizon.

GLEN SHIRA, SCOTTISH HIGHLANDS, LATE OCTOBER 1716

As Rob Roy and a handful of his men kept watch in a barn they had converted to a temporary gaol, the hills and farms around Glen Shira began to glow with the samghnagans, or bonfires, of Samhain. Lit to protect the people from the fair folk, as the faeries prefer to be called, and other creatures who might otherwise conspire to make for a horrible harvest or otherwise bring misery to the good people of the Highlands, the fires were a cause for celebration and dancing as well.

While the clans' ablest young warriors saw to the slaughter and burning of the sacrificial cattle and children carved turnips, or neeps, into Jack o lanterns, the clan elders told long, inspiring tales in verse of the victories won by the great Scottish warriors—from whom they personally claimed ancestry—over the creatures and demons of the underworld.

Pausing his whittling of a piece of ash he was fashioning into a cross for his youngest son, Robin Og, who had just entered his tenth month, Rob looked skyward and prayed to the ancestors that he might borrow some of their strength on this night, for nothing over the past few weeks had gone quite right.

It had begun with the robbery and kidnapping of John Graham, factor to Rob's sworn enemy, the Duke of Montrose, who had just collected his employer's rents. Graham had been responsible, two years prior, for the burning of Rob's farm and the molestation of Rob's wife Mary, a grievous act that Graham had participated in with full vigor with his men.

Rob shot the bastard a look as he sat in the makeshift gaol, a smug smile on his face that Rob would not mind carving away with a scythe.

The plan had been to secure a ransom from Montrose for his primary man, a sum—along with the stolen rents—that would offset some of the reversals Rob had recently faced in his cattle business. It would go a long way as well toward making up for other losses that had come with backing—for the most part—the earl of Mar John Erskine and the Old Pretender in their failed campaigns against the English army. Losses that had exponentially increased after the pair had fled Scotland for greener pastures in France, leaving Rob and other leaders of the Jacobite clans to bear the burden alone.

The plan had been fair, just, and sound.

Until Montrose sent word that no ransom would be paid. Furthermore, as he had done in the past, the duke was proposing that, in order for Rob to escape the full force of his wrath, he send a letter to King George in England detailing the nefarious operations of John Campbell, Second Duke of Argyll, who was not in fact the king's ally but an agent for the Jacobite cause.

As he also had in the past, Rob had refused, knowing that Argyll would come to his aid, taking Graham off his hands and protecting him from whatever it was Montrose had planned.

Argyll's politics were none of Rob's business. As long as he was useful, he was a friend.

Judging by the knock at the door, his friend was once again as good as his word.

"Mae rescuer's at the door," Graham said, standing from the putrid strands of straw that had been his bed for thirteen mostly sleepless nights. "Pray ye, let 'im in soo I caen see fer maeself joost what a traitor ye are, Rob Roy MacGraegor."

Waving the half-carved cross at the door, Rob watched as Duncan MacDonald opened it, revealing the duke of Argyll and a slight man with wild red hair and eyes that looked as though he might very well be possessed by one of the Samhain spirits the neeps and samghnagans were supposed to keep away.

"Maery Samhain tae ye, Rob," the duke exclaimed. "Mae next yair's harvest bae greater still than this one's." Peering into the cell with a look of disgust, he added, "I see the baistard's noot too worse fer wair. Raedy tae goo back tae yer maester, Graham? I am sure hae has missed his mongrel."

Taking the duke to the side, Rob whispered, "Whoos that thair wit' ye? Hae looks nay a' dere, if ye ken?" As he spoke, the little man began to mumble a tune, his feet moving out of time with it in an odd little jig. "Doo ye see haim? Hae is noo doot aff his haid!"

"That mae bae, Rob," the duke answered. "Boot hae has baen a help tae mae, an' I think tae ye as weel, by spyin' on that feartie baistard Montrose."

"Ye haev mae attention."

"Haes name is Finlay Fletcher. Haes a barber bae trade. An' hae overhaird James Stuart an' I in a maetin' in Scone Castle at the turnin' a' the year—information hae took tae Montrose."

Rob shook his head. Were he given the choice, he would never have kidnapped Graham. The mud was getting deeper around his ankles with every passing moment. "Soo what is hae doon hair wit' yoo?"

"Hae wanted soomthing froom Montrose that the connivin' baistard was noot weelin' tae give."

"Soomthin' ye air, noo doot."

Argyll nodded. "As weel yoo. I knoo ye haev noo love fer the Murrays a' Scone."

"That bae troo 'nuff."

"One a' Murray's brood took a fancy tae Finlay's baetrothed, an' has kaept hair a prisoner in the castle fer over a yair."

Rob was beginning to understand. "An' Montrose has moor thaen a few bis'ness deals goon wit' the Murrays…"

"Ye ken weel 'nuff. Once Finlay was refused, the smart lad, weel past sair, came tae mae. An' noo I am coomin' tae ye. I weel take Graham off yer hands, sure 'nuff… an' ye weel look after Finlay an' doo all ye caen tae get his love back tae haim, agreed?"

Looking at Graham, still standing smug in his cell and then at the wild-eyed, flaming-haired barber, who had stopped dancing but was now starting to sing at the top of his lungs, Rob shook the duke's hand. "Aye, I doo indeed. If ye caen get that boggin' bampot Graham oot a' mae sight soo I caen get a moog a' ale an' a hunk a' mutton befoor thair goon."

As Duncan unfastened the door to the cell, Rob approached his new charge. "Finlay, is it? What say ye tae a mug an' a bowl a' soomthin' warm, eh?"

In response, Finlay, who had stopped his singing as Duncan led Graham out into the open and he recognized who it was that had been standing in the shadows of the cell, again started up his song and odd little jig as he followed Rob out the door.

"Mae lady is lost in the Tower a Scone... la diddy la diddy da diddy da do..."

He had added several verses as the year had marched on— enough to last him for as long as he needed until his beloved was home and he would be compelled to sing out his sadness no more.

Colonel William Rhett was accustomed to working with powerful men.

But there was something about Absalom Ravenskald that the former slaver and ivory trader found wholly unsettling.

The scene before him, down in the hold of the *Henry*, did not aid in altering his perceptions.

Standing in a spreading pool of blood, the origin of which was two Portuguese fisherman—or what little recognizable was left of them—tied to a post beneath the sputtering light of two nearly exhausted lanterns.

Ravenskald was meticulous and methodical, and his intricate work with razor and cobbler's pliers had gone on for most of the night.

The Portuguese had a resounding reputation as a hearty, stubborn breed with a high threshold for pain, and these two had not been a disappointment to Absalom at all.

The *Henry* and *Sea Nymph* had been sailing near the Cape Fear River two days before when a ship bearing the flag of the colony of Virginia had hailed them.

On board was Absalom Ravenskald, whom Rhett knew only by reputation.

Looking at what remained of the Portuguese, he wished it had stayed that way.

"I do not know what I shall tell the men tasked with cleaning this carnage from the post and decking," Rhett said, the statement in no way an exaggeration.

Dropping his hideous, sadistic tools into a bucket brimming with bloody rags and various parts and pieces that had come into the world attached to the corpses before them, Ravenskald smiled. "You are the captain. Tell them nothing! If their God has blessed them with a modicum of sense, they will know that, to ask a question, hazard a comment, or even hesitate in the slightest to do what they have been instructed, they will meet a similar fate. Really, Rhett—I had heard such promising things regarding your appetite for just this sort of work... and yet here you stand, as thoroughly disappointing as Moseley, Vail, and their pitiful little *family*... What you witnessed here is art at a sublime and practiced level. As to your doubt about the necessity of my methods, I secured the information those useless men in the Abermarle could not."

Rhett could not argue that the outcome had been exactly what Ravenskald desired. It would not have been more of a success in that sense if the Portuguese had been carrying the object Ravenskald referred to as the Tiber Vial on their person when a half dozen of Rhett's crew had brought them on board.

How Ravenskald had come by the information that had led him to these two insignificant fishermen from the inconsequential and unincorporated town of Beaufort, whose city plan had only been laid three years before, following the Family-engineered Tuscarora War, he had not asked and his guest had not volunteered. Ravenskald had simply requested a detail of six armed men to accompany him to the shore once they passed through Topsail Inlet.

Rhett had wisely complied. Though no Ravenskald had held any formal rank or title, he knew that governors, generals, and even kings and popes did their bidding without question.

They had returned several hours later with the Portuguese, already beaten and bloody, in tow.

"I am finished here, *Colonel*," Ravenskald said, not yet bothering to wash the dried, encrusted blood and tissue from his hands. Rhett stood in amazement at how Ravenskald had somehow made a rank worthy of considerable honor and respect sound like something a whore would mutter to fool an incompetent lover into thinking he was cock of the walk. "I will need a longboat and half a dozen men. Different than those who helped secure our prey." Rhett was sure Ravenskald was going to spit on the corpses, but he mercifully refrained. Perhaps it was a sign of how precious he thought his fluids were. "No one man should know too much."

Taking his cue from this last remark, although waiting until Ravenskald had gone on deck to do so, Rhett, removing his coat and rolling up his sleeves, decided it was best to do the disposal work himself.

Sometimes it was a form of insurance to be one of the few to know a secret, and with the Family falling out of favor—which he hoped included that smug son of a whore, Colonel Moore—Rhett intended to make the most of the one he now possessed.

FORT OF NASSAU, NEW PROVIDENCE, BAHAMAS,

ALL HALLOW'S EVE, 1716

Benjamin Hornigold had been born of an even temper and rarely given to worry. It was not that he was a man of God. He had amused himself as a child attending church in Bristol, England by making drawings of the minister and ladies of the port city in compromising positions in the hymnals with a smuggled bit of charcoal and took from the basket as much or more than his father dropped in it as it was passed along the pew every Sunday. Childhood folly aside, Hornigold did not indulge in the gloom, doom, and superstitions that turned many a man of the sea old before their time.

It was true that the early whitening of his beard had earned him the unfortunate nickname of Grandpa before he was forty, but a man played what he was dealt and made the most of it. He had accomplished much as a privateer and as the commodore of the Republic of Pirates.

Let them call him what they would, as long as they let him lead.

He had fought for New Providence, for all of the Bahamas, throughout the War of Spanish Succession, writing endless letters to the House of Lords and the English Admiralty for money and provisions to keep the fort in good repair despite monthly—at times weekly—attacks by the Spanish and French. Not a single response nor coin had come. The islands, forgotten and left to fend for themselves when Europe's no longer feuding rulers had signed the Treaty of Utrecht, had endured the final affront, and he had acted accordingly.

But Hornigold was wise enough to know that his adopted home did not have the ports, plantations, and possibilities like Jamaica, Barbados, and other islands more hotly contested by the European empires because of what each could yield for their coffers.

Instead of idle lamenting, he had seized the chance to escape notice and build something lasting, something that would give the men beneath him a voice, a future, and a reason to keep on fighting.

He had simply run out of time.

Edward, William, and others said he had been too trusting, too eager to accept new captains and crews. They were all too happy to speak the name of Levasseur as though the word itself dripped with deadly venom.

And now the vote the Frenchman had so unceremoniously called for—nominating the popular and egalitarian Samuel Bellamy instead of himself in a master chessman's move—was only two days from happening. Hornigold had no idea how it would play out. He would not lower himself to campaigning for a position he had not so much earned as created out of nothing and Bellamy and Levasseur had gone out in search of prizes—in opposite directions, if the rumors were true—rather than stumping in the taverns or otherwise trying to gather needed votes.

Perhaps their overconfidence would be their undoing. Perhaps good sense would prevail and the crews would see Hornigold's edict against attacking English ships for the sensible course of action that it was.

A republic without allies was no republic at all. Not one that would last the storms that had only been hinted at with a few flashes of far off lightning but would no doubt soon envelope them all in thunder, wind, and rain. The Royal African and East India companies would not allow the Caribbean pirates to cut into their profits to any greater degree without making a response. And the Royal Navy would go wherever it was told by the lords who ran those companies and therefore the whole of Britannia herself.

Such were his thoughts as he heard a knock on his door in the fort. Thinking it was Edward or William, he said "Enter" without looking up.

The voice he heard surprised him.

"I just need a few moments a' the commodore's time, if he shall be so kind."

Looking up, Hornigold saw before him Henry Jennings, the partner of the greatest threat to New Providence by a considerable margin—the surly, unpredictable Captain Vane.

This was no doubt another of his stabs at power.

"I am surprised ye were let into the fort," Hornigold said, not bothering to stand or offer a drink.

"Yer men tried to turn me away, Gran'pa, but I told 'em what I have come ta tell ye an' before ye here I stand."

"Then I shall listen. Rum?"

Waving off the offer, Jennings took a seat. "Vane an' me have had a severe difference of opinion. These past weeks I have been on my own, with several dozen loyal crew in a ship that needs careenin', refittin', an' repair. I hear tell ye have been challenged an' the vote is soon upon ye. Give me a place amongst yer crews an' my men an' I will stand with ye an' fer ye. We may not have the numbers ta ensure the vote will fall yer way, but we shall support ye ta the end."

Taking his time by packing and lighting his pipe, allowing Jennings's surprising offer to linger in the air to be assessed, Hornigold leaned back in his chair, not wanting to give the appearance of being eager to accept.

"I have heard whispers that Vane has come into considerable funds—a hidden treasure pilfered through God knows what nefarious means. That he is recruiting and intends to come back after us as soon as he is able. He may have spies amongst us. How do I know that ye are not amongst their number?"

"Ye have no way to know," Jennings answered, his nostrils twitching at the smell of the rich tobacco burning in Hornigold's pipe. Pulling his own from his pocket, he asked, "Would ye be willin' ta share some a' yer weed? I have been out fer nigh on a week."

Sliding his pouch across the desk, Hornigold softened. To go a week without tobacco. Things must be poor for Jennings indeed.

"Ye and your men must be willing to sign and abide by the Articles. To not attack English ships. Or Dutch. Ye will of course retain your captaincy and autonomy, provided ye honor the Articles."

Lighting his pipe, and taking a powerful drag, the smoke lingering deep inside him for a considerable minute before he expelled it, Jennings let his eyes drift upward as it relaxed him. "Aye, Gran'pa. I can do more than that. I can tell ye all I know about what Vane thinks he is chasin', an' about that devil Devon Ross. But I warn ye—tis a tale like none ye ever heard, I heartily promise ye that."

Pulling a bottle of rum from a shelf behind him, Hornigold smiled. "My ears would welcome such a story. Do tell on and spare me no detail."

FORT OF NASSAU, NEW PROVIDENCE, BAHAMAS,

LATER THAT DAY

The conditions and circumstances that lead men to choose a life of piracy, to go "on the account," to join the Brethren of the Sea, to commit to a "short and merry life," and to carry the label of *hostis humani generis*—enemies against all humankind—are as varied as the men whose stories are linked by and are the lifeblood of this tale.

It is wise to let them tell it through their doing, so we shall keep this brief.

The forces arrayed against them, as you have and will continue to see, were many. They were targets of propaganda, character assassination, and outright lies. Colony newspapers like the *Boston News-Letter*, thought nothing of printing whatever sold copies and kept them in good stead with their masters. For many pirates, as the noose tightened and they ultimately lived their lives with nothing to lose, the stereotypes created by a few and propagated by those who wished to destroy them became all that history would know of their kind.

Captain Edward Thache is perhaps the most misunderstood of all. Statistically, other pirates were more successful in terms of ships taken and treasure collected. Bartholomew Roberts, whose story rarely intertwines with those unfolding here, quickly comes to mind. Samuel Bellamy enjoyed more success at a quicker rate as well. And yet Edward Thache is the pirate most remember.

But it was not always destined to be. Thache, at the onset, had no greater ambition than to serve a higher cause to which to contribute his skills and, if need be, his blood, striving toward an ideal of equality, fraternity, and liberty.

It was for this reason that he had joined Benjamin Hornigold in his vision for the Republic of Pirates. And why, as much as he admired and respected Samuel Bellamy, he could not support him in the upcoming vote.

Now, with Sam sitting across from him, having surprised him with an impossible request, he had but one chance to make his friend see reason and avert what he knew would be the undoing of all for which they had worked. And that meant not only the republic in New Providence but the support they could give to the Old Pretender.

"This is not easy, Sam. I hope ye see that."

Ye shall have to do better than that, Edward told himself. *Just look at the way he glares.*

"I..."

Sam put up his hand. "I should not have come to see you, Edward. I realize that. Ye are quite the success. Already upgraded to an eight-gun sloop. And a crew of... what? Ninety? Surely if ye could operate without the constraints—"

"I have!" Edward answered, immediately regretting raising his voice. He knew well enough that was no way to reach a man like Samuel Bellamy. "And so did ye. I will not speak of certain outside influences—"

"Which I appreciate."

"—but ye know how I feel on the matter. How I feel about the unwise action that damaged the *Marianne*. That lost a man his life. Ye made an oath, Sam."

Sam raised a brow. "As did ye. To a larger cause than Hornigold's weak little dream. New Providence is a base of operations, nothing more. The ideals we uphold—ideals I know we share, ye and me—are not to serve one man's ambition, but the whole of the world. And if that means taking English ships, or making alliances with less than perfect men... We must do so. Anything else is naïve."

Biting back his words, which would have ended the encounter most unkindly, Edward leaned back, taking the measure of the man before him. Was he right? Was Edward being naïve? Was he hiding in New Providence, afraid to face the larger consequences of expanded operations—of eventually having to face the might of the Royal Navy, whose prowess and ruthlessness he understood, having served beneath its captains, commodores, and admirals?

And if he was, was he wrong to do so?

"Sam... listen to me. I know ye are a man of great courage, of even greater heart. But what about Goody? What about when the time comes for ye to return to Cape Cod, once ye have made yer fortune and secured yer reputation? Will ye be able to face her—to face her father—if ye have shed unnecessary, innocent blood? If ye have become the very thing we fight against, in order to overcome it? Because I am certain that is where this is headed."

His visage softening for the first time, Sam leaned forward, placing a hand on Edward's knee. "Perhaps ye are right in some of what ye say. I fall asleep each night, thinking of Goody, of the man whom she shall marry. As for her father... his actions against Xiang Yu make him, in my estimation, less than nothing—an unfortunate fact that will have to be navigated carefully upon my return. So let us not weight with an overindulgence of emotion an already heavy conversation. There are forces at work, arrayed against us, which I do not understand. Otherworldly. Perhaps demonic. Secrets abound. Quests for objects that have already led to ugly actions. Things that I never would have thought possible. But we can only hope to control them if we are in control. Hornigold has not the respect nor the alliances necessary to do so. So, I ask ye again, Edward. Will ye give me your support?"

Sam could be persuasive. Edward had often witnessed it. And he could see where they clearly agreed.

And he knew as well where they did not.

"Abraxas Abriendo is not to be trusted," he began, searching for something that might turn Sam from his plan. "And his loyalty to La Buse will not last. For he has no loyalty. I knew him when we were boys. Ye must trust me. I can control him. I already have to some degree. But not if Levasseur is given unbridled power."

"And ye think I will allow that?"

Edward matched Sam's angry tone with his own. "Now who is being naïve! He runs ye in the hunt, Sam, like a master does his dogs. I will not allow him any more power. He will not run the Flying Gang like he runs his little flotilla—regardless of if ye prevail in the vote and carry the title of commodore."

A shadow passed over Sam's face as he stood. "I will overlook your insults because of the particular circumstances from which they stem. We need each other, Edward. I cannot afford to count ye as my enemy. They are already far too numerous. If ye will not support me in the vote, I ask that ye not turn against me. That ye continue to fight for the cause and honor the oath to which ye swore. And, most of all, that ye refrain from blocking my path."

Remaining in his chair, Edward tried his best to smile. "Agreed. And in return, I shall expect ye to do the same."

PART SIX:

OF THE CANNON AND THE QUILL

To the credit of all of those involved, no matter their allegiance or personal disposition, the vote the previous evening was conducted in an orderly, fair, and uncontested manner.

Edward Thache, sitting in the bow of the sloop *Adventure*, preparing to depart with twenty-nine others, *Captain* Hornigold included, could not dispute that fact, as much as he might wish to.

The outcome was as Edward Thache had feared... although the final tally of the votes was so overwhelmingly in favor of a new commodore and the slow death of Hornigold's vision for a true republic of pirates that Edward had found himself in a precarious position. He had made no demands on the crew of the *Marauder II*, and more than two thirds had voted for Bellamy. Henry Jennings, whom Edward had no choice but to welcome back into the fold, mustered even less of his own men to cast their vote as he had.

Edward wished he could say that Levasseur had coerced a crucial percentage of the men to vote for Samuel Bellamy, but there was no evidence to support it. Even the fact that he had arrived the previous night having recruited dozens of new men in order to ensure the vote would go his way had been unethical but not illegal. There had been no provision made for how long a man had to be a signatory of the Articles before he could vote, an unforgivable oversight for which Edward took a considerable share of misplaced responsibility. In the final analysis, knowing their victory was assured, Levasseur had been the very model of grace and charm.

As much as a Frenchman could be, given his natural traits.

And so it was that Samuel Bellamy, at twenty-seven years of age, was voted commodore of the Flying Gang. His speech following the tally of the votes and the announcement by William Howard, senior quartermaster amongst the crews—who did an admirable job of hiding his disappointment as he read out the results—was everything Edward would have expected based on their conversation two days before.

"Good men of New Providence, of the Bahamas, of the Caribbean, and of the world!" he began, from halfway up the mast of the *Marianne* as nearly three hundred men lined the decks of the ships around him. "I thank ye for your faith in a new future. I look at ye—men from England and Africa; from Ireland, Scotland, and

Wales; from France, Spain, and Portugal. From Denmark and Norway. And my old, dear friend, Xiang Yu, all the way from China. I assure ye that I shall not let ye down. We shall expand our operations—that is clearly what ye want—but we shall abide by the rules that have governed us so well as far as pay, conduct, and expectation. We humbly thank Captain Hornigold for the Articles of which I speak. And we shall not be guilty of impressment like the bulldog Royal Navy, although, should a ship require the services of a carpenter or surgeon, it is permissible to fill this need, whether the man is willing or not. The commodore's role shall at times be lonely and fraught with difficult decisions. Those who trust me and believe in our cause have dubbed me the 'Robin Hood of the Seas,' while those from whom we pull their unearned wealth have taken to calling me 'Black Sam Bellamy, the Scourge of the Seven Seas'! I tell ye this—I shall answer to either, though one shall be met with a mug and the other with a sword!"

Pausing to allow the assembled men a hearty series of cheers, Sam trained his eyes on Hornigold, standing between Edward and William. Just behind them stood Henry Jennings, looking as though he had backed the wrong horse.

Accommodations would be made should Jennings deign to ask, for Hornigold had not shared whatever information Vane's former partner had no doubt shared with him and Sam was keen to acquire it.

But back to the task at hand. This would be the most difficult moment for Sam to manage—the true indicator of a seamless transfer of power. He had rehearsed it, keeping it to himself, despite Levasseur's and Paulsgrave's constant questioning prior to the vote.

Quieting the crowd with an ease that did not escape Edward's eyes and ears, Sam continued, his tone quieter and more solemn. "The future of the Flying Gang and the larger consideration of the prosperity of all the Brethren of the Sea must be duly considered, and without delay. I hereby offer Captain Hornigold and any man who wishes to go with him the sloop *Adventure* in place of the *St. Marie*, which is too important a vessel to sacrifice, and enough provisions from our stores to get where they desire to go. I further decree that whatever weapons they possess shall go with them as well. Cannonball and powder are precious, but they shall have enough of each to service their six cannon in the case of an engagement with our common enemies. I deem this just and fair. What say ye?"

The positive response to Sam's generosity and evenhandedness washed over the assembly like the waves of an autumn storm.

So it was that the course-changing events of the previous day had concluded.

Looking at the twenty-seven men around him—which included William Howard and Conall MacBlaquart, for whom the constant danger and feigned loyalties of being a spy on Bellamy's ship had taken a toll from which he had asked Edward the prior evening to be released—Edward knew not where they were headed, nor what they would do when they arrived.

Henry Jennings had urged them to head for Jamaica, where the new governor, Peter Heywood, might be willing to offer patronage would they agree to track and kill Charles Vane. Hornigold, however, much to Edward's relief, for he had no wish to return to his childhood home, had declined, knowing they were in no position to bargain with the strength required to assure that Heywood would not betray them to higher authorities.

What Jennings would ultimately do was unclear. All Edward knew was that he had declined a spot on *Adventure*.

Calling the men to their stations as Hornigold climbed aboard, Edward moved to help his captain over the gunwale. "I saw ye in parlay with Bellamy and Williams. May I ask the substance of your discussion?"

"Ye may ask me anything, Edward. I am grateful for all ye have done. Please be assured, ye shall be back in command of a ship of your own as soon as it can be managed. Our very lives depend upon it." Watching their limited crew go about their tasks with skill and determination, he said, "As to the parlay. I simply wished them well and suggested they watch their backs, for I fear the Royal Navy and others will take advantage of a shift of power once the news of recent events has reached them."

Turning his attention to the hoisting of the anchor and final preparations to leave port, Edward caught a flash of sunlight from the *Postillion*, anchored to starboard. Standing on the quarterdeck was Abraxas Abriendo, his cursed mirror grasped in his left hand— light emanating from it in all directions—a look of spiteful glee upon his pockmarked face.

And in his right, which he waved briefly above his head before tucking it into his cape, was a thin length of wood, stained red, carved into the shape of a woman's delicate hand and lower arm.

Edward felt his own hands clench at the sight, though he knew not why. All he could say if pressed was that he knew the hand was a means to power and could not be allowed to linger long with its current possessor.

Such were his thoughts as the men of the *Adventure* left New Providence, in search of the necessary prizes to secure themselves a strengthened position and a suitable port of call.

As Dr. Friedrich Reinhardt punched the button for the twenty-third floor of TRG Tower or, as the inner circle privileged enough to have an access code called it, Solomon's Temple, he replayed the events of the previous thirteen hours.

Looking at them from yet another angle, Friedrich came to the uncomfortable conclusion that there was no chance he could spin them far enough away from the awaiting cudgel in an office beyond the elevator to avoid a serious blow to his distinguished career. Despite his training at Columbia and Stanford, his internships and consulting contracts with everyone from DARPA to RAND to the deepest secret divisions of the Pentagon, and his current position as head of special projects at Quarry Peak Psychiatric Hospital, Friedrich was about to join the ranks of the woefully unprotected.

Having had as his patients—voluntary and otherwise—the upper echelons in politics, economics, and the global military–industrial–intelligence complex, he knew the consequences of failure all too well, though always second hand. He had lost count of how many times he had manipulated men's minds—for it was still ultimately a male-dominated world—to aid them in achieving the aims of the elite who kept him more than comfortable as they continued to fund his work.

As the elevator opened, Friedrich—in no rush to enter the office just down the hall—stepped out and stood before one of the bulletproof, shatterproof windows just across the way to look out over the seven-mile surveillance state known as Storm Haven.

It had been three years earlier, in the aftermath of Superstorm Mammon—a "catastrophic weather event" as one of the Weather Channel's blue-jacketed storm chasers had dubbed it—that TRG had purchased this devastated swath of land in affluent Monmouth County for a premium price in order to develop a prototypical city of the future.

Putting all of their considerable financial and technological resources behind its design and construction—including input from Friedrich on the psychology of place and urban landscaping—TRG had turned useless marshland that had been draining local resources for decades in the aftermath of each once or twice yearly hurricane into the headquarters of their multinational juggernaut. All around Solomon's Temple were dozens of support complexes laid out in sacred geometric patterns for their thousands of employees and testing centers for a variety of state of the art surveillance systems and smart technologies.

Similar communities, all under the aegis of TRG, were planned for twenty-seven other cities deemed too crime-ridden, run down, and drug-invested to be saved by any other means. Each would have its own nuclear power facility, although that project was still a decade away from completion.

The corporate oligarchy–controlled chambers of Congress and the boardrooms of the Big Eight banks were hailing Storm Haven's design and philosophy as America's new religion. All that they had learned from the corporate cooptation and regulation of New Orleans in the aftermath of HAARP-enhanced Hurricane Katrina in 2005 had been applied to this little slice of surveillance-state heaven.

Now Friedrich, no longer able to stall, was about to enter the inner sanctum of its undisputed God.

The Holy of Holies in this modern Solomon's Temple.

Knocking lightly, but not awaiting an answer—he had been here half a dozen times under far better circumstances—Friedrich entered with a smile carefully cultivated to disarm preconceived aggression, confidently proclaiming, "I do not see this as the disaster others are proclaiming it to be, Mister Rave—"

Looking at the figure across the desk, Friedrich choked back the name, which was no longer accurate.

Instead of the CEO and chairman of the board of TRG, Friedrich was looking into the lizard-like eyes of his unofficial supervisor, Xavier Hearst, head of the most technologically advanced projects currently funded by the ignorant taxpayers of the Reinhardt family's adopted homeland.

"Frank. I wish I could say it was nice to see you. Close the door."

Trying not to show his anger at the slight, Friedrich—*Frank* was the name he had used from the time he was a teenager to ease bullying and promote his social integration, a lie reserved now only for outer professional circles and published papers—did as he was told. Willing his face back into a smile, he turned and approached the block of basalt carved into an ornate desk that served as Solomon's barrier against having his underlings getting too close.

"I am curious, Frank," Hearst continued, "as to exactly how you intend to convince us that this is not a complete and utter disaster."

Calling up the text he had rehearsed and stored away for ready access in his genius-level brain, Friedrich said, in a single even breath, "While the illegal retrieval of Kirstine MacGregor by unknown assailants late last night is no doubt unfortunate, the mirror machine sessions gave us all that we need… Rather, all that we could get from her, Mister Hearst."

Hearst's reptilian eyes remained impassive. Cold. Licking his lips with his sharply tapered tongue, he hissed, "The only reason you are here instead of strapped to your own machine is because of the impressive level of infiltration. We are clearly dealing with special forces–level planning and execution. It will all be analyzed and necessary improvements made. The list of potential perpetrators is of course short. It is our technology, our training modalities, our weapons and tactics, and our physical and mental enhancements imprinted all over this infiltration. We shall in time turn these data to our advantage."

Friedrich, proceeding off script, which was less than ideal, replied, "And so, as I said, this was far from a disaster. I personally sealed the sectors of Doctor MacGregor's mind pertinent to our interests from all who might attempt to open them. I am confident we can proceed to further phases without her. She may very well mislead them."

Without changing posture or demeanor, Hearst said, "You should hope you are correct, Frank. I would hate to see you teaching freshman seminar at some state college somewhere, struggling for tenure in the morass of 'publish or perish.'"

Pushing the image of a patched-elbow tweed coat and dented Peugeot from his mind, Friedrich decided he could afford to push a little further. "I was expecting to speak with—"

Standing to his full height of five and a half feet tall—although he seemed much taller—Hearst clicked his tongue against his teeth. "Someone higher up? Ah… Solomon the Wise… Do not be an idiot, Frank. He does not reward expertly spun mistakes, nor does he suffer fools such as yourself. No Ravenskald ever has. None ever will. Come here for a moment. I want to show you something."

Moving diagonally across the room to meet Hearst by a dimly lit glass display cabinet in a far corner of the office, Friedrich saw a simple bone-handled knife seemingly suspended in midair. Looking below it, he could see two delicately crafted gold supports arising from the red velvet bottom of the box.

"Do you know what this is?" Hearst asked, simply because there was no way Friedrich could, and seeing the doctor flail gave this barely human lizard-thing immense and exquisite pleasure.

Rather than vocalize his ignorance, Friedrich waited for Hearst to enlighten him.

"It is the blade that Abraham would have used—that some say he *did* use—to sacrifice Isaac to his God thousands of years ago. It is here as a reminder for us all that we are continually being tested. And failure will mean death." Pointing to the door, he added, "You may return, for now, to your duties at Quarry Peak. I want the 3D mapping of what you retrieved from MacGregor's mind by end of business tomorrow."

As Friedrich turned to leave, Hearst hissed, "And be sure to include the communications from the psychic intruder. I am most interested in discerning what my old adversary is attempting to accomplish."

Heading for the elevator, Friedrich resisted the urge to wipe the sweat from his brow or to adjust his collar to let the sweat that had pooled there run down his back.

There were cameras everywhere. Hearst and Solomon Ravenskald himself were no doubt watching him walk the hallway from behind the basalt desk.

He had no idea how Hearst knew about the communications from "PF." He had made no mention of the intruder in any of his reports. He had told no one on his team—not even Nurse Anita Stiles, the closest thing he had to a confidante, insufferable though she was.

Perhaps the simple life of a professor would be preferable to the fetid pool of viper-handlers within which I now swim, he thought, as the elevator opened, inviting Friedrich into its vertical jaws.

If such a position existed, Olivier Levasseur would be the undisputed king of St. Croix—the largest and most important of the cluster of Caribbean islands Columbus had named *Santa Úrsula y las Once Mil Vírgenes* in 1493.

Although Levasseur did not believe the story told to all good Catholics that the Huns had slaughtered Saint Ursula and eleven thousand other virgins as they made their pilgrimage to Rome, there was no question that this island was of the greatest strategic significance to the Star Quorum and those tasked to protect them— the illustrious Knights of Malta.

This sacred task had led the Order of Knights of the Hospital of Saint John, initially formed in Jerusalem in 1099 and known by the shorter name of Knights Hospitaller, to relocate to Malta in 1530, where the Star Quorum had chosen to have their meetings.

In 1651, in response to the growing turmoil in the Caribbean, the Knights of Malta had delegated a portion of their forces to St. Croix, one of four islands they had purchased from the French.

And so it was that in Christiansted Harbor, easily defended and crucial to the island's sugar trade and true, secret purpose, the Knights had built the stronghold in which Levasseur now stood.

Having sold St. Croix in the mid-1660s to avoid the mounting scrutiny of the council of Catholic leaders from throughout the world that the Knights of Malta had sworn themselves to defend—who had moved their meetings to the island when the stronghold was complete—they had enlisted agents from France, Italy, and Spain to monitor their interests in the Virgin Islands, as the lazy English called them.

Olivier Levasseur was one of their primary agents and, at the moment, arguably the most powerful.

Two weeks ago, he and Bellamy had taken a ship named the *Bonetta*, under the captaincy of Abijah Savage, whose passengers were traveling from Jamaica to Antigua. This was no random capture—taking passage on the ship were Cardinal Alberoni and a young Franciscan monk named Guillermo Vincolaré, whose actual destination was the fort on St. Croix.

Rather than remove only the two of them and provoke unnecessary questions, Levasseur and Bellamy had taken hostage all two hundred passengers, which required inventing a pretext. Suspicion of treason by senior members of its crew against the government of France was chosen to explain why the pair of pirates had taken the *Bonetta* despite its sails being struck "so they flapped like laundry"—the traditional and expected-to-be-honored sign of surrender.

The mission had yielded unexpected pleasures beyond the honor of aiding Cardinal Alberoni, who held a seat on the Star Quorum along with Cardinal de Fleury, Levasseur's primary patron. For instance, there were the two boys grappling, as all boys will, on the white-sanded beach just below him.

The first, for whom Cardinal Alberoni declared Caesar to be a most fitting name during the interrupted journey from Jamaica because of his proud, defiant demeanor, was a boy from the tribe of Chief Dagaakutsu on the Gold Coast of Africa. Sold into slavery at Port Royal to then governor Archibald Hamilton, Caesar had quickly proven himself unmanageable to Hamilton's replacement. Before he could be shipped off to Carolina or some sugar plantation island where he would be overworked and dead within a handful of months, one of the Star Quorum's agents, who knew of Caesar's knowledge of the ancient religion of Obeah—his grandfather being a practitioner who had fallen out of favor with Dagaakutsu over a disagreement about something called the Jumbee—had arranged for his passage on the *Bonetta.*

The second was a ten-year-old English boy named John King who, in the midst of the pirates' takeover of the ship, loudly announced to his mother that if he was not permitted to join the pirates rather than be a hostage, he would be happy to beat her for one and all to see.

Levasseur shortly after installed this entertaining pair of firebrands as cabin boys on the *Postillion*, which was being careened, along with the *St. Marie* and *Oiseau de Proie*, while the *Marianne* defended the entrance to the harbor.

From down the hall, Levasseur heard the door to the meeting chamber open. Bowing to the inhabitants before heading toward the French captain was Abraxas Abriendo, the black mirror and the object with which he had taunted Edward Thache as the banished crew left New Providence—called the Fatima Hand—grasped tightly in his sausage-like fingers.

"What news from zee Quorum, weezard?" Levasseur asked.

"They are still meeting with Alberoni and the monk," Abraxas replied. "But it is as you thought—the Quorum knows the whereabouts of the Baptist Bowl and we will almost surely be tasked with retrieving it. If, that is, we can regain their full faith and trust."

Levasseur groaned. "Zey are angered over zee treasure stolen from zee far side of zee island by Vane, *oui*?"

"*Oui*. Although it was an insignificant amount in the grander scheme of what the Quorum is worth, it was a breach of secrecy on the part of Hamilton, a man they fully trusted. Add to that the trespass on this most important island, and the incompetence displayed by yourself and the rest of the New Providence pirates by not killing the tiger when he was just a kitten, after storming and plundering the Spaniards' fort in Florida."

Levasseur once again groaned. "Zat fort was long before my time, weezard. And you are wrong—Vane ees *le puce*, not *le tigre*. I shall brutally dispense of him between my thumb and forefinger when zee time ees ripe, as a child would zee flea that he ees. I know zee moods of zee Quorum. They cannot afford to do weethout us. We shall regain zehr favor and have zee opportunity to retrieve zee skull of zee *baptiste*. Which means we shall soon control four of zee twelve sacred objects. And our agents know the locations of at least two more."

Exhaling garlic while flopping himself on the ledge where Levasseur sat, Abraxas shook his head. "Until we can open this," he said, holding out the Fatima Hand, "we should say we have three... we are not sure the Joseph Scroll still remains inside. Though you are correct—both the Abraham Blade and the Tiber Vial could soon be in hand. And, under the right conditions, this mirror will tell us the locations of the Sheba Comb and Magdalene Balm. It is believed this young monk Guillermo can be of assistance, which is why he is here. The boy has *dreams*, you know..."

"As do we all, Abraxas," Levasseur responded. Looking down the hall toward the council chamber, he added, agitated, "Zey must be quick weeth whatever decisions need to be made. *Capitaine* Bellamy weel not be weeling to hold zees two hundred hostages for much longer. Not once the careening is *fini*."

"He may become a liability you cannot afford, La Buse."

"*Oui, oui, mon weezard*. I know zees all too well."

"**Y**e pipe doon noo, ye hair?… Ye damned numpty roaster… Ye weel see us all daid befoor yer throo…"

For the past two weeks, ever since the Duke of Argyll had taken John Graham off his hands in exchange for his agreeing to aid the source of his scolding—the barber Finlay Fletcher—in the retrieval of his betrothed from the castle within which they now hid with a few of his most trusted men, Rob Roy MacGregor had been suffering the repeated singing of the song Finlay had once again begun:

"Mae lady she feasts on a baeggar man's bones... la diddy la diddy da diddy da do..."

"I weel noot ask ye again, ye wee odd man—stop that singin'!"

"Guid gear cooms in small bulk," Finlay replied, though he did not start the song again.

"Noo thain," Rob said, motioning the four men crouched beside him deeper into the shadows. "Ewan. Lachlan. Ye see this throo an' I weel see tae it Argyll has ye made men a' the Order a' the Thistle. Many a fine knight has been lost as of late in this damned rebellion… Why, our very oon James, Earl a' Perth, as weel as Gordon an' Melfort."

Ewan Cameron whistled low, placing his hand on Rob's arm. "Nay befoor yoo, Rob. If any man stands tall tae their motto, 'Wha daurs meddle wi' mae?' it is ye."

Rob shook his head. "Nay MacGregor weel bae named any time soon, dae ken?"

"What aboot Dooncan MacDonald hair?" Lachlan Campbell asked. "He has served ye weel, Rob. Better than any man has."

"Ack… I donnae hair that shite, Lachlan," Duncan hissed. "What has drawin' swords shoulder tae shoulder wit' a lot a' numpty nobles gotten any of oos? Eh?"

"It is nay matter," Rob said. "We haev oor plan an' that's where oor brains moost bae. Ewan, Lachlan—ye create a ruckus that weel draw the guards froom in front a' the wee lass' chambers. I weel fetch her quick while ye keep 'em busy an' weel bae celaebraetin' in Glen Shira wit' a wee dram afoor midnight."

Lachlan Campbell laughed. "Again I ask ye, Rob—What aboot Dooncan MacDonald hair? How doos hae figure in all a' this grand schaemin' a' yoors? An' where weel this barber of oors bae?"

Drawing his dirk, Duncan stood and peered down the hall. "Oor shrewd duke didnae joost send oos here on a count a' his loov a' good romance. The Murrays haev joost received a shipment a' arms, which the barber—who knoos thair precise location—weel bae aidin' yoo in collectin' fer oor cause. Ken?"

Standing up and drawing his sword and pistol, Lachlan laughed again. "Finally soomthin' makes sense in all a' this carryin' on weer aboot! Weel bae naidin' all the weapons we can get after that damned Disarmin' Act."

Ewan and Rob nodded in agreement. On 1 November, the act, passed by the Parliament of Great Britain months earlier, came into effect, its purpose being to prevent any clansmen in the Highlands from having "in his or their custody, use, or bear, broad sword, poignard, whinger, or durk, side pistol, gun, or other warlike weapon."

Joining his men with both his weapons drawn, Rob said, not waiting for an answer, "Time is wastin'. So let's git aboot oor bis'ness."

L ord John Carteret dipped his quill into the pot of ink on the ornate desk in the Council Chamber behind King George's throne room, careful to get just the right amount on the meticulously shaven tip.

Two copies of a document detailing a preliminary alliance with France lay on the desk before the king, ready for his signature. At its core was the guarantee that Britain would back France against the increasingly vocal claims coming from Spain by Philip the Fifth that the French throne was rightfully his.

The Duke of Orleans's minister, the Abbé Guillaume Dubois, who was clearly anxious to conclude their business so that he could make his return to France, had just signed the copies that lay before the king.

Lord Carteret was just as happy to have him do so, and with all haste. One of Carteret's greatest advantages in maintaining a close relationship with the king was the fact that he was one of the few nobles in the English court who spoke German. George was also fluent in French, which meant that Lord Carteret, although he had managed the negotiations with the Duke of Orleans and his agents while George and his son had been in Germany the previous summer, had stood to the side as Abbé Dubois and George had spoken only to one another for a good part of the morning.

Always prepared, Carteret had made sure to have one of the Mammon Lodge members fluent in French present at the meeting.

He would be dining at Carteret's home in an hour.

Also in attendance was Andrew Colson. Carteret would deal with him soon enough.

Handing the quill to King George, Lord Carteret stood at his shoulder as the monarch signed the documents, standing almost immediately.

His German mistress awaited him elsewhere in the castle.

The dozen or so ministers and attendants began to file out of the room as the Abbé Dubois accepted one copy and the king's personal secretary handed Lord Carteret the other. After they had nodded their goodbyes, Lord Carteret met Andrew Colson at the door as the latter was attempting to exit.

"A word, Andrew, if you please." Not awaiting an answer, Carteret closed and locked the door, indicating that Colson should sit where the king had been a moment before.

"I would not be so bold," Colson answered, remaining in his position by the door.

"Oh, but you would," Carteret answered. "And you have. I have received the most interesting series of reports from Captain Ellis Brand of His Majesty's Royal Navy from his position near Scotland. He has been busy rounding up Scottish Masons. At my request. They have told him the most interesting things about both the Masonic Lodges in London and George Seton. *Most* interesting… Do you care to comment, Andrew?"

Not giving Carteret the least indication by face or gesture of how he was taking this news—although he would pass a restless night of twitching hands and a heart that would not stop its hard, insistent beating—Colson answered, "I do not. Surely you will not dare to kill me here in the king's Council Chamber with so many witnesses to our being the last two left in the room on such an auspicious day. So I am not sure where we stand, My Lord. I truly do not."

"Then let me enlighten you. I expect your resignation from the board of the Royal African Company by midday tomorrow. You are of course also prohibited from attending any gatherings of the Mammon Lodge. You are hereby banished. Stripped of all rights and benefits. Which is dangerous ground on which to stand, considering that Mammon owns your soul." Pausing a moment to let that fact sink in, Carteret continued. "And know this, Andrew. From this instant on, I consider you one of my greatest enemies. Which is a select list of miscreants that includes George Seton—whom I will track down and punish—and Henry Bolingbroke. I control this city. Soon I shall make considerably more of the key decisions that will affect all of Britain and further consolidate and strengthen the power of the Mammon Lodge and its chief benefactors. You shall not be safe here. The Masons may be banding together under Anthony Sayer, but they will not be able to protect you. No one can."

Moving closer to the door, Colson said, "Is that all?"

Unlocking the door and stepping aside, Carteret answered, "I am serious, Andrew. Sacrificing your bleeding, broken body to Mammon is something I look forward to with every fiber of my being. I shall only delay the gratification of that act for so long. Even now, I can feel Master Mammon's hunger for your flesh. My god, how you have disappointed me. Then again, you never were anywhere near the man your father was."

Walking through the throne room and out its side door into the courtyard of the palace, Colson began contemplating his next moves, for they would be key to his survival.

He knew his life in London was now all but over. He had been preparing for this inevitability for months. He had already transferred many of his assets to locations outside the city. His agents would sell his home and other properties within days to buyers secured through the Masons. At present, he would use a secure route to reach a safe house provided by Grand Master Anthony Sayer who was presently out of the country but whose closest advisors were prepared to help Andrew with anything he should need.

Of all the threats and disparaging remarks Carteret had made, the one most hurtful to Andrew was the remark about his father, because it was the truest. Despite all he had seen as a member of the Inner Circle of the Mammon Lodge, Andrew knew that there were other forces—equal or maybe greater—that would protect him. If he did not, he would never have had the courage for betrayal. Carteret would not expend considerable energy on tracking him once he left the city. He could not afford to—not with all of the other mounting challenges he faced from within and from without.

As he made his way to the safe house, an image began to haunt him. An image of a young boy—a farmer's son—stoically taking blows from Andrew's father's cane held in his hands in a castle in Exeter. Afterward, his father had berated him for not breaking the boy's spirit on the spot. For allowing the boy—and his father—to leave with some small remainder of their dignity.

Their relationship had only deteriorated from there.

What had become of that boy, Colson had heard only rumors for many years. It was not until recently that the Royal African Company's network of agents had made him aware of Samuel Bellamy's activities in the Caribbean.

Samuel Bellamy, who was partially to blame for the indignities Andrew had suffered from his father and Lord Carteret.

Andrew had much to do, but he would not allow a farmer's son to outshine him. Not for a moment. Not for a day.

It was time he set things right.

Twenty-four hours can feel like a lifetime.

Shifting his position for the half-dozenth time since he lay down in his new bed, Commodore Samuel Bellamy could sense that much-needed sleep simply would not come.

His mind was afire with all that had happened since the previous evening, when he had first stood upon the deck of his new flagship, the twenty-six-gun *Sultana*, which had surrendered to him after a brief exchange of fire following a four-hour chase not far from where they now lay anchored.

Sitting in parley with the captain, Sam had learned that the British ship was providing protection for the five hundred Dutch overseeing three thousand African slaves working the sugarcane and other plantations on St. Thomas.

"Well then," he had said, courteously sampling the local rum the captain offered, "they will simply have to settle for land defenses. One of my captains, Paulsgrave Williams, will bring ye and your crew to the harbor on the *Marianne*. Should ye resist in any way, Captain…"

The prudent seaman had assured him there was nothing to fear from his crew and he was as good as his word.

It was only a few hours later that Sam had received a message that the thirty-two-gun Fifth Rate HMS *Scarborough*, under the command of the formidable Captain Francis Hume, while in pursuit of Bellamy and his cohorts based on old intelligence that they were careening on St. Croix, had destroyed six ships under the command of Commodore John Martel.

Feeling a debt to Martel, a former fellow privateer—a capable seaman who had also assisted Levasseur on more than one occasion in a tough spot during the War for Spanish Succession—Bellamy had set sail for St. Croix, where Martel's crew of one hundred and thirty had sought refuge near the fort on Christiansted Harbor. Upon arrival, as he was sorting the men for assignment in his own flotilla—having sent word for Levasseur and Xiang Yu to return with all haste—Sam was summoned to the fort.

The Star Quorum wished to speak with him.

This was most unexpected. Sam had been busy overseeing careening and coordinating patrols when they had first reached St. Croix. The powerful Catholic council had not invited him to their chambers, and he had not asked. He was content to allow Olivier,

Abraxas, and their group of religious advisors to conduct their business with no interference or questions from him.

At the time he received the summons, he had already been awake for thirty-six hours. A rough stubble coated his usually clean-shaven face, his hair was a knotty tangle he tied hastily back with a length of faded ribbon, and his clothes were wrinkled and damp. He was aware he was giving off a subtle but pungent odor.

No doubt the Star Quorum would not invite him to stand too close.

Straightening his belt and baldric as the sun shone down from the mid-morning sky, Sam put John Martel in charge of the organizational operation. Before heading for the fort, he looked out into the bay. The masts of the *Postillion* and *Oiseau de Proie* were barely visible on the horizon. They were still several hours away.

Entering the hall that led to the council's chambers, Sam was met and escorted by four men whose tabards of red, with a white cross upon the torso, indicated that they were Knights of Malta.

The chamber itself was simple. Seven high-backed wooden chairs, cushioned, but without carvings or other adornment, were arranged on a low platform in a semi-circle. The stone floor and walls were clean but not polished or painted. Around the four walls hung dozens of shields of various shapes and sizes, filled with all manner of sigils and heraldic devices.

As the quartet of knights led Sam to the platform, a door in a darkened back corner opened and seven men entered, filling the chairs without making eye contact with him or speaking to each other.

When they had taken their seats, a grey-robed Franciscan monk came through the door and approached Sam, nodding to the knights to depart.

"Commodore Bellamy, welcome." The monk had a light Sicilian accent, pleasant to Sam's ears. "My name is Guillermo Vincolaré. On behalf of the Star Quorum, I welcome you here today. It is of the utmost importance that you do not speak to a single soul about what we share with you here today, nor share the names of the men who speak to you the messages for which they have summoned you here to receive. It is both a privilege and an honor to stand before these wise, stalwart men, whose names and positions I shall now make known to you."

Each acknowledging Sam in their own way as their names were called—be it a wave of the hand, nod of the head, or a slight bow from where they sat—the seven members of the Star Quorum were as follows:

The first four seats were occupied by Ramón Perellós y Rocafull, noble from Aragon and Grand Master of the Knights of Malta; Archibald Sinclair, descendant of Henry St. Clair and advisor to what remained of the Knights Templar; Anthony Sayer, Grand Master of the newly united Free Mason grand lodge in London; and Michaelangelo Tamborini, Superior General, Society of Jesus.

Those who held the remaining seats were red-robed Cardinals all, one of which, André-Hercule de Fleury, Sam knew. He had given Bellamy the oath on the *Expedition* less than two years before. The other two were Giulio Alberoni, advisor to the king and queen of Spain and Filippo Antonio Gualterio, advisor to the Old Pretender, James Francis Edward Stuart.

The introductions made, Guillermo invited Sam to sit in a chair brought forward by two attendants. When he had done so and the two attendants had retreated through the side door, which he heard lock as it was closed, Cardinal de Fleury stood. "Samuel Bellamy. It is good to hear, my son, that the faith placed in you by Paulsgrave Williams and subsequently by myself has paid great dividends to our cause. Your election as commander of the fleet at New Providence and effectively Nassau and all of the Bahamas puts you in a unique position to continue to shape events. It is for this reason that we have seized upon your unforeseen presence here today—unforeseen by all but one—to take you into our confidence. I apologize that we did not speak when you were last on the island. As Ecclesiastes chapter three tells us, 'For everything there is a season, and a time for every purpose under heaven.' Your time is now, Samuel. Do you accept this, absent details, as a show of faith to this council?"

Although he was exhausted and overwhelmed by the previous evening and morning's events, Sam did not feel weary, nor unsure. Eyes wide, he had replied, "Yes, Your Eminence. Let me continue to be your instrument."

He then had listened, taking it all in—much of which would take days to consider and process—as hour upon hour passed away.

Levasseur—whether cagey or cautious, it mattered not—who had been waiting for him as he exited the fort, did not ask where he had been (he surely knew) or what was said (he surely knew not). They then completed their business with John Martel and his crew before sailing back to St. Thomas for supplies before going their separate ways.

Looking at a nearly full moon out the window of his new quarters on the *Sultana*, Sam considered all that he had heard.

He was no longer the boy in Exeter accepting blows from a tyrant's cane.

Now, at last, he would be the one to deliver the blows.

GLEN SHIRA, SCOTTISH HIGHLANDS, LATE NOVEMBER 1716

Rob Roy MacGregor and his wife, Mary, had just finished feeding the livestock on the far side of their barn when they heard the splintering of wood and the shouts of a shrill voice ordering a thorough search of their home.

"Ye stay hair, Mary, ye ken?" Rob ordered, drawing his claymore and fetching a pair of pistols from a box near the barn. "Ye take one a' these an' stay safe behind the stone wall hair."

Taking the pistol but not turning toward the place that Rob had directed her to go, Mary answered, "I cannae doo as ye ask, hoosband. Ye ken fool weel which wolf is at the door. I owe that bastaird a debt a' blood, I doo."

Knowing it was pointless to argue, Rob nodded, crouching down as he closed the distance between the barn and his house, indicating that Mary should do the same.

He knew what the intruders were looking for and that, when they did not find it, they would burn the structure down, as they had in Perthshire years before.

Reaching the stone wall ten feet from the house, Rob was relieved to see Ewan and Lachlan approaching from the other side. Motioning them to wait for him before they entered, Rob cocked his pistol as one of Montrose's men emerged from the doorway.

"Ye hold yerself still noo, ye eater of shite, ye ken? I weel split yer skull like an egg!"

"We knoo ye haev stolen a cache of arms froom the Murrays a' Scone," Montrose's man shouted, as he was joined in the yard by eight others, all heavily armed. "That, an' soomethin' else, Rob Campbell—soomethin' Laird Murray's nephew is keen tae get back, safe an' sound."

Before Rob could answer, the man was falling forward, a spray of blood emerging from the socket where his right eye had previously witnessed his version of the world.

"Safe an' sound, eh? As safe an' sound as ye air noo, in't that right?"

Though the assassin did not emerge from the shadow of the doorway, Rob knew full well who it was, and why he had spoken what he did.

Rob and his two men—by now joined by a dozen others— leapt the stone walls around the house, training their pistols and muskets—some of those stolen from the Murrays, though the others were safely hidden within a hill an hour's ride away in Balquhidder.

"We weel noot fire if ye doant!" one of Montrose's men answered, dropping his musket and indicating to the others to do the same.

Keeping his pistol trained on the man who spoke the words, Rob approached, followed by Ewan, Lachlan, and the rest.

"Ye haev murdered one a' the Duke of Montrose's own baest men," the man continued. "Anoother a' Lord Murray's nephews—recently coom froom Glasgow tae lairn the fam'ly trade."

"I am weel an' trooly sorry fer the wee lad," Mary answered, stepping up to the man with her pistol cocked and aimed at his temple. "Boot ye nae knoo what lies concealed in the darkness beyond that doorway. A lass once fine a' shape an' visage, once sound an' sane a' mind, made mad bae rape an' threats an' deprivation o'er the course a' many a moonth. 'Twas hair betrothed shot the cur. Caen ye blame him?"

So it had been that the ugly, heartbreaking truth had been revealed when Rob had entered the room in Scone Palace where Finlay Fletcher's bride to be had been kept a prisoner and plaything of another of Lord Murray's nephews, until she had finally snapped.

There were moments during their initial retreat that Rob was sure that Finlay would give them up with his shrieks and wails as he loaded the tragic couple into the wagon beside the cache of pilfered weapons.

The tragic strains of Finlay's tortured song had started within minutes and had rarely ended since.

New verses all the time, as he stroked her hacked-up hair and scarred and hollowed cheeks as she lay on a bed staring at the floor joists above her or slumped in a chair staring at the wall.

And those were the more peaceful of the moments since their sad return. The moments when a man other than Finlay was nowhere near. For when one was, his broken betrothed, whose name they learned was Rowan, pointed, screamed, and clawed until her throat was torn and hoarse and her exhausted body collapsed.

As Montrose's men moved off, carrying the body of Lord Murray's nephew with them, after agreeing to tell the duke he died in a fight fair and square, Rob kicked dirt over the pool of blood before the door while Mary entered the cottage and threw open the concealed door to their root cellar to check on Rowan.

Not long after, Finlay emerged, still holding the pistol he had used to kill the man he very well might have thought was Murray's first nephew himself.

And if he had not, it mattered to Rob not a wit.

As he covered the last of the blood, Rob heard a verse he had never heard before:

"Mae lady was raped in the Tower a Scone... la diddy la diddy da diddy da do...

Beaten an' bled an' starved an' alone... la diddy la diddy da diddy da do..."

Though he had come close, both on that day at Scone and many nights after, Rob finally allowed himself to weep. For Finlay and Rowan, for his own bonny Mary, and for the many others who had suffered at the whims of the savage "nobility."

Letting the hot, insistent tears fall into his beard without wiping them away, Rob swore in silence that he would kill Lord Murray's other nephew.

And should it bring a war, it mattered not a whit.

CHESAPEAKE, VIRGINIA, JANUARY 1717

Lieutenant Robert Maynard was sloppily, unapologetically, unappealingly intoxicated.

Sitting at a back table in a seedy sailors' tavern called The Busted Anchor, he pushed away the whore stroking his unshaven cheek and whispering all manner of unappealing ideas in his ear and ordered another pitcher of ale.

"Belay that order, and leave us both alone."

Willing his eyes to merge the two human-shaped shadows before him into one, Maynard choked down an erupting swell of acid and waved the solidifying apparition over.

"How did ye find me? And what do ye want, *Captain* Brand?" Although those were the words he intended, it sounded like a nursery rhyme flatly intoned while the child chewed on gauze.

"I have not the foggiest idea what ye are saying, Robert. And it is honestly no matter. If Gordon finds ye like this, he shall do far, far worse than he already has. At least ye are not in uniform. But look at ye, man. A complete and utter disgrace."

Looking down at the bile-flecked homespun shirt that covered his odorous body, Maynard tried to remember where he had gotten it and where he had left his uniform.

Nothing came to mind.

He did recall, through a steadily worsening headache, that he had arrived at the tavern a few days before, his recent pay in hand, in a torrential, biting rain. Standing soaked to the skin in the doorway—in uniform, he was almost sure—he secured a room and a bowl of soup and requested that he be left *utterly* alone for the duration of his stay.

Though he had slackened the "utterly" now and again, taking the pleasures of the tavern-keeper's daughter that evening in his room and allowing the other whore—apparently no relation—to keep him company at table as he ate and drank and mumbled, Maynard had by and large shot a "stay away" glare at any and all who approached.

By the following evening, no one bothered to try.

Putting a chair from the table at such a distance as to not have to smell Maynard's body or breath, Brand said, "Robert. I do not have much time. Nor do ye. So I shall say what is most important, and then pay one of these serving girls to get ye bathed and dressed. If they cannot locate your uniform, I shall arrange to have one delivered.

"I leave on the morning tide as the newly installed commander of the HMS *Lyme*, which is, as ye are no doubt aware, a thirty-two-gun Sixth-Rate frigate, sure and sleek of line, with an excellent reputation. I have tried my damnedest to have ye reassigned to my staff, but Gordon will not have it. Easy man! Ye are liable to bust your hand!"

Brand's warning was in response to Maynard's taking a half-filled pewter plate from a pile beside him and slamming it hard against the table.

His anger was understandable. The Admiralty had left Maynard in the cold while they richly rewarded Brand. True to his word, Lord John Carteret had secured Brand's captaincy of the *Lyme* in return for the valuable information he had retrieved from the Scottish Masons and other rebels he had questioned and at times subjected to torture.

A few had expired, not up to the rigor with which he had completed his task.

"Ye were instrumental in getting what was needed, Robert. Our benefactor knows this well. As does The Family in the Albemarle. They shall be most valuable allies now that our reassignment to Virginia has at last been secured. As will Lieutenant Governor Spotswood, who is most anxious to meet ye. They shall not forget what ye have done. Unfortunately, as ye know, neither will Captain Gordon."

Trying to speak and finding himself unable, Maynard drove his fist half-heartedly into the wall on which he leaned. Infuriated by his alleged insubordination and secretiveness and further incensed by his obvious allegiance to the captain of another vessel, Gordon had blocked Maynard's promotion to captain, which would have secured him Brand's former ship, the HMS *Garland*, a thirty-two-gun Fifth Rate Ship of the Line, and cleared the way for the two men to work together, unfettered.

"So ye must be patient, Robert," Brand said, standing and waving over one of the whores. "And more than that, ye must be impeccable in the execution of your duties on the *Pearl*. *That* is how we get ye out from under. Nod if ye understand. I am anxious to be gone from this hellhole before I am seen by someone who matters."

Managing to raise his head and then to let it fall, Maynard did not resist when both the tavern owner's daughter and the non-related whore pulled him up from the table and turned him in the direction of his room upstairs.

Whatever he had to do. No matter how much crow he had to eat or bile he must swallow, Maynard would do it.

He would get his captaincy yet.

The Highlands had never felt as foreign to Ailish MacDonald as they did as she stood in the snow on the shore of Loch Fyne on a frigid January morning, two thick wool shawls doing nothing to keep the cold from sinking into the joints of her shoulders and crawling like a hungry specter up the nape of her neck.

Grasping an oblong stone, flat on one side, in her blue, protesting fingers, Ailish concentrated on the spot in the lake where the ice had been thinnest. She had spent the better part of an hour throwing stone after stone at it, breaking it away until she had created a sufficient opening for her task.

To skip the stone six times.

In memory of Angus. In penance for the letter she never should have sent. As an offering, a healing, for the broken lives of Rowan and her half-mad barber, Finlay Fletcher, whose outbursts had only increased since the incident with Montrose's men outside the MacGregors' cottage. For Mary, who Montrose's men had so sorely abused years earlier without the slightest hesitation. For Rob Roy, whose homes had been burned, lands confiscated, cattle stolen, and spirit hammered upon with such ferocity for so long she did not know how he still managed to stand so straight.

Bringing her arm into position like Duncan had shown her at the shore of Loch Voil before they had packed their things and come to Glen Shira from Balquhidder, Ailish cocked her wrist, letting the oblong stone shift slightly to the ends of her frozen fingers.

"Tha's noot hoo ye doo that."

Stopping her arm mid-toss, Ailish closed her eyes and wished the intruder away.

James MacGregor had been appearing all too often at inconvenient times and in undesirable places since they had made the move.

"Are yoo gonna turn 'round, lass?"

Ailish's decision to go with Rob Roy's family had been at the prodding of her cousin Duncan, who had settled into his role as her protector with an intensity for which she could not wholly account by the sole fact that they were kin.

He had not been the same since his return from the Caribbean. Without either of them putting it into words, they had agreed to share a silent grief, the depths of which only the other could understand.

James had moved closer. She could feel his breath on her ear.

"Weel?"

Keeping hold of the stone, Ailish turned around, taking two steps back as she pulled her shawls tighter around her.

"I wish tae bae left aloone, James Campbell," she said, not caring about nor trying to hide the look of disdain on her face.

James stood his ground. "Coom now, Ailish. Ye haev nae reason tae blow sooch a cold wind upon mae. Whoot haev I doon? I cannae figure it oot. An', honestly, lass… We air MacGregors hair. Soo doan call mae a Campbell. It is nairly as big an insult as MacDonald."

"Yoor nae a MacGregor, James. I noo ye made it haird fer Angus. Ev'ry moment, ev'ry day. An' I bet yoo figured in his be'en sent away."

Pursing his lips and nodding, James said, "So this is aboot Angus, eh? Forget 'im, lass. He is nae worth a tear. Mae da raised him an' chose him—laird knoos why—tae doo a man's work fer oor clan an' he betrayed oos. Haev soom sense. Dooncan did ye a favoor."

Before she could stop him, James had Ailish in his arms. Although she was no weakling, given to hard work and looking after herself, Ailish found herself unable to move.

If only she could, she still gripped the oblong stone.

"It is time we were married, lass. I haev baen patient, boot it is coomin' tae an end. I weel soon haev what I deserve, an' I need a wife. Loocky fer yoo, tis yoo, lass."

Pressing her arms against his with all that she had in her, Ailish hissed, "Yoo unhand mae, ye bowfin jakey! Yoo smeel a' whiskey! I weel nae marry yoo. I swear it!"

Crushing her arms against her sides, James kissed her, his teeth pressing hard against her lips. "Aye, lass," he said, flicking his tongue against a bubble of blood that had formed on her lower lip. "Ye weel make a fain, spirited wife. Weel haev half a doozen bairns befoor waer thairty!"

Adjusting his left arm so he could grasp the back of her head with his right, James again brought his whiskey- and blood-tinged lips hard against hers as Ailish closed her eyes.

Then she felt him yanked away.

"I weel keel yoo, yoo bastard! Tooch hair again an' see if I jaest."

Opening her eyes, Ailish saw James sprawled on the frozen ground, Duncan's claymore at his neck.

"Yoo haev nae idea what yer on aboot," James said, though the fear in his voice was clear.

Pressing the tip of the claymore into James's flesh so it drew a bit of blood, Duncan replied, "One clean shirt weel doo ye, shood yoo tooch Ailish ever again." He moved the sword away and James leapt to his feet.

"Cannae promise yoo that, yoo MacDonald bastaird," he said, backing away. "She weel bae mae wife. An' yer murderin' mae coosin made it so."

Why Duncan did not throw James back upon the ground or run him through, Ailish could not guess. Perhaps it was for the same reason she did not throw the stone she still held at his head.

James is right. We are party tae Angus's murder, she thought. Another would be more than they could bear.

"Yoo all right, lass?" Duncan asked after James had run away.

"Aye, Dooncan. Thanks tae yoo."

As Ailish sought safety in his arms, Duncan came a tongue's tip from telling her the truth.

Instead, he walked her home in silence and cursed his coward's heart.

Standing within the impressive outermost room of the subterranean temple of the Mammon Lodge in Dublin, Ireland, two weeks earlier, Lord John Carteret could not help but feel a twinge of envy. Despite announcing his arrival, he found himself unceremoniously ignored. Cautioning himself against an overhasty show of temper, he had occupied himself with an examination of his surroundings. The repurposed cairn stones the builder of the two-story dwelling just above—who had been a speaker in the Irish House of Commons—had chosen with such care for this temple had caused quite the stir. The hired workers and villagers had raised their voices in warning and derision against the desecration and ghostly retribution that would surely be at hand, but the builder did not care.

On the contrary… such things were precisely the point.

Rumors of another, even more energetically potent temple somewhere in the far north of the Americas aside, the Mammon Lodge of Dublin was the secret site where the most powerful of the winged demon's inducted representatives gathered to make their sacrifices and requests.

Lord Carteret had long expected an invite—he had more than earned it—although, when it finally arrived, three weeks earlier, it was not so much an invite as a *summons*:

Carteret—
Your presence required in Dublin by Waning Gibbous Moon.
Bring the Blade. Prepare to stay a fortnight.
AR

The Grand Master who had sent it was obviously less than pleased, meaning he thought that Mammon must be as well.

How dare the bastard be so bold.

And the request to bring the Abraham Blade… The sole permission to wield it was Carteret's alone.

The Lodge in Dublin had its own ancient object—said to be the magical staff of the High Priest Aaron himself—so why did they want him to bring the Blade?

Answers had not been forthcoming, a situation with which Lord John Carteret was both unaccustomed and uncomfortable. Some twenty minutes after his arrival at the Lodge's house in

Dublin, he had been greeted by one of the Grand Master's acolytes, a nervous young thing—mostly scarred skin and long bones—who was unable or unwilling to look him in the eye as he bowed too often and tripped on his robes with laughable rapidity.

This was the sum of the hospitality the greatest confirmed Mammon Lodge on Earth had to offer a fellow Master?

For the next eleven days, stripped of his fine suit of clothes and given an itchy, bug-filled hair suit—no more than a length of molded filth with a hole cut for his head—Carteret sat in a cell without a window, subsisting on a small bowl of rice and two cups of water per day.

He was no doubt being prepared—but for what?

His only comfort was the Abraham Blade beside him, which had yet to be confiscated, no less mentioned.

Any time he asked for audience with the Grand Master, his scrawny source of daily sustenance quickly shook his head and whisked himself away, the keys on his cloak jangling as he went.

On the twelfth day, the acolyte did not come at all. Nor did food or drink.

Carteret was beginning to grow weary of the Grand Master's game.

Good thing for all involved, he thought, as the sun rose on the thirteenth day, *I am due to leave tomorrow. Whatever he is planning, it has to happen soon.*

And it did.

First, the acolyte handed him a coarse but comparatively comfortable cloak of brown-dyed, unadorned wool with which to replace the hair suit. As Carteret peeled the ugly garment from his body, he saw it had caused a rash over most of his torso, punctuated at points by the bites of a variety of insects. Standing and stretching as the cell was unlocked and opened, Carteret moved forward as the arm of the acolyte indicated he should take the Abraham Blade and exit the cell.

As they passed half a dozen cells on either side of them, Carteret tried to peer into the blackness to see what trials and tortures their inhabitants were enduring. Although he knew they were there—he had heard plenty of their moans, screams, and pleadings the previous twelve days and nights—each cell was so dark, so visually impenetrable, that his curiosity was not curtailed with facts.

As they approached an arched doorway at the end of the hall, Carteret heard a familiar, comforting sound: *"Wa hay-nah sa ma ka Dominus. Mu-kah do hay-nah ka. Tach ma, tach mu, sa mu sa Dominus. Co-mama sa. Co-mama sa Dominus…"*

A ceremony, and no doubt sacrifice, was under way. Carteret, suitably prepared and put in his place, was no doubt going to be the guest of honor.

As he had entered the temple proper, Carteret saw that it was much like the one over which he presided beneath his house in London. The altar was larger, although the carvings above it were exact in every respect.

As three dozen black-robed figures arrayed themselves around the altar— behind which stood the Grand Master in ornate blood-red robes fastened with a woven gold belt, the tassels of which hung nearly to the floor—Lord Carteret saw why the altar was three times larger than his own.

Led into the room by another dozen of the black-hooded figures were half a dozen children, ranging in age from barely able to walk to those still in the midst of puberty. Only one had the dark hue and features of an African—the rest were an array of skin tones, hair colors and styles, and body types. They shuffled along, the pairs of priests accompanying them not holding their arms so much as guiding them to assure they stayed in a line.

As the priests brought the children before the altar, the chanting grew louder.

"Wa hay-nah sa ma ka Dominus. Mu-kah do hay-nah ka. Tach ma, tach mu, sa mu sa Dominus. Co-mama sa. Co-mama sa Dominus…"

The loose rags each of the children were draped in were pulled to the ground as the chant continued to swell, reverberating off the walls and quickening the pace of Carteret's blood.

As the chant reached an almost eardrum-splitting crescendo, the six pairs of priests laid the children on the altar in twos, where their throats were slit, quickly and cleanly, and their blood drained into golden bowls through a series of channels carved into the stone.

As the Grand Master slit the final throat—Carteret noticing the simple, wood-handled knife, nothing like the impressive Abraham Blade—all present, including Carteret, shouted out in ecstasy.

With a slight nod of the head, the Grand Master set the four-dozen priests into motion to remove the bodies and clear the room. As they filed out, he lowered the hood that had covered his face, revealing long, corn-colored hair gathered in complicated braids and a long beard, similarly braided at the extremities, gathered halfway down by a weave of golden thread.

"Lord Carteret. Master of the Mammon Lodge of London. I see you have brought the blade as I requested. Excellent."

The voice of the Grand Master had the no doubt exact timbre and lilt of the Scandinavian warriors who ravaged the monks of Lindsfarne after arriving in their clinker-built, dragon-headed longships in the early summer of 793.

Carteret was certain that it was this man's family, the Ravenskalds, whom had been behind the raid and benefitted most from the religious relics carried off.

The staff the Grand Master now grasped as he rounded the altar—said to be that of the Israelite priest and brother of Moses, Aaron—might have been one of them.

"Might I call you John?" the Grand Master asked, stretching out his long, pale fingers to indicate that his guest should hand him the Abraham Blade.

Not yet acquiescing, Carteret responded, "Might I call you Adonijah?"

Under other circumstances—perhaps if they were standing in Carteret's home temple instead of this one—he might have thought the Grand Master's laugh pleasant and even inviting.

But here, at this moment, with Carteret weakened and alone, it was not.

"You forget yourself, John," Ravenskald answered, placing his hand on the Abraham Blade and gently pulling it toward him. "Your close relationship with England's wrongful king and supervision of a minor lodge do not entitle you to call me anything but Grand Master. Nor do they entitle you to refuse my requests as you have just done with this knife nor to speak unless I request it. I am not impressed—nor are our superiors—with how you have handled events in Scotland, the Caribbean, or the American colonies. My brother Absalom would just as soon sacrifice the lot of you, beginning anew with better prospects."

It was in that moment that Lord John Carteret, so used to being in charge, was grateful to be here alone, absent witnesses to this cruel humiliation.

"You have questions," Ravenskald said, gazing into Carteret's soul with a pair of blue-grey eyes that could easily turn a lake into ice if their owner chose to do so. "I shall allow you to ask them. But be quick and expect a terse response, for there is much we must do before the coming of the dawn."

"Then let us make this easy," Carteret said, his primary goal to not let Ravenskald see his fear. "Why am I here, what right have you to the blade, and what do you intend to do with me?"

"Ah… is that *all* you want to know?"

"Actually," Carteret answered, drawing strength from his ability to sound as though he were still at peace inside, "I wonder as well about the sacrifice of the six children I just witnessed. It goes against our code."

Ravenskald nodded. "For the rituals for which *your* lodge is approved. But there are also others—more powerful than Mammon—on whose strength the Chosen of us draw."

Not anticipating this answer, Carteret felt a cold sweat begin to form on the back of his neck. "Moloch," he whispered. "The bodies will be set aflame."

"They already are," Ravenskald replied, shifting his hands on the staff so it was exactly horizontal, even with his waist. "Soon you shall smell them. Should Moloch leave a scrap or two behind, I will be sure to have them included with your parting evening meal. Now, to your other three queries. You are here because you require strengthening. Tempering. Your will is strong, but your execution is weak. My right to the blade should hinge solely on the fact that I, your superior in every aspect, asked that you bring it to me. But, you are not completely without use, so I am willing to grant you a boon. Events are moving rapidly—the Star Quorum and their ancient army have increased their activity as of late—and I no longer deemed it safe in your care. There is another reason, which you soon shall see. As to your final question…"

What happened next took merely seconds. As much as he had seen, Carteret would at times in the future be more inclined to dismiss it as hallucination than an actual event.

Spinning the staff in his right hand with incredible speed, Ravenskald let his eyes roll back in their sockets, which shone an unnatural white as he intoned in a language with which Carteret was not familiar. As the speed of the spinning increased, Ravenskald shifted the Abraham Blade in his left hand so that the blade was facing down.

Raising his right hand above his head, Ravenskald closed his fist tighter, so the staff stopped its spin, positioned on a vertical axis in front of him. Running the Abraham Blade along the lower third so that it produced a deep gash, Ravenskald opened his hand as the staff became a writhing serpent whose fangs were quickly, painfully lodged in the soft flesh between Carteret's shoulder and neck.

As his vision blurred and heart began to pound—rapidly, thunderously—in his ears, Carteret looked at Ravenskald for an explanation.

He could feel his life force draining away. As he fell to the floor, Ravenskald cradled him in his arms as Mary did her Jesus in Michelangelo's *Pietà*.

"John. Listen to me closely. I needed the blade to transform the staff," Ravenskald whispered, stroking Carteret's forehead as he felt his limbs go numb. "The venom of the serpent, the *tanin*, is necessary for your further transformation. It will mix with Mammon's own. You will thank me in the end."

As Carteret tried to remain conscious—he knew sleep would lead to death—he heard Ravenskald whispering the call to Mammon. *"Wa hay-nah sa ma ka Mammon. Mu-kah do hay-nah ka. Tach ma, tach mu, sa mu sa Mammon. Co-mama sa. Co-mama sa Mammon...* We call upon Mammon... Dark angel of prosperity and gold... We devoted servants call upon your favor. May this earthly realm be yours... *"Wa hay-nah sa ma ka Mammon. Mu-kah do hay-nah ka..."*

And then their great and glorious benefactor was upon them, its leathery black wings folding over both of their bodies as the dark demon's long, forked tongue lapped at the wound the *tanin* had made.

As Mammon sucked and drank, Carteret, whose hands he could now move, grasped both of Ravenskald's own.

"Thank you, Grand Master," he whispered, giving in to Mammon's need, as he felt healing and more begin to course through his torso and into his limbs.

"You may call me Adonijah. For now we are truly brothers."

In the two months since Edward Thache—temporarily demoted to sailing master—had departed New Providence on Benjamin Hornigold's *Adventure* with twenty-nine others following the vote that had displaced the commodore as leader of the Flying Gang, he had undergone bouts of profound loss of hope followed by resurgent and fierce commitment.

He had carefully watched over Hornigold, Quartermaster William Howard, and the others—most especially Conall MacBlaquart—taking comfort in the fact that, although each had faced the same flipping of position and mindset, they had done it with enough of a stagger that someone was always able to find sufficient faith and focus to prop up and rally the others.

As the four sets of two bells that signaled the end of the middle watch rang out in the silence and stillness of the sea, Edward filled his flask with rum from the barrel in the officers' mess and climbed on deck to meet Conall, who would be descending the ratlines within seconds.

The once-awkward Highlander, now grown into an able, seasoned sailor, had stayed on task and been the best of the crew since that early November day.

But Edward could also see that, ever since they had held parlay with a ship out of Glasgow a few days earlier, something was eating at Conall that went well beyond their current set of circumstances.

Not that those circumstances were insufficient to keep each and every one of them fully occupied without additional burdens. Insisting on caution, Captain Hornigold had chosen as their prey only those ships that he deemed as easy targets. Survival was paramount. Although he had sent a few expeditions out as emissaries to various Jacobite strongholds he felt that he could trust, most were solidly backing Levasseur and Bellamy. This was no time to go to war with their clearly stronger foes.

Edward's disappointment in their current pace and course of action was considerable. He had hoped to be once again in command of a ship of his own by this time and to have other captains recruited to enough of a flotilla for them to have regained some of the ground they had lost.

Or water, as it were.

Enjoying the feel of the crisp evening air, Edward looked up into a bright, star-filled sky, against which was the shadow of the descending watchman, right on time, a book and quill stuck in the back of his belt.

"Evenin' to ye, Conall," he said, offering the flask. "I brought ye a 'wee dram' as ye would say."

Accepting the offering with a half-smile edged with sadness, Conall said, "Yer timin' couldnae bae baetter, Maister Thache. I donnae suppose ye haev anythin' tae eat as weel?"

Letting out a laugh, Edward shook his head. "We shall remedy that in a moment. There is hot soup an' a fresh loaf in the galley happily waitin' on ye. But I thought we could sit and have a word about the cloud that is over your head."

Taking a long pull on the flask and handing it back, Conall said, "Thank ye. I didnae ken I was bein' soo obvious aboot it. I am indeed sair aboot news froom hoom. Boot it weel nae interfere wit' mae dooties."

Motioning for Conall to sit on one of two sea chests near the quarterdeck, Edward sat upon the other. "It is not about the execution of yer duties. Ye have been beyond reproach. I am askin' as a friend."

Surprised by what he heard—Mister Thache was not what one would call naturally disposed to such sentiments—Conall paused for a moment in thought, wishing to choose his words with care. "One a' the men on that ship outta Glasgow is froom mae village back hoom. Balquhidder. Prettiest land ye would ever wish tae see. Loch Voil, oop in the Highlands... I couldnae wait tae leave, an' all I wish fer lately is tae bae back. Doo ye ken?"

"I do not," Edward answered. "I left Spanish Town, Jamaica because there was nothin' left for me, an' it is obvious to me there is now even less. But that is no matter—do continue with your tale..."

"I knoo I was nae supposed tae, boot I asked after Ailish. That bae the lass I lost. Mae kinsman nae recognized mae wit' this long beard an' a better filled-oot frame... An' his answer..."

Before Conall could ask, Edward handed him back the flask, which he nearly drained in his discomfort at having to talk about what was gnawing at his innards. "Do not be embarrassed," Edward said. "I know little of love, but I do not dismiss it as a noble, worthy quest."

Nodding with an understanding only the brokenhearted have, Conall continued. "She is bein' courted bae mae coosin' James—"

"The one that has caused ye all the trouble."

"Aye."

"Surely she would not—"

"He didnae say. Boot she mae haev nae choice. Mae ooncle has power. Influence. An' that means soo doos James. As the oldest—an' a damned clever schemer—hae is nae all bum an' parsley. He is fain at playin' the wee hen that never layed away… Meanin'—"

"He is good at playin' innocent. I ken ye," Edward said with a smile.

"Aye. Yer nae talkin' mince, Maister Thache. I am nae sayin' Ailish would talk tae mae—after all, I am daid far as she kens, which makes maetters awkward tae say the least—so, tae bae here, so far froom hair, an' nae able tae doo anythin' while that foul coo-kisser gets his way…"

Seeing the gleam of a tear lit by moonlight in Conall's eye, Edward half regretted the course he had set them on. Although now, so deeply into the meat of the matter as they were, he had to see it through.

"You must remain dead, Conall. There are larger matters to consider. But even if there were not, changin' tack would only put ye an' her in danger. I have known far too many like this James… bullies ye do not run afoul of. Not without a solid plan and considerable backin'." He placed his hand on Conall's arm. "I once had occasion to make the acquaintance of a Zulu from the south of the African continent. They have a sayin' for a trusted friend. 'Once they take yer hand, they hold it unto Death.' I am offerin' my hand, Conall MacBlaquart, if ye catch my meanin'."

Taking Edward's offered hand, Conall replied, "I doo, Maister Thache. An' I thank ye fer it."

Applying just enough pressure for Conall to know just how deeply he meant it, Edward removed his hand and stood. "We should eat. All that rum will soon enough set yer brains to swimmin' if ye do not get some grub. But know this… the time is soon at hand for outstanding accounts to be squared. We are embarking on a reckonin'. I do not understand the magnitude of the forces in play around us… I regret how I handled Commodore Bellamy's alliance with La Bouche… not that I approve, but there was more—much more—that I should have learned from them about the Star Quorum and these damned objects Abraxas Abriendo goes on and on about. Regardless, I know this beyond doubt—ye an' I were meant to meet. To pledge our service to one another. In the months to come, our partnership will reveal itself in larger detail, but it is clear that each must play his part. I do not know what ye saw in that mirror, but I know it weighs on ye. I shall be the cannon and ye shall be the quill. Put that journal of yours to the best use ye can. This story in which we appear must honestly, truthfully be told. No matter the cost, my friend. And ye are the one who must tell it.

"It shall matter more than ye ken."

Finis (fer noo...)

ABOUT THE AUTHOR

Joey Madia is a novelist, screenwriter, historical educator, playwright, actor, and director. He also writes narratives and designs the puzzles for Escape Rooms, based on literature and historical events. He is founding editor of www.newmystics.com, a literary site created in 2002 that houses the work of over 120 writers and artists from around the world. His website is newmystics.com/joey. He also has profiles at Stage 32 (where he is a frequent blogger), Instagram, Facebook, Goodreads, Film Freeway, IMDb, and OnStellar.

www.ingramcontent.com/pod-product-compliance
Lightning Source LLC
Chambersburg PA
CBHW021219260626
47172CB00002B/502